CW00920728

Autobiography

I am a 60 year old ex engineer, born in Liverpool in the fifties. One of
eight children to Albert and Edna. Married now for thirty-six years to my
beautiful wife Fran and four grown up children. I have never written a
book until made redundant and then only to help fight off the
depression that accompanies it. To read a book is a wonderful thing, to
write one is an adventure into the unknown.

Synopsis

The great Braer approached the boy, he reached out with his
giant front paw and touched Daniel on the shoulder, and then he
spoke to him in a strong and yet mellow voice. "I am yours and you
are mine, I am your protector and your friend and together we will
overcome all that is put before us." When the great beast removed his
paw, Daniel found that he had left a small imprint on his skin.
Daniel and his friend Emma travel through unknown dangers,
guarded and guided by Daniels friend Trayan a master trainer in the
art of Brannai. The trio of friends hunted and their skills tested to the
limit as they battle through tournaments and trials that ultimately lead
to a destiny that had been set out years before.

Brannai

Pete Stulberg

Copyright 2010 by Pete Stulberg

Brannai

BRANNAI

With grateful thanks to all those who have helped me on this journey.
Special thanks to my son Daniel who, without his support, this book
would have remained just a dream!

Brannai

THE KINGDOM OF ARNORST

Prologue

BRANNAI

Philip stood; his leather jerkin was his only protection as he braced himself against the storm. The rain drove into his face, matting his blonde hair against his head and all around, the darkness was closing in. There was a loud clap of thunder followed by a sheet of lightening that lit up the night sky; silhouetting the outline of the trees, lighting them up like monsters with long raking fingers. He looked up and to his left was his friend, Taitu. He was fifteen feet tall when standing on his hind legs, powerful and majestic with his silvery fur wet against his body.

The great ape stood on all fours; his back arched in a perfect pose. His breathing was heavy and he bled from the cuts to his arms and chest, but for now there was no time for pain and he turned his head and with his piercingly blue eyes, he looked down at Philip.

Philip steadied himself, then spoke to Taitu, "one last effort my friend, this is our time, our victory." Taitu looked across at his advisory, "He will be Lord of the Brannai no more," and he spoke with a strong and determined voice.

The land and the grass had turned to mud in the downpour and across from Philip, Torek waited. His face twisted with rage as he stood in disbelief. How can a common person even challenge his title? This peasant, with his monkey, dares to wrestle his mantle from me; I will bring him down, humiliate him and destroy his beast. He looked up at Kaldeira, "You will finish this, or so help me I will finish you".

Kaldeira looked down at Torek, he too was breathing heavy for the battle had not gone well and he stood there with heavy cuts from his neck and arms. "My lord," he said as he bowed his head, but his voice was labored and for the first time, full of uncertainty. Torek drew his sword and raised it to the stormy sky, "now kill him." The great beast took off, throwing mud and grass high in the air as he charged at Taitu. It was a terrifying sight, standing the same height as Taitu with two powerful claws on a body supported by six legs. His long tail had a curved sting and now the human muscular upper body contorted with rage and he screamed as he ran.

Taitu raised himself to his full height and in a raw fury; he beat his chest and roared, revealing the two sharp fangs in the upper jaw of his powerful head.

"My friend, wait for him, let him come on, then bring the pain." Philip looked at the charging animal as he spoke, but did not waver in his conviction.

The Kaldeira struck out with his left claw, but Taitu had seen it coming and had moved to the right were he grabbed the other one in his giant hand and then landed a huge blow across the jaw of the beast. Kaldeira reeled his head back then struck out with his right hand and at the same time attacked with his huge right claw. Taitu was in full flow and he roared as he jumped and spun in the air kicking out with his feet. This time it caught Kaldeira across the back sending him falling to the floor.

"Now," shouted Philip and the great ape landed gracefully on the floor and instantly pounced on his fallen advisory were he rained blow upon hideous blow down onto Kaldeira's head, pummeling him into the floor.

Torek looked on in disbelief and screamed out at the top of his voice. He had a look of pure evil and it seemed that all the blood in his anguished body had risen to his face.

Taitu stood over Kaldeira, placed one foot upon his back, and beat his chest in victory as he roared. Philip dropped to his knees, the tension releasing from his body. He raised his arms to the sky and sighed, he had won.

Lord Torek now screamed out in horror, "Kill him. Kill Philip," and with the life flowing out of him, Kaldeira whipped out his tail and his sting pierced Philip in the chest, then, the great beast vanished in a shower of silver light.

Taitu let out a roar that would have brought down the gates of hell; he turned and charged at Torek slipping and sliding in his fury to reach him.

Brannai

Torek was breathing heavy but now he gathered himself and stood tall to face the charging ape. Then he simply laughed, with his face pointing to the heavens, he laughed, as Taitu came on. Then when the ape was only a few paces away and as he gathered himself for the fatal blow, he vanished in a shower of silver light.

BEGINNING

In the land of Arnorst far to the south lies the small village of Dantaal, quiet and unassuming in the heart of beautiful woodland. The people there are simple folk, hardworking and honest, farmers mostly by trade. On the outskirts of the village is a farm run by a mother and her son.

Kate was a stout woman, tall with long black hair graying in the roots. She had strong, yet elegant hands; the softness of which had been ground away through long hours working on her farm, but in her face, she retained a beauty from her youth. Her son Daniel was sixteen although you could not tell by looking at him, his young looks betrayed his years, although his good physique and bright blue eyes and thick wavy blonde hair would see him grow into a handsome man.

"Daniel!" Shouted Kate, "Daniel, we need provisions from the village, I've got to milk the cows and then I'll prepare something to eat, get out of bed." It was a beautiful spring morning but Daniel was still in bed although he answered his mother promptly and politely, "fine mother, I'll be there in a minute". His room was small with bare walls and beams, a single table with a mirror and a jug and basin for necessities. On the wall was a hook where his breeches hung and on the floor beneath them where his shoes.

Daniel jumped out of the bed and then went and washed himself in a basin of cold water. As he dried himself, he slowly walked over and stood in front of the mirror. He looked himself up and down, then, stood on his toes imagining himself the same size as the other boys his age in the village, Daniel sighed and went to the hook on the wall were he pulled on his breeches and threw over a ragged shirt and then went to see his mother.

"Don't be too long son, after milking I'll prepare us some cheese and bread, fresh from the oven." The smell of the fresh bread travelled through the wood and always put an extra spring in his step when he returned from an errand.

Brannai

This day he set off as usual along the dusty path that wound through the open fields and then took a small detour through the edge of Barrow wood. The air was crisp and clean and his breath was still visible as he exhaled and as he walked, he took in all the sights and sounds that this beautiful land had to offer.

This day was like any other, maybe so, he thought, but something was there, small, at the back of his thoughts, but there nonetheless. He travelled on, passed the old oak and along the dusty path that wound its way through the edge of Barrow wood and the warm sun shone off his blonde, scruffy hair. He knew most of the wood well, with its trees and animals, he knew where the old hawk had made its nest, and the pool where the largest fish in town could be caught, and yet on this day he was unusually weary, not scared, but alive, tingling all over and very alert.

As he travelled along, he became aware of something not quite in sight but yet there in the shadows. His step quickened and his heart pumped faster and faster, his eyes darted between every bush and tree searching for whatever it was. Quicker and quicker he ran, unaware of where he was going, half running half tripping as he went, he was being corralled like prey, driven into the deeper parts of the wood where he had never been. The shadow was nearer now, more visible, a pair of bright yellow eyes flashed in the distance and there was a pulse of strong breath in the air and the low haunting sound of a beast with only one thing on its mind. Daniel's pulse rose and his hands began to sweat. He ran faster and faster searching frantically as he went. He ran with no direction crashing into branches until, crack! He had caught his step on a branch and fell to the floor. The young boy was agile, he rolled and stood up in one quick movement, and there he found himself in a clearing, alone, that is, except for the beast that now hid some fifty paces from his very position.

The beast would not come into the open, instead it stalked menacingly through the trees, treading carefully as it went. It moved with a purpose, rubbing its side on the trees as it passed them always keeping itself in the shadow. Its breath was pulsing fast from its gaping jaws, showing the banks of sharp yellow teeth and saliva was drooling onto the forest floor as it moved. Its sides were heaving in and out and its claws were primed and ready. Daniel looked around and spotted a large branch on the floor, he tried to bend down to pick it up but his feet faltered and he stumbled, but still, he tried to pick up the branch as he did so. He could not take his eyes off the beast as he searched with his hands. Then finally, he grabbed the stick and lifted it in front of his eyes.

Slowly the beast revealed itself. It stepped out into the patchy sunlight showing its matted black fur, enormous paws and long sharp claws, a Wolf, with one intention, evil. It eyed Daniel up, moving gracefully into position, its head quite still, level as it moved, and its large yellow eyes focused on the boy. Daniel was shaking, the branch in his hands became heavy and his step labored. The wolf, who was all the time moving closer and closer, matched every step he took. Then, suddenly it howled, and the noise echoed through the trees. It turned its head to look straight at the boy, and then it growled loudly as it ran, churning up the floor as it did so.

Daniel froze with fear in the face of the charging beast, then when it was a few steps away it pounced; jumping high in the air. The boy pulled the branch in his hand back, ready to strike, every bone in his little body, shaking. Suddenly there was a deafening roar and a claw slashed out and ripped through the wolf's throat, killing it in an instant and leaving it bloodied and motionless on the floor.

The boy stood back in disbelief, for there; standing in front of him was an animal, tall and majestic, perched on its hind legs. It had the body similar to a polar bear, but not the color. With thick hazel fur and enormous claws, that it held out in front, still dripping with blood. Daniel looked up at the huge beast and saw the most piercing blue eyes looking at him and a wild face that somehow calmed his insides, and then it vanished right before him. Daniel did not know what to do; he looked down at the wolf at his feet and ran south out of the wood as fast as his legs would carry him. Quickly he managed to find the path that led to his home, and his mother. He ran up the path and burst through the door. "Mother, mother," he shouted and was stopped in his tracks.

There sitting at the table was Kate and opposite sat a stranger, an old man dressed in the clothes of a traveler with an old cloak wrapped around his shoulders, his hair thick and matted and tied at the back with a piece of cloth. He had an aged face, rough and rugged though he also possessed a kindly demeanor. "Good morning Daniel," he said, "my name is Trayan and I knew your father."

BRAER

Daniel looked to his mother then back to Trayan. "You say you knew my father, that can't be true, I have no father, there is just me and mother, and we live here alone."

"Tell me," said Trayan, "what happened in the wood", Daniel looked shocked at the question, then his mother spoke, "Daniel," she said, "we have lived here these past sixteen years, happy years, I have loved you as much as any mother could," and she spoke with a sincerity and sadness in her voice. "I will always consider you my son," and she wept.
 Daniel shook, he had never seen his mother cry, she had always been strong for him, and he ran to console her. She raised her hand and stopped his approach, then gathered herself before she continued. "Trayan came to me when you were a babe, wrapped in a blanket and carried in a basket, he asked me to look after you and raise you as my own, how could I refuse you were so beautiful. When he left he said he would return around your sixteenth birthday to reclaim you".

"I don't want to go with him," said Daniel, "who will look after you, you need me here, the pigs, the cows, the…the," but his mother stopped him again. "Son it is time to let go, you must go with Trayan, you are destined for great things," and she stood up went over to him and took him by the hand and led him over to where Trayan was sitting. Kate then took Daniels hand, placed it on top of Trayan's, and then kissed the boy on his forehead.

Kate helped him pack. She loaded the table with fresh fruit and cheese and some hot bread from the oven, then wrapped it in a chequered cloth as only a mother could. She thanked Trayan and hoped he would look after her son, then she kissed Daniel one last time and the pair left. Kate stood at the gate to her farm and watched until they were out of site, then felt immersed in a great emptiness, and fell down onto the ground and cried.

The two new friends now followed the path along the fields and out until it met the Barrow wood and as they travelled Trayan spoke to the boy.

"So tell me what happened just before I arrived." Daniel told of his fight with the great wolf, how out of nowhere a mighty beast had just appeared and saved him. "What you saw," said Trayan, "was a Braer, they are one of many magical creatures that live in this land, but remember," he said, "they do not appear to anyone or anywhere for that matter. This Braer is yours, it is your Brannai, your protector and your soul and it will die for you."

"If it is my protector why have I only seen it now, why not last spring when Joshua and the others cornered me in Drays' field and beat me because of my size?" Trayan did not falter in his step as he answered the boy, "All Brannai do not appear to their trainers until their sixteenth year, it is a time when your mind and body change and you can become more aware."

Trayan explained to Daniel that he is a trainer of Brannai and that he does not own one, he said that Brannai do not appear to anyone, his or her carefully chosen owners only appear in special areas called arenas. "Now" he said, "it is time to meet yours."

They walked for several miles until they reached a part of the wood the boy did not know, and yet felt familiar. Daniel soon realized the wolf had attacked him earlier in this very same part of the wood. Daniel took Trayan over to the body of the wolf; it was still there fresh on the floor.

Trayan looked at the boy and put his arm around his shoulder, then he said, "The Brannai came to you because you were in trouble, now I want him to appear again," and he took Daniel away from the body and then to the clearing were he stood behind him with his hands on the boys shoulders. "Now close your eyes and open your mind, think of the Braer and picture him before you. Now, open your eyes." Daniel did so and when he opened them, there before him stood Braer. The beast was on all fours and he prowled majestically before him before turning to face Daniel, "I am Braer," he said, and his voice was powerful and at the same time calming, "I am yours and you are mine and together we shall overcome all that is put before us."

Daniel was amazed, "you can speak," he said.

"All Brannai can speak," replied Braer. Then he stepped nearer to Daniel until they were only a small space apart, he reached out with his giant paw and touched the boy on the shoulder. As he did Daniel could feel Braer's heartbeat within him, and he could feel the strength of the animal flowing through his body and he knew instantly that they were one.

When the Braer's paw was taken away it left a mark, a small paw print the size of a penny, and so a great friendship was set up, which no man would ever break.

"We will spend some time near these woods," explained Trayan. "It will give you time to get to know your beast."

Therefore, Trayan and the young trainer made camp.

Trayan set up a tent and set Daniel the task of collecting some firewood. The tent was a thin canvass sheet supported by wooden poles transported in a sack carried on the back. It had guy-ropes that supported at the ends with small wooden stakes driven into the soft ground.

Trayan was adept at living in the wild, over time, he would show the boy how to fashion a bow with string from the innards of an animal. Wood from a certain branch, that would bend but would not break to make a bow, but for now, they settled down to a meal of berries and cold meats, warmed by the glow of a blazing fire.

The question had been burning in Daniel's mind ever since their first meeting, "tell me about my father." Trayan turned to the boy and saw the worried look in his eyes and his heart went out to him.

"Your father's name was Philip, but he liked to call himself Barras, he thought it spread a little fear or respect into his opponents, what do you think? What would you like to call him?" Without hesitation Daniel replied, "Philip."

"Interesting," uttered Trayan and then he continued.

"He was a great Brannai master and he owned two great beasts and he won many victories," Trayan paused as Daniel interrupted again, "You said you knew him, how did my father die?" Trayan stalled at such a delicate matter, then gathered himself and looked at the boy; the truth he thought was what his father would want him to hear

"He was betrayed by another Brannai master by the name of Torek. Know one thing Daniel, the Brannai are here to do battle, to honor and to protect, but they are as one with their trainers, what the trainer is, the Brannai will become, such was the case with Torek. He was a dark trainer but the trait he hid from Philip until it was too late.

During a fight, Philip battled Torek and won but when Torek's beast was all but defeated and Philip's guard was down, he set his beast on Philip and slain him. Brannai are noble creatures and will not harm their trainers, but as I said, Torek was dark and his beast became the same."

Daniel looked at Trayan with tears in his eyes, "When I face this Torek I will not make the same mistake as my father."

Trayan looked sympathetically at the boy as he said, "It was through your father that I met Kate, your mother has done you proud and I think Philip would be pleased at the young man you have become, now, goodnight Daniel," and with that he ushered the boy off to bed.

That night Daniels dreams filled with images of his mother, alone on the farm and he tossed and turned.
When morning broke Daniel emerged from his tent with his head full of questions. Trayan was already up and making a hot drink by the fire. Daniel moved over and sat on a log by the old man who had cupped the warm drink in his hands to fend off the fresh morning air.

They did not speak for some time and it was Trayan, who broke the ice,

"Today you start your training."

"I thought you trained the Brannai," replied Daniel.

"I do, but as the trainer grows stronger so does the Brannai, it will take on your strengths and weaknesses. You must feed off each other and grow together, now it is time to run and build up those puny muscle's of yours."

He made him run for several hours, stopping only for a short rest and some water. He gave him heavy loads of logs to lift and exercised him until he was sore to the bones. When Daniel felt he was at the end Trayan took him to the clearing.

"Now, just because you are tired, does not mean you cannot control yourself. Let go of the fatigue close your eyes and relax. Now summon your Braer."

Daniel did so and when he opened his eyes, Braer was standing before him. Together they turned and faced Trayan who had took up a position some fifty paces away. "Prepare yourself," said Trayan, and with a clap of his hands above his head, he shouted "Bransar." There was a flash of light and suddenly there beside him stood a, well to Daniel it looked like a small donkey. Piebald with a mass of black fur on top of its head that looked just like someone had placed it there. The animal looked at Braer and sat down on its backside completely unimpressed with the whole event.

"Daniel!" cried Trayan, "This is your first battle, this is Bransar and you must defeat him with Braer."

Daniel looked at Braer and then at the Bransar and thought the whole episode would be a waste of time, I mean, what a mismatch, he thought.

"Braer!" cried Daniel "Attack!"
The Braer roared and charged at the little animal, who continued to sit unimpressed. Braer began to get up some speed as he closed in on his opponent.

"Bransar, tangle!" shouted Trayan, and out from the animal shot long roots, they hit Braer in the legs and sent him tumbling to the ground, "Snare" said Trayan, and the roots wrapped themselves around Braer's neck leaving him struggling to breathe. "Bransar, release" said Trayan, and before he could do anything else Daniel had raced to Braer and had dropped beside him.

"Braer, Braer!" he cried but in an instant, the powerful beast disappeared in a shower of silver light.

Trayan clapped his hands above his head and the Bransar vanished.

"Walk with me," said Trayan.

"What did you think when you saw the Bransar?"

Daniel thought, then said, "The animal was unassuming, pitiful I think, I looked at Braer then at him and I laughed to myself, this will be easy, so I charged".

"Would you charge again if the two Brannai were matched once more," said Trayan. "No" said Daniel quietly.

"Then you have already begun to learn," he put his arm around the boys shoulder and led him back to the camp.

After a hot meal of Rabbit, stew and a good night's sleep Daniel awoke fresh and alive. Before breakfast, the boy went over to Trayan and in an excited mood he asked, "I should like to try again against the Bransar." So once again, the two Brannai faced each other.

"Braer, listen to me," said Daniel, "when you attack this time I want you to be ready for those roots, be agile when you run. Look for the roots and try to move away from them," The great Braer attacked again, this time he saw the roots as they came at him and he dodged them. Left and then right until he pounced and swiped at the beast with his great claw catching it across the head, and the small donkey toppled to the ground and then disappeared in a shower of silver light.

Braer stood on its hind legs and gave out a mighty roar and Daniel ran over and hugged the great beast. "Well done," said Trayan. "Now show me your Braer's strengths." The Braer had a mighty roar, which he could direct, bending small trees and branches in its wake. He had his great strength and powerful claws. When he charged nothing could stand in its way. "Let me show you something," said Trayan. He stood Braer and Daniel side by side "now concentrate," he said, "see that tree stump some ten paces away, I want both of you to think of standing next to it, concentrate very hard." All of a sudden, Braer disappeared and reappeared next to the stump, as he did so Daniel felt a weakness come over him and he went down on one knee. Braer came over to where the boy had been standing, "Are you alright, what is the matter." Trayan eased Daniel and Braer and said, "only when both Brannai and trainer are strong can you achieve such a fate, if you are not, the weaker will feel the effect," even so Trayan was proud of what the boy had achieved and he saw a special bond forming between them.

TORK

The following weeks where made up of hard training for Daniel and competition for the Brannai and his trainer. Trayan worked them hard, getting the boy to identify weakness and strengths in the animals he fought and of his own Braer. Both Daniel and the Brannai went from strength to strength and now and then, in between the training, you could catch the two of them walking through the wood, talking and playing. Sometimes Braer would let Daniel ride on his back, and Daniel would climb trees and throw fruit, which they would share under a tree. Altogether, Daniel thought that this was the best time of his life.

One clear night as he lay under the open sky he drifted off to sleep and dreamt of his mother and the smell of the baking of fresh bread as he would return on an errand to the farm, then her smiling face as they sat together and told stories of the events of that day.

It was time to move on, they packed their camp and Daniel and Braer said farewell, for they would not meet again until they reached another arena.

Trayan told Daniel that they would head north to the village of Tork where they would pick up some provisions. "Are there any arenas along the way?" asked Daniel, to which Trayan answered, "As far I am aware no, but an arena can sometimes appear were none have been before." He said that the Brannai and the arenas revolve to the magic of the land and if the need or balance dictates it then one will appear. "Is that what happened to me?" said Daniel, "yes," replied Trayan, "When I placed you in the care of your mother, there were no arenas in the area. Then, when I travelled down to see you because it was the sixteenth year, I felt the change in the air; it appears that the magic of the land dictated that you and your Brannai should meet earlier than expected." Trayan looked at the boy and thought to himself, the fates were taking a hand in the boy's life. He just hoped that it would not end the same way as his fathers.

They reached the village of Tork in good time and both Daniel and Trayan were in good spirits when they entered. Tork was a small village, though larger than Dantaal. It had the usual necessities that one of that size would have, a butchers, bakers and grocers and of course an inn where Daniel and Trayan decided to book in for the night. There were plenty of people around and quite a few of similar age to Daniel. Trayan decided to go for provisions, just the excuse the boy needed to set off and explore. It was a pleasant village and the people there were friendly, as were most people of the south of Arnorst. Daniel would politely say hello to people he passed and they would always answer back. The day was bright and warm as spring had arrived in earnest, there were buds on the trees and birds were preparing for the arrival of their new families.

Through the center of the town ran the river Lud, and as the weather was warm Daniel found that there were children swimming. They were jumping off the bank and seemed to be having a great time. He decided to himself that it looked a great idea and once he had stripped off to his breeches, he jumped in. Water held no fears for him for he was a strong swimmer, but when he entered, he found that it retained a touch of winter about it and he squealed in delight. He found the water refreshing and invigorating and it alerted all the senses in his body. Suddenly there was a great splash right next to him as someone jumped in. "bombs away," came the cry. When the person emerged, Daniel saw another boy of the same age as himself and the two started laughing. They splashed, played, and took turns jumping in and out of the water until, tired out they lay down on the bank.

"I'm Ben," said the boy, "Daniel," replied Daniel and the 2 exchanged stories. "Where you from," asked Ben.

"Dantaal," replied Daniel. "You are a long way from home."

"I am travelling with a friend, we are heading north."

"I love the water, don't you? "Ben appeared to ignore Daniels previous statement. Daniel agreed, before they both were interrupted by a call from nearby.

"Ben, mother says you are to come home it's time for dinner." Daniel and Ben turned their heads and there standing before them was a girl.

She was a pretty girl, Daniel thought, taller than him. (Although everybody his age was) with shoulder length brown hair and matching brown eyes and a clear complexion. Ben turned to Daniel, "this is my sister Emma, what's up sis." Emma replied but her gaze dwelled on Daniel.

"Mum says you are to come home for dinner."

"Would you like to come?" asked Ben as he turned and faced Daniel. Daniel thought it a great idea and agreed.

Ben's home was a modest stone house for the area although larger than Daniels was. It had two rooms downstairs, a kitchen and dining room, the latter of which was set with a le at one end. The le was plainly set for four with a large bowl of stew in the middle and freshly baked bread in a wicker basket beside it. Ben sat opposite his mother, who sat at the end of the le. She was a pretty woman with auburn hair and the faintest sprinkling of freckles on her pale skin.

Daniel sat opposite Ben's sister Emma. "Ben tells me you're from the south," said his mother. "What are you doing in Tork"? "Oh! I am just travelling north with my friend, we have just stopped here for provisions, this stew is great," he said as he as he tucked in to a bowl, happy to change the conversation and the pre-occupation Emma had with him. "I saw a mark on your shoulder," Emma said, "Strange, it looks like a paw, is it a birth mark."

"Err yes," replied Daniel, happy that Emma had already given him a reply. Nothing more of interest passed and the meal ended pleasantly. Finally, Daniel begged his leave and made the inn to meet up with Trayan.

TAITU

The following morning Daniel helped Trayan with the new provisions. For his endeavors he ended with the task of carrying them on his back, to build up the puny muscles in his legs, Trayan had told him. The two headed out of the town and headed along a dusty path used by travelers before them. As they walked they exchanged stories of their time in Tork, Daniel told of his meeting with Ben and of the dinner at his house.

The countryside was beautiful as they passed by, the grass was taking on the green of summer and flowers were starting to bud. Trayan decided to stop for a short break and so they sat down on the grass just off the path. They unpacked some coffee for Trayan and a snack of fruit and biscuits and took in the spring sunshine.

Then the peace shattered with the emergence of a figure in the distance heading their way. Trayan noticed it first and it was the fact the old man raised his hand to look, and cover the glare of the sun, that made Daniel turn his head and look as well. Slowly the figure came into view, "Emma! What are you doing here, is everything fine, Ben, your Mother?" Daniel looked worried.

"Everything's fine," said Emma, "it is always fine, fine and boring, that's why I'm here. I want to go with you, I know who you are and I want some adventure to, oh don't worry ive left a note explaining all, and anyway it's not the first time ive ran away."

Trayan stood and spoke in a stern voice, "That is not possible, were we are headed could be Dangerous, especially for you."

Emma immediately became agitated, "you mean for a girl, don't you, well let me tell you I am as good as any boy and I can prove it."

Daniel stood and spoke directly to Emma. "Look, you can't come were we are headed you have to be, well sort of special."

Emma grew furious, "you mean special like this," and she rolled up her sleeve to reveal a small paw print on her arm about the size of a penny. Trayan took his gaze away from the two teenagers and lifted his head slightly. He looked around at the fields and then he closed his eyes, he could feel a change in the air.

Daniel and Emma were now arguing and finally Emma shouted at Daniel, "right then let's see what you have got."

Daniel did not want to fight the girl but that was not what she had in mind. She took a few steps back from Daniel and closed her eyes. Unexpectedly a large monkey appeared next to Emma. It had dense black fur and powerful arms and the most piercing blue eyes. Both Emma and the ape stared hard at Daniel.

Daniel was taken aback by the whole episode, he took several steps backwards and then looked across at Trayan. Trayan gave him the slightest of nods and then stepped to the side to watch.

Daniel closed his eyes and summoned Braer. Daniel looked at his Braer and said, "Get ready to fight." The great beast gave a mighty roar and turned to face their opponents. Daniel turned to Braer and said, "Remember the Bransar, you must be ready for anything". "Braer replied, "I shall never forget", and with that he roared into an attack.

Emma looked to the monkey, "Taitu, get ready," and the Taitu replied, "I shall bring the lumbering beast down."

Taitu allowed Braer to run at him and when he was close, enough Braer swiped at the Taitu with its mighty claw. Taitu had anticipated the strike, had leapt high in the air, and as it rolled it gave a sharp blow with its hand and caught Braer on the side of the head, then landed gracefully on the floor. Braer swiped at the ape several times each time the animal simply moved out of the way. Daniel was watching and now he recalled Braer back to him. Daniel and Braer both faced their opponents again and Daniel noted smugness on Emma's face. He turned to Braer and said, "You know what to do."

"You are not strong enough", replied Braer, but Daniel was insistent and so once again Braer attacked.

He charged at Taitu, but when he was about ten paces away, he vanished and re appeared beside Taitu and he struck out with his paw.

Taitu had somehow sensed where Braer would be and had picked up a loose branch on the floor and had jumped and spun in the air bringing it down on Braer's head. Braer roared with the blow and struck out wildly with its claw, luckily catching Taitu across his chest.

Taitu stumbled back and Braer seized his chance and smashed the branch in its hand with one mighty bite. "Enough," shouted Trayan and stepped between the two adversaries. "You have both done well now ask your Brannai to leave."

He looked across at Daniel and Emma and calmed them both down. He called the two trainers over and sat them on the grass. "Twice the magic of this land has summoned an arena, once for Daniel and now for this girl. It seems that you are destined to join us, but know this, it has been your decision." Then he stood and beckoned them to follow. As they walked, Trayan looked to Emma and said, "Tell me how you knew an arena would appear."

"I didn't," she replied, "I was just angry and I wanted to prove myself." Daniel interrupted them, "how do you know when you are in an arena." Trayan turned to Daniel as they walked along the dusty path and said, "Well, here an arena just appeared but if you think back to the time in the wood when the wolf hunted you, you say you tripped when you were running, what made you trip?" Daniel thought for a moment then answered the old man. "I tripped on a branch," he said.

Trayan stopped walking and looked hard at the boy, "think back, what made you trip?" Daniel went back in his mind to the chase in the wood and the fright immediately built up in him. He pictured himself running through the trees clattering into branches along the way, and then suddenly he felt it, a small sharp pain in his stomach. He opened his eyes and with realization he looked at Trayan, "there was a pain in my stomach that is what made me trip," he said.

"What you felt was the crossing of the threshold, the boundary of the arena, all trainers can feel it," and with that he turned and walked on.

They turned and took a northwest heading, Trayan said he would like to stay in the south for a while and that it would give Emma and Daniel time to get to know one another. They walked for sometime through the meadows and fields of the south until they came across another arena, it was small and probably overlooked by most but it sought the purpose of branding Braer against Taitu for some friendly practice. Braer would cast his might and strength against the intelligence of Taitu and his uncanny ability to know where Braer would attack was a site to behold. The two Brannai became good friends during their battles, sometimes Braer would win, sometimes Taitu, but always the foursome would laugh and make up at the end.

During one such battle, in the arena at Mills Wash, a barren marshland were Seldom grew and few wild animals could be seen, Trayan sat on a mound of dry earth overlooking them, to ponder their tactics, when far off in the distance he noticed a glint on the land, it was there for an instant, and then it went. Probably the sun reflecting on a patch of water he thought, but then it happened again. He followed the sparkle on and off as it drifted across the horizon until it happened no more. He came down from the mound and called the two trainers to him. "It is time to break camp," he said. "I think we might head west to the town on Brien, we can pick up some more supplies there."

BRIEN

The trio of travelers set off once more and they reached the town of Brien within three days. Daniel knew why Trayan had called it a town, it was much larger than Dantaal and Tork and it bustled with life. It had a small harbor were a ship was moored and cargo was being unloaded by hoist and tackle. The workers on the quayside sang songs as they worked pulling and lifting the loads from overseas. The whole thing was breathtaking, Daniel had never even seen the sea, and the ship was a thing of pure beauty. To begin with, they stayed close to Trayan, trusting his judgment in this strange but exciting place, as they sought a place to stay. "This will do," said Trayan. "I've stayed here before, I know the landlady, Maggie, but be careful, she'll shower you with kindness."

As they entered a jolly, middle-aged woman, on the plumper side of life came to meet them. She recognized Trayan instantly and came running over.

"Trayan," I've not seen you in years, how are ya'?" and she gave him a great hug and kiss. "Who might this be? Not yours I hope," she said as she looked at the two teenagers. Daniel and Emma both fell instantly in love with the woman, "Come inside, I've got some hot stew on the stove, and you can tell me all about your travels." She helped Daniel off with his pack and they all sat down by a blazing fire. Trayan told of his travels through the land of Arnorst, and both Daniel and Emma listened intensely.

"You still playin' with those magical animals of yours?" said Maggie, "What they called Brunnies?" which sent Emma and Daniel into heaps of laughter. They finished telling stories and were well stocked up on helpings of the tasty stew and then after an hour or so Daniel and Emma decided to explore the town.

"Be careful!" called Trayan as they left the inn. After the children had left, Maggie brought over a tankard of ale and sat with Trayan. "So, why are you really here?" she asked. Nothing much missed old Maggie McKenzie and if you wanted to know anything about who's who, or what is new in town, she was the one to go and see, precisely why Trayan had come to the Ship inn in Brien.

"Tell me, have you noticed anyone new in town lately? Outsiders, particularly from the north?" asked Trayan.

 Maggie noted that she had not, but she had heard from other travelers of a few lone soldiers as far south as the river Godwen. "Why?" she said. "You're not in trouble are' ya?"

"No, not me, but the boy, he's the son of Phillip." Maggie grimaced and looked serious for the first time.

Daniel and Emma wandered through the streets looking through every shop along the way were they found a butchers with whole pigs hanging in the window and strings of sausages hanging around their necks. They went inside and found a small le in the corner, set for three with three little pigs stuffed and sitting in chairs, as if to eat dinner. Emma thought this hilarious, and the two laughed along with the owners. They said their farewells and moved on through the town. Daniel asked Emma to go back to the harbor so that he could look at the great ship.

There they listened to the men as they unloaded the ship and worked on the quayside. The whole town seemed alive with excitement and Daniel now saw why. He bent down and picked up a hand written poster that had dropped on the floor. "Look!" he pointed out to Emma, "It say's: Welcome to the Annual Brien festival! And look, a Brannai tournament for novice trainers." Emma looked to Daniel and the two of them ran excitedly back through the town to see Trayan.

Trayan was still at the inn when the two-rushed in. "A tournament, here!" cried Daniel, "and it says it's for novice trainers."

"Can we enter," They both said together.

"It is why I brought you here," answered Trayan, and he smiled at the two then added, "We have three days to prepare; the tournament is to be held at Boggs's Creek. We will be up early each morning to prepare, plus it will give you a chance to exercise your Brannai, and you will be able to see your competition."

The excitement was almost too much to bear when they woke the next morning. They came running down the stairs like a couple of excited schoolchildren on their last day of school. They sat down to a breakfast of porridge that Maggie had made for them, and they gorged it down in no time at all. Trayan on the other hand, sat and ate the porridge at a more distinguished pace. Maggie had already prepared them a packed lunch each placed in a wicker basket. "Come then," said Trayan as he stood and moved to the door, and the three said their goodbyes to Maggie and headed off to the edge of town.

They approached Boggs's Creek from over a hill and the first thing they noticed was the temporary stand that built by the town's joiners. It stood out on the east side of a roped off area surrounded by canvass flags mounted upon poles. The colors were bright and they shone in the spring sunshine.

Inside the arena, people were already gathering, there was a mixture of teenage boys and girls, and some a little older. There was a small section just before an opening in the rope, were four chairs placed alongside an old wooden table. Four elderly men sat at the table taking the names of the day's participants and their Brannai. Daniel and Emma both stepped up and signed their names, and then they passed through the opening in the rope. As they went through, both Daniel and Emma felt a small sharp pain in their stomachs as they crossed the threshold. Trayan told them that as they became stronger and more experienced, this pain would decrease in size.

"Such beautiful Brannai," exclaimed Emma and she immersed herself into a world of her own. All around, trainers had set up their own space, had summoned their own Brannai, and were starting to put them through their paces. There was such a variety of magical animals that Emma could not contain herself. "This is why I came." She immersed herself so much in the moment; she forgot to summon her Taitu as she walked around the arena looking at all the different animals. There was a wolf-life creature, silvery grey in color and with a white bushy tail, and she could not believe her eyes when its trainer put it through a test attack, and it split into two, running between trees as it charged.

Further, along, she noticed a beautiful bird perched on a tree stump, some paces away from where she was. It was about the size of a swan, with two extraordinary long tail feathers with what appeared to be flowers on the end. It was a truly beautiful bird standing there, stretching its pale blue wings out wide as though it was getting ready for its first flight.

Emma was aghast at the sights she was witnessing, suddenly she stopped and turned and noticed there in the distance, Daniel, she concentrated on the young man. He did not appear to take any notice of what was going on around him; instead, he was talking to Braer, directing him in his attacks and defenses, helping him with how to roll out of harm's way.

She noticed the dedication in the boy and the love he had for his Braer and she came to her senses about Taitu, which she now summoned c9mencing her own training. The training at the tournament went on for the next three days as Daniel continued extensive exercises on himself and his Braer. He would only stop to take instruction from Trayan, and then the morning of the tournament arrived.

They all came downstairs in good spirits and sat down to a breakfast of bacon, eggs and fresh bread prepared by Maggie. "Are you coming to watch," said Emma as she swallowed her last piece of bacon.

"Wouldn't miss it for the world," uttered Maggie "I've got tickets for the east stand next to Trayan."

Emma and Daniel both looked at Trayan and they both spoke together "Are you not going to be with us,"

Trayan replied, "No, as the other trainers you will be on your own, but know this you must trust your Brannai as they trust you."

All four finished their breakfast and headed out of the inn and into the streets. There was excitement at every corner, whole families with baskets full of packed lunches and children carrying carvings of their favorite Brannai were all heading in the same direction. The tournament planned for midday, and so as it was early they decided to stop off at the food market, decked out in flags and banners. There were rice's, chicken, spicy food and potatoes. So much choice, the people were there in numbers. There was cold ale for the men and fruit juices for the children; everyone seemed to be having fun. Even the shopkeepers had dressed up in their finest overalls and had set up displays in their shop windows.

At about 11 o'clock Trayan decided that they should head to the arena and prepare for the event. On the way, Maggie said it looked like the biggest tournament so far.
"Do you have this every year," asked Emma.
"No dear," replied Maggie "Every five, this is my eighth."
After that, she and Trayan left for the stands that left Emma and Daniel to head for the judges le and to sign their names. They were handed Their first opponents by an old judge who had graying hair, bald on top and yet tied with a pony behind his head. The man looked quite old to the children however when he spoke his voice sounded young and vibrant and he directed them to their respected waiting positions.

They were both separated and sent to a roped off waiting area. Two other boys a similar age to himself joined Daniel. He shook their hands and wished them good luck, and he meant it. One by one, the referee called them out, and Daniel could hear the roars of the bouts as they continued. Daniel was excited and yet he felt extremely confident, he could see the crowd raise and cheer when something happened and he could feel an inner calmness within himself. Soon he stood alone, until a small overweight judge with a baldhead and blushed face came up and told him to get ready as he was up next.
Daniel felt a pride rise inside him and he could feel alertness all over his body as he stepped through the rope onto the arena. Sided on the right was the east stand full of a packed and cheering crowd, in the centre was a clearing with a few bushes dotted about a patchy grassland. A wooded

area with dense pine trees stood to the left and about fifty paces away stood a boy.

He was facing upright and proud towards the crowds taking in all of their applause with his hands raised above his head in acknowledgement. The boy was taller than Daniel with thick wavy black hair, and a muscular physique.

A judge stepped forward dressed in fine garments and turned to face the stand. "Ladies and gentlemen" He shouted, and the crowd cheered instantly.

"On the left from the town of Dantaal we have, Daniel with his Braer, and on my right we have Joshua from Talek with his Kedra. Maggie looked to Trayan "What is a Kedra."

"A Kedra is a magnificent beast similar to a wolf yet larger in size, it has great speed and powerful jaws, one Kedra is a terrifying sight as it runs towards you, but it has a trick up its sleeve which you must prepare yourself for when the bout begins."

The judge then turned and faced the trainers "Gentlemen" He cried, "Summon your Brannai!" As the two beasts appeared the crowd, wooed, cheered, and small children who stood at the side sat on their fathers shoulders for a better view. "On the count of three you may begin."

Daniel looked at Braer "Be ready my friend,"

Braer looked back to Daniel and replied, "I am always ready."

One! Two! Three!
The Wolf set off and the ground churned high in the air as it sped off, and it made straight for the centre where Daniel was standing.

Braer let out a mighty roar and met the Kedra with a charge of his own. When the two adversaries where half distance something strange happened.

The wolf howled as it ran and then quite suddenly a mist formed around it, hiding its form and out of the mist shot a patch of bright light that dispersed the mist and from there shot two wolves, one took the left flank and the other took the right.

This made Braer stall but Daniel Immediately took charge.

"Braer" He cried,

"Face the one on the left and charge at him."

Braer did so and the wolf to the right closed in. However, Braer was swift and he reached the wolf on the left before its partner could help.

The wolf pounced high in the air.

Braer stood on its hind legs, roared and then gave a mighty swipe, catching the animal on the side of his head sending it reeling to the floor. Then he turned and faced its mate and roared, the force of the roar was such that it sent it the beast tumbling backwards.

The wolf rolled and when it stood up it cowered and whimpered like a common dog. Then it simply vanished in a shower of silver. The crowd cheered wildly and Daniel and Braer took it all in, round one was theirs.

Emma too had progressed to the next round. She had faced a flowertail, a large Swan like bird, which had soared overhead, its magnificent pale blue wings spread as wide as an eagle's. There had been a loud crack! In addition, the bird had snapped its tail like a whip releasing a shower of spores down to where Taitu had stood. Taitu had anticipated the attack and in the shower of spores that fell, he had quickly rolled and moved to the trees. It climbed up and out to one of the far branches as the great bird turned in its flight. Taitu had then bent one of the branches and when the bird had flew past it released the branch smashing it in its side causing it to crash to the ground where it disappeared in a shower of silver.

The two friends fought twice more, each defeating their opponents, until in the early evening of that spring day; they faced each other in the final of the tournament, outside the town of Brien.

Braer stood to one side of the area, powerful, strong and majestic. On the other was Taitu, focused yet intelligent and sublime. The trainers stood either end of the great arena. Daniel, contemplated the battle ahead, and yet he felt quietly confident as his Braer simply stood, silently beside him.

Emma had tied her hair back in a pony and had rolled her sleeves three quarters of the way up her arm. She stood nervously next to her Taitu and felt the butterflies in her stomach. The crowd shouted and cheered as the old judge with the ponytail appeared on a rostrum. He raised both his arms aloft and waved them down to quell the noise of the crowd. Then he took a loudspeaker and introduced the final event of the day.

"Today we have seen a great tournament, with excellent young trainers and magnificent Brannai; all the battles have now led us to this moment." The crowd cheered and hats thrown prematurely into the air.

"We have seen the next generation of champions, right here in Brien, and without any further ado I give you your finalists."

Trayan looked across to Maggie, "this should be good, they know each other very well but who of the two can hold their nerve."

The other participants of the day sat in the front row of the stand and they all clapped along with the rest of the crowd. Daniel remained through the announcement and his Braer raised its nose to the air and sniffed, trying to get the scent of Taitu. Emma on the other hand became fidgety and Taitu started to look around at the crowd.

Then the judge introduced the two finalists. "From the town of Dantaal I give you Daniel and his Braer."Once again, the cheering went up.

"And From the town of Tork I give you Emma and her Taitu." The cheering went on for several minutes until the judge quelled their enthusiasm and turned to face the two teenagers.

"Trainers, he shouted, on the count of three.

"One,"

Daniel pictured in his mind the battles that had taken place between Braer and Taitu.

"Two!"

He could see how Taitu was always ready for his attacks.

"Three!" He looked to Braer and spoke softly to him. Braer stood on his hind legs and let out a mighty roar. Emma looked at Taitu and they both held ready for Braer's attack.
Only, Braer did not attack. It simply went onto all fours and stalked Taitu from side to side, giving a glance to its rival every now and then. The crowd were quiet and Trayan leaned back in his chair and smiled.

Emma raised her head and looked over at Daniel who did not move, nor did he change his blank expression. She was utterly confused and it showed in Taitu, who began to shout and jump up and down in panic.

"If his Brannai is scared mine is not," she shouted out, and she ordered Taitu to attack. The great ape beat its chest and charged letting out an almighty roar as it did so.

Braer stood on its hind legs but did not move forward. Taitu was wild and it shook its head from side to side, as it ran at the mighty Braer. When the ape was about ten paces away, Braer vanished and re-appeared in front of Taitu. There it took a great swipe with its giant paw catching Taitu across the head, sending it reeling sideward, were it rolled to the floor. Braer quickly followed up and attacked the monkey with a series of strikes from his two front paws, until the fight was over and Taitu vanished in a shower of silver light.

The crowd went wild with emotion shouting and stamping their feet on the wooden decks. Trayan and Maggie both stood and clapped loudly, joining in with the celebrations.

The ceremony for the champions was held shortly afterwards. The podium dressed in a banner depicting the town of Brien, represented by a coat of arms consisting of a green shield crossed by silver and the words of the town's motto in Latin. There where flagsticks in each corner decorated in bright fabrics and as is tradition in Brien, victory a wreath hung on hooks from the wooden supports.

Daniel, Emma and another girl by the name of Becky, from Brien, climbed the short set of stairs to rapturous applause from the crowd and introduced one at a time in reverse order. When the judge, who was dressed in his finest robes of green and silver called out third place, the home reception was deafening.

Then Emma climbed the steps to warm applause and finally Daniel, who had the Reith placed on his head by the judge and a purse of silver placed in his hands.

There was so much celebration and cheering that no one noticed the lone figure of a man at the side of the stands. He was dressed in a long travelling cloak, dark in color with patches of mud splattered around the hem. The hood was raised but beneath it you could make out the hard, rugged face of an assassin.

A LUCKY ESCAPE

After the ceremony, the crowd dispersed quickly and orderly, Daniel and Emma both met up with Trayan and Maggie and together they headed back to the inn. Trayan was quick to praise Emma for reaching the final and was pleased with Daniel as well. "That was a clever ploy of yours, to wait for Taitu to attack first then to make your own move," he told Daniel.

"Well I was not sure whether it would work, but every time we attacked him before, he was always ready for us, so I thought maybe he could not know what we were doing if he was too busy with his own attack."

Emma moved towards Daniel and spoke directly at him for the first time since the final. "You are going to become a great trainer; you beat us fair and square." Then she held out her hand in friendship. Daniel ignored her hand and gave Emma a great hug.

Maggie set out a table full of food to help celebrate the day's events. A large pan of her famous stew and a basket either end of the table full of hot bread. She also set out some cold meats and a cheese board, complimented with a tankard of ale for Trayan and homemade lemonade for the two victors. The party and the stories went on for several hours into the evening, until they all became tired and went to bed.

The children were late out of bed the following morning and when they came down the stairs Trayan and Maggie were already at the le enjoying a breakfast of bacon and eggs.

Daniel and Emma were both in high spirits, Daniel for his victory but Emma also, for she felt she had done well reaching the final, a fact reiterated by Trayan who said she had done her and Taitu proud. After the meal Trayan told Maggie that they would be leaving that morning, he said they were going to head east and try to pick up the river Lud then head north and cross the Godwen at Briers Bridge. The two teenagers were sad to be leaving Maggie for she had been a great host and they had fallen in love with her personality, not to mention her cooking. The farewells were said and an abundance of hugs given out, especially from Maggie.

They left the town of Brien behind them but the memories had planted firmly in their memories. They did not take the main road out of Brien instead Trayan took them through the countryside, passing through rolling hills of green grass dotted with the blooms of spring and it was well into the evening when the weather finally broke and the heavens opened up.

Trayan found a small wood and set up tent in a small clearing near its center. The camp was a modest affair, two tents, one for Trayan and Daniel and the other for Emma. They built them around two fallen trees that had decayed but made excellent benches, with a fire in the middle. Trayan had set a tripod above the flames with a pot of boiling water on the go. It amazed Daniel how, even in the rain, Trayan could manage to find dry tinder. Around the camp, there was a thin scattering of trees, now thick with the leaves of summer, providing shelter from the worst of the rain. In-between the trees were thick bushes giving excellent cover against the winds. There would be no hot meal that evening, the rain was too heavy and so cold meat and bread washed down with a mug of hot tea was the order of the day.

The fire was kept burning through the evening, its glow became a comforting feature. Trayan told Daniel and Emma that they would stay there until the weather broke; they were as he put it, in no hurry. They sat through that evening in their tents. The doors pulled open, telling stories to each other about the tournament in Brien. You could not get a word in edgeways when Emma started talking about all the wondrous Brannai she had seen.

"Did you see that Vior how gorgeous was he, or she for all I know and that Gostyre what speed." ("How anyone could say a giant Bat was gorgeous was beyond him thought Daniel.")She would have talked none stop, all night if Daniel had not interrupted her. "Will we head for another town," he said sharply to Trayan.

"If you mean another tournament, then no," replied Trayan, "you both need to train, to grow stronger for your next opponents."

Daniel looked to Trayan, "does that mean we will be fighting better trainers."

Trayan took a sip of tea, "maybe, let's take one step at a time." The rain came down even heavier and they decided to close their tents and settle down for the night. Emma wrapped herself tightly in a blanket and listened to the rain pattering on the canvass until peacefully she drifted off to sleep.

Morning came with broken rays of sunshine dancing through the leaves of the trees and reaching through the gaps left in the tent doorways. Trayan was up first, as he always was and was out tending to the fire and looking around for some dry wood. "Is there anything I can help with," asked Daniel.

Trayan looked at the boy and gave him the task of stripping the wet bark off branches to use as firewood, while he tried to light a fire and maybe start some breakfast.

On the edge of the small wood a rider approached, he came unheard and unnoticed using the nightlight and the heavy rain as cover. He dismounted and loosely tied his horse to a branch using a tried and tested quick release knot. He was soaked through to the bone, a predicament he was used to and did not mind, what was more important was the target and he knew exactly where that was. The horse was silent as the rider reached for his weapon of choice, the crossbow; he lowered his hood and headed for camp.

Trayan had managed to start a fire and had already boiled the water for some tea. Emma woke up to the smell of bacon and was soon dressed and now she headed out for breakfast.

"Good morning, nice of you to join us." Trayan smiled, as he continued cooking the bacon, he knew it was the one thing that would tempt Emma out of her warm bed. Trayan was kneeling over the fire and he now looked up at the skies, "looks like it is going to be a nice day."

Before Emma could sit and enjoy breakfast, she had the chore of hanging out the wet clothes.

Finally, they all sat down and enjoyed freshly cooked bacon and bread rolls accompanied with a mug of hot tea. Emma started to talk about the Brien tournament and the wonderful Brannai, but Daniel straight away raised his hands over his ears and cried out "no more, please, no more, I cannot take any more descriptions of your wonderful Brannai."

Emma looked shocked at her friend's outburst and was about to stand up and say something when both Daniel and Trayan started to laugh aloud. She turned to the old man, then back to Daniel and laughed along with them.

She approached Daniel, who now stood up and held out his hands in front, to fend her off.

"You," she said and she managed to get close to him and gave him a gentle push.

Daniel was laughing so loud that when she pushed him he lost his footing and tripped stumbling backwards.

Suddenly there was a loud thud and an arrow embedded itself in a tree right were Daniel had stood.

Trayan was first to react, he turned his head and immediately looked at the arrow embedded in the tree, and then he worked out the direction from where it came. "DOWN, NOW," he screamed, and directed the pair behind a fallen log, which would give them the most protection. They did not need telling twice, just in time, as they fell on the floor, another arrow stuck itself in the log that they had just dived behind. Trayan ran to his pack and took out his bow; quickly he knocked an arrow on the string and took up a position behind a tree, facing the direction of this new threat.

"Keep your heads down," he shouted to Daniel and Emma. He was not a soldier but he was also not afraid of anyone and he was a dammed good shot with a bow.

Trayan noticed that the arrow had come from a crossbow, the weapon of a soldier. He looked to the trees in the distance and could make out movement, not from a person but from the branches and leaves.

The person had fled. Trayan looked to the two children. "Daniel, Emma, I want you to stay down and do not follow." He set off after the assassin. He kept his bow held high and an arrow knocked as he ran, looking ahead for signs of the path taken by this soldier. He ran, but was cautious as he did so, stooping to miss low branches as he went. Then he heard hooves, just ahead. He came out of the trees and into the open just in time to see a lone figure on a horse disappear over a hill.

When Trayan returned to the camp he found Emma still behind the fallen log, but Daniel was up at the edge of the clearing, on watch. "Has he gone, who was he?" said Emma in a very frightened voice.

"I am not sure," replied Trayan and he went to the bolt that was stuck in the tree. He pulled it out and looked it over.

"Why was he shooting at us," said Daniel.

"I do not think he was shooting at us, I think he was shooting at you. I believe he was a soldier and I also think he will be in the pay of Torek." Daniel looked at Trayan, "The same Torek who killed my father." "I believe so," replied Trayan and he sat down on the fallen log.

"When your father fought him, Torek was undefeated, lord of all the lands and a king amongst the Brannai trainers. He could not live with the fact that a commoner had defeated him, and now, I believe he does not want you to grow into that same powerful figure.

Brannai

Daniel sat down on the log next to his friend and looked over at him as he said, "I think I would like to become that powerful figure, for my father."

Trayan put an arm around the boy and hugged him, then scuffed Daniels hair and prepared to break camp. "We will head for the Regal Mountains, there is someone there I think you should meet."

Brannai

VOICES IN THE BAY

They broke camp and headed north, keeping away from any paths or roads. The pace they now kept was a little sharper and for the first hour or so, the three friends kept their eyes on the horizon. After a short while Emma spoke up, "who is it we are going to see and how far are these mountains."

Trayan did not take his eyes off the path ahead when he answered. "The man's name is Thomas and he was the old king's man at arms and a good friend, as far as the mountains are concerned we should be there in about ten days."

"Could we not buy some horses," asked Emma.

Trayan looked annoyed as he answered, "Horses have enough burdens without carrying the likes of us around," and he quickened the pace as though it was a punishment. Daniel and Emma both looked at each other and said nothing but hurried along in silence.

The land around them was beginning to fill with all the sounds and sights of an early summer. Beautiful rolling hills full of green grass and new blooms were all around them as they passed through the southern region of Arnorst. There were buzzard's overhead, circling, looking for a rabbit or vole and the skies were a clear blue with the odd fluffy white cloud drifting along.

The trio travelled the land looking out for any farms, were the owners would offer lodgings, and they would stay in the out buildings for safety. When they did not come across any dwellings, Trayan looked to the woods for protection against any prying eyes. Slowly the great mountains came into view, their snow covered peaks reaching to the heavens and jutting into the clouds.

Trayan deliberately picked a path that took in no arenas; he wanted to avoid any delays in reaching his friend Thomas.

After the fourth days travel, they came to the southern edge of Lake Tey, a vast expanse of fresh water just south of the Regal Mountains. The fish eagles replaced Buzzards and water birds, such as ducks, waders and gulls.

The area around the southern coastline brimmed with small coves and outcrops of rocky hills and it was at one of these coves that they decided to set up camp for the evening.

It was a lovely sight to see the gentle waves wash ashore and hear the gulls overhead. If Trayan did not know, better he would swear he was at the edge of the great sea. They set up the two tents away from the water's edge, on the grass surrounded by low hills and the area felt protected against the elements.

The mood in the camp was melancholy; it had been four days since the attack in the wood. Trayan set them a firm pace and was always vigilant to the surrounding lands, looking for travelers and strangers. Daniel missed Braer, the warmth of his fur and the great strength that flowed through him whenever he was near. Emma too, missed her Brannai, she was expecting more contact with the magical beasts than she was experiencing right now.

Trayan set out the camp for the evening and insisted on a small fire, you never know who is watching he had said and we must keep, he was about to say vigilant but both Daniel and Emma said it aloud for him. This small outburst seemed to break the tension that had built up between Trayan and the children since the events in the wood and they all laughed and settled down to their evening meal. The scene was very relaxing, sat around the flames of the fire with the small waves lapping the shore.

"How long until we reach the Mountains," said Emma as she sipped a hot cup of tea?

"It should take four more days travel although our journey will take us along the coastline for some miles and we may take in some fishing." For Trayan it had been a long time since he had cut the two children some slack and he believed it was about time they had some rest and play. The three travelers retired early, ready for an early start and Emma and Daniel went to sleep happier than of late.

Daniel woke up in the very early hours of the morning as Trayan shook him in his bed, and his finger was over his lips, suggesting silence. Once up, they went to Emma's tent and ushered her out of her slumber in the same way. Trayan beckoned them out of the camp and had them follow him a short way up the coast. They came to a small hill and Trayan crawled to the top and looked back. He put his finger to his lips and beckoned Daniel and Emma up, but waved them to keep low.

At the top of the hill, they peered over and watched silently as below them sat three soldiers sitting around a blazing fire. They could make out the three figures clearly. One of the men was short but very broad; he had a beard and a baldhead. The other two were similar in height and stature you could almost make them out to be kin. One man, who bent low over the fire, was a little thinner than the other of similar height and had long scraggy hair, however, it was the third, dressed in a long cloak with the hood down around his shoulders that appeared to do all the talking.

Hills surrounded the small cove, making a natural amphitheater and the voices of the three soldiers carried clearly to the trio on the hill.

The person sat bent over the fire asked, "What does lord Torek want with the boy." The other, dressed in the long cloak, answered. "I am not privy to that sort of information; all I know is that he will pay highly for the boy."

"What of the others "asked the smaller as he spat into the fire.

The soldier in the cloak looked up from the flames; his face tormented by the heat as he said, in a low and definite tone. "The old man is to be killed, the girl, he has other plans for her."

Trayan tapped Daniel and Emma on the shoulders and brought them down the hill, then led them back to camp. They quietly gathered up their belongings without anyone saying a word, then packed away the tents and headed north along the banks of the great lake.

They walked a few miles keeping the lake on their right and the further north they went the more uneven the ground became.

"Will this Thomas be able to help us?"Asked Daniel, and the tone in his voice suggested he was concerned.

"I am hoping he will be able to help you," replied Trayan and he scuffed Daniels hair.

The sun was high in the sky by midday and from their raised position on the hills, the views were breathtaking across the lake and the surrounding countryside. If they looked north the Regal Mountains with their snow, peaked tops became clearer and set against the tranquil waters of Lake Tey they were a magnificent sight.

Trayan was looking for something, the children could tell, and then as they rounded a jut of headland, he stopped. "This is it, there is a cave just over that rise," and he pointed to a section of rocky outcrop some three hundred meters away. The cave was small but Trayan decided it would keep them from prying eyes. There was enough room for all of them but not the tents and so they made beds on the rocky floor. Daniel looked around, it was quite dry and once the fire lit and the blankets laid out, it felt I little like a home. Trayan cut some nearby branches and placed them at the entrance to hide the glow of the fire.

They felt at ease for the first time since early that morning and they enjoyed an evening meal and some hot tea before settling down for the night. Daniel lay on his back looking up at the cave roof and watched the shadows cast by the fire Dancing on the surface of the rocks. He could not help but think of the soldier at the cove and his words lingered in his mind, kill the old man- plans for the girl, until he drifted off to sleep.
Emma was the first of the children to wake and as she turned in her bed, she saw Trayan sitting by the entrance, looking into the distance. She got

up and went to sit next to the old man. Trayan looked at her and put a fatherly arm around her shoulder and she laid her head on his arm.

Trayan spoke softly "If you look you can see the mountains and to the right, there is a path that will take us through the peaks and into a valley."

"How long," enquired Emma in a very wary tone.

"Two days, no more," said Trayan and he was true to his word.

THOMAS SHERIDAN

The journey had been long and hard but finally they came to the foot of the mountains. Daniel and Emma both looked up at the peaks above them and wondered at their power and size. Trees covered the land around the mountains, mostly pine, alive with life. Squirrels were busy climbing the trunks and all around there were different birdcalls echoing through the branches. Trayan led them upwards along old paths long forgotten by men and through breaks in the crags only goats would know. They seemed to climb forever with no end to the rocky sides, onwards and upwards they went until they came upon a break in the terrain. Suddenly as if from no-where, the land opened up beneath them.

There below lay an unspoilt valley, beautiful and green with a small river, moving like a serpent down its center. They began their decent and wondered at the green rolling hills in the middle of such majestic peaks. After a while, Trayan pointed out a small house built close to the river, it was there that the trio now headed.

They approached the house slowly and in full view and when they were near to the entrance, an arrow that fell some five paces from their feet, stopping them. Trayan raised his arms and asked Daniel and Emma not to worry. "It is just his welcome, "he told them, and then he stopped and stood still. Emma and Daniel looked around and there from over a small mound in the land strode a man. He looked a little older than Trayan but was heavy built, tall with stout legs and large powerful arms, the sort you would find on farmers who had spent their days in the fields. When he drew near, Emma noticed he was completely bald and was holding a bow with an arrow knocked on its string.

Finally, the man came close enough into view to see his face. He was rough, battle hardened with a scar on the left side of his forehead but as soon as he noticed Trayan, he gave out a hearty laugh that bellowed around the valley. "Trayan, my old friend, after all these years," then the two hugged like lost brothers.

"Are you not going to introduce me," said Thomas. Trayan placed an arm around Emma, "She is a fine trainer and her name is Emma." "She's a pretty one too," acknowledged Thomas, to which Emma blushed. Trayan then turned to Daniel, "This is Philips son, Daniel," to which Thomas went suddenly serious. "Then you must be in trouble, come inside and we will talk."

The house was of basic construction built for convenience and not luxury. Inside there was a fireplace with a blazing fire on the go, the walls were plain and decorated with crossbows and swords. Hanging on one wall, were a pair of large axes that looked too large to lift and by the fire stood a hand built rocking chair. Once inside Trayan and Thomas sat at the small hand built wooden table and left Daniel and Emma to warm each other by the fire.

"Tell me how I can be of service," asked Thomas.

Trayan told of the attack in the wood and of the meeting with the three soldiers at Lake Tey. "You know the history between Philip and Lord Torek; I believe he does not want the boy to grow as powerful as his father."

Thomas sat back in his chair, "why don't you just take the boy away?" he said, unconvincingly.

Trayan cut straight back, "you know he would track the boy down sooner or later, no, I must train him in the art of the Brannai, however I cannot train him properly to defend himself."

"That is where I come in." Thomas looked hard at Trayan, then stood at went around the table to stand in front of him.

"My friend, the pleasure will be all mine, anything to help bring that charlatan down." Then he grabbed Trayan in a great bear hug.

Daniel and Emma were watching through the whole conversation and now they looked at each other and smiled.

The evening passed off with a good meal of rabbit stew provided for by the very proud Thomas. Daniel and Emma were entertained all evening with stories of war and honor supplied raucously by the exuberant Thomas until late into the evening when they all retired for bed.

The following morning brought bright sunshine and the rays bounced in through the wooden windows. It was a beautiful late spring day in the picturesque hidden valley. Thomas and Trayan were already sitting at the table enjoying tea and bread when Daniel and Emma joined them. "Trayan tells me you two are trainers; tell me what are your beasts."
Daniel told Thomas that his was a Braer and Emma followed by naming Taitu. "A Taitu," exclaimed Thomas, "that was Philips Brannai, powerful beast he was, stood nearly fifteen feet tall. Scared the crap out of me he did, when it beat its chest it sounded like thunder." This started Daniel and Emma laughing, for how could such a man as Thomas be scared of Brannai.

Thomas looked at Trayan, "have you told them." Both Daniel and Emma looked to Trayan with excited smiles on their faces and Trayan answered their queries. "Just upstream, to the far end of the valley, lies an arena."

Daniel and Emma could not hide their excitement and they whooped and laughed, for they had not seen their friends Braer and Taitu for many days. Trayan interrupted their shouts with a calm and assertive voice. "I will be taking Emma this morning, we will travel to the arena but Daniel will remain here with Thomas, he has much work to do."

Trayan left later that morning with Emma and that left Daniel with Thomas. "Come," said Thomas, "let us see what you are made of."
He took Daniel to a level patch of grass by the water's edge. "You will have to learn to use a sword, I can teach you the moves, but you will find it hard to master a real one until you gain some height and strength." With that, he produced two wooden ones, ideal for maneuverability, but ones that would still hurt if they caught you on the fingers or head. Thomas taught Daniel basic defensive moves to begin with, parry, block and then, the just do not be there maneuver where you roll under a blade swiped wildly at your head.

Daniel became an enthusiastic and quick learner, only struggling when Thomas gave him a real sword, the weight of which showed him for what he was, small for his age. Thomas fashioned him a bow, smaller and less powerful than a normal one, but one the boy could handle. However, he could not do the same with the sword. He simply did not have the resources.

Daniel knew the moves but the weight made him slow. However, in both weapons the boy began to excel under the guidance of Thomas.

Thomas gave Daniel daily exercises designed to build up his arms and legs and after two weeks, both Trayan and Thomas agreed that the boy was progressing nicely. It was now that Trayan decided to give Daniel a break and all four set off one fine morning for the arena.

They travelled along the edge of the mountain stream following its winding path as it made its way through the trees and hills. Towards the end of the valley, they came upon a clearing where the trees lined an area around a flat section of grassy land. Daniel and Emma felt the sharp pain in their stomachs as they came through the trees into the open space and they smiled.

Daniel was first to summon his Braer as Trayan and Thomas sat down on a grassy mound. Braer could sense the newfound confidence in the boy and he stood before him and gently bowed. Daniel simply ran and hugged the great beast around the waist. Trayan and Thomas watched as Daniel and Emma walked side by side talking and playing with their friends.

"He has a fine animal, strong and powerful, and yet it seems strange to me that the Taitu is with Emma and not the boy," Remarked Thomas. "They do not choose their Brannai my friend, it is the Brannai who choose them and those two are made for each other."

"What of the girl," asked Thomas?

"Emma? She too will be a fine trainer but her destiny lies down a different road," and Trayan simply smiled at his friend.

That evening they all sat around the le to enjoy a supper of roasted deer and the last of Thomas's ale, warmed by the glow of a blazing fire. Emma brought up the question as she looked over at Thomas. "You have a great life here; the valley has everything, beautiful trees, animals and seclusion from the world beyond. Do you intend to spend the rest of your days here?"

Thomas looked up from his meal and then wiped his mouth with a cloth. "I have seen many battles and have led a full and exciting life. This, valley, gives me the peace and tranquility I have searched for since the death of the old King and yes, I think I will see out my days here."

Trayan looked at his old friend with a pride inside him. "We will not keep you from it, my friend." He said, "How long before the boy will be ready."

Thomas simply stated, "He is ready, I can do no more he just needs time to grow and to strengthen," and then he reached across, touched Daniel on the shoulder, and smiled. Trayan sat back in his chair, "we leave tomorrow."

The following day Trayan, Daniel and Emma packed their belongings and met outside the house. They all said there farewells and made to leave but Thomas stopped them.

"Wait," he shouted and he turned and ran inside. When he came out he was carrying a sword and now he presented it to Daniel. "When you can wield it you will know you have grown into the body of a man, use it wisely," and Daniel put it in his pack with his bow and shook the hands of his friend. Thomas looked to Trayan, "where will you go."

"I think we might head east to the border town of Doran, they hold a tournament this time of year and it is time we were back on track."

DORAN

They all left and headed out of the valley and back along the old track that passed through the mountain peaks. The warmth of the valley was replaced by the chill of the high mountains and they had to wrap up warm at least until they reached the lower slopes were the bare rock was replaced by woodland. There the heat of the sun returned to them and so did the beauty of the late spring.

The land was thick with fir trees, fresh grass and all around animals were preparing for the trials of summer, and birdsong was alive in the air.
It was here that they sat and talked. Trayan showed Daniel and Emma pictures he had drew over the years, pictures of Brannai, with listings of their strengths and attacks. Daniel studied them closely trying to memorize each one and Emma could not believe the quality of the drawings that the old man had produced.

She looked at the old man in awe and asked, "How did you become a trainer."

Trayan did not look at all put out by the question and he answered in a calm voice. "For me, I think it was in me from an early age. When I was young I could summon them, from dreams they would talk to me always inviting me to see them. It was not until I was about twelve years old that I realized they were a part of the land, something to be cherished and not to be owned," and he smiled over at the girl.

They set off once more and it was not long before the encountered a river.

"This has made its way down from the mountains and is full of the finest trout in the land."As Trayan spoke, he went searching the nearby trees and soon returned with three cut down branches. "At lake Tey I promised you some fishing, we were, distracted then. Now, take these and find a spot for yourselves."

He handed them some line and hooks that he had fashioned when they were in the valley visiting Thomas.

Daniel found himself a spot on a rock that jutted out in the running water, while Emma sat on the bank downstream from Daniel and cast her bait of bread into the river under an overhanging willow tree.

Trayan had set his line up on a makeshift tripod and had lain down on the grass and there he lit up an old pipe. For several hours, they sat and enjoyed the warm sun and the tranquil surroundings, after which time Trayan set up a fire to cook their catch. They each returned to show what they had caught. Trayan threw down two fat shiny fish and smiled as he did so. Daniel threw down his rod and said the whole thing had been a waste of time, to which Trayan and Emma both laughed aloud.

"I'll bet you did not do much better." Said Daniel, to which Emma threw down three large and shiny silvery fish. Trayan laughed even louder than before and Daniel turned away.

They set up their tents and enjoyed a fish supper, a meal they all cherished for there is none finer than the one you have caught yourself. That evening they slept under the stars and felt the warmth of the early summer.

They set off the next day and followed the path or the river for several miles until they parted ways, the river headed south and the party went east to the town of Doran.

Doran in many ways was similar to Brien except being inland it had no harbor. However, the approach to the town teamed with travelers. People who had come solely for the upcoming festival and the town were ready for them.

There was a placard, placed at the town's main entrance proclaiming, the festival of Doran and the holding of the twenty fifth-anniversary Brannai tournament.

There were canvas flags and banners across every street stretching from house to house and Daniel and Emma beamed at the excitement. Trayan placed his arms around both of them, "next to Kingdale, this is one of the biggest tournaments in the land. There are different levels and trainers come from far and wide to test their skills."

"Does that mean we will fight at another level? "In addition, Daniel looked excited as he spoke.

"Although you have done very well so far, you are still only sixteen and as such are still a novice and must carry on learning and gaining experience."

They stopped at an old wooden building, two stories high with great wooden beams rising from the floor up to the windows and then across to the roof. There was also a hand painted wooden sign hanging from the front, of a large green frog standing upright holding a walking stick.

"Here we are, the Crooked Frog, finest Inn in town," and Trayan led them through the front door. Arthur, the proprietor, met them straight away. He was a short, portly sort of fellow with hair only at the sides and back but he had a bright and jolly face and a plump demeanor.

"Here for the festival or the tournament," he said in a very upbeat and happy sort of voice.

Daniel answered enthusiastically, "The tournament of course, we are trainers."

Arthur turned and shouted to someone inside the inn. "Hey, Bessie we've got two more."

Out of the back came a short, portly sort of woman the double of Arthur only with short black curly hair. She beamed a huge smile in their direction, "is that right, well you are the third. There is another staying here with you, full of himself he is. You will no doubt meet him later, reckons he is going to win the whole thing. Dinners in half an hour," she added before heading back inside.

Daniel and Trayan booked into one room high in the attic, while Emma had a room to herself. Daniel went to the window to look outside. The streets were busy with people going back and forth and the houses opposite decked out in banners and flags. Down the street and up to the left Daniel could just make out the flags on the top of the stand around the arena and he pointed them out to Trayan.

Emma on the other hand had a first floor single room and she was delighted with it. She had her own wardrobe and side le with a mirror on top. Her bed sat in a thick quilt, stitched in different colored squares and she flopped up and down on it several times.

Later they all met in the dining room for the evening meal. The table set for eight people, decked out in a beautiful chequered tablecloth. There was a vase of flowers in the center of the table and breadbaskets at either end.

Daniel and Trayan sat together at one end of the table and Emma sat opposite Daniel. One by one the other guests came down, a married couple from a village to the south of Doran and two young people a little older than Daniel and from the town of Brien itself. They all took their seats and it left just one empty chair at the head of the le next to Emma.

Then the final guest came skipping down the stairs and entered the dining room. He was a tall, thin lad about the same age as Daniel. His jet-black hair combed neatly into a side part and his pale skin made him look unwell. What was unusual about him was the way he held himself. His nose was long and pointed, he held it at an upturned angle, and he spoke in a very posh upper class voice.

He went and sat at the final spare chair. "Colin, Colin Parkes," he said and he looked straight at Emma. "From Pallet Copse just outside of Bedding, where all the finest trainers come from and of course I include myself in that statement." "I might add," he continued, "that you are looking at the next tournament champion, novice, but not for long, my Bransar and I are quite unbeatable." Emma was speechless.

Colin then added, "And you are." Emma cleared her throat and gave out her name as politely as she could. Colin then looked across at Daniel. "I see you are here with your father, come to watch have we, well I can tell you, you are in for a real treat, my tactics are second to none."

Just then, Bessie came in carrying a large bowl of freshly made stew and she sat it down in the center of the le.

"Ah," said Colin, "at last, help ourselves shall we?" In addition, he picked up a ladle and waded into the stew. "No time to be shy," he added, to nobody in particular.

The meal passed quickly with no one able to get a word in edgeways and Daniel, Emma and Trayan were relieved when they were able to leave. They made their way over to the large fire with mugs of hot chocolate.

"Come on dad." Said Daniel to Trayan, who tried to cuff the boy around the head but missed because Daniel had ducked. Daniel and Emma laughed and Trayan soon joined in.

"Can you believe him," said Emma in astonishment, "he is so full of himself, I just want to." However, she could not finish her sentence through pure frustration. Colin was the attention of the conversation for the rest of the evening until after some hours and another hot chocolate they finally retired to bed.

The following morning greeted them with bright sunshine that put a spring in the step of the already happy Arthur and Bessie. The pair sang together as they prepared the morning breakfast and their happy mood was infectious. All of the guests seemed to have a smile on their faces, that is, except Colin. He just picked up a slice of toast and a quick glass of fresh juice before he decided he had to go and prepare for his upcoming victories.

Daniel, Emma and Trayan on the other hand sat down at the le and enjoyed some wonderful scrambled eggs, bacon and toast. After such a hearty breakfast, Trayan decided it would be a good idea to go and register with the judges.

They set off through the town, passing shops with highly decorated windows showing off their wares and then they passed through the market place, which at that time of the early morning only filled with the owners preparing for the day ahead. Finally, they arrived at the arena, what a site it was.

It sat on the edge of the town in a dip in the land, surrounded by natural hilly viewpoints. On one side, nearest to the town was the main stand with canvass flags posted on the top seats and already there were people gathering. The arena itself was a mixture of grassland and tall fir trees. Dotted around the trees were large boulders that looked as though someone had individually placed them there.

The judge's area was next to the main stand and it was here that the trio now headed.

There were three judges sat at a long oak le, two men and a woman. The two men were brothers and had the same thick wavy red hair and pale complexions, but when they stood, there was a difference in height.

However, the woman beckoned them forward. She was a slim, late middle-aged woman with mousy colored hair and a very stern look about her. As soon as Daniel and Emma approached the table, she spoke. "Can I have your names and your Brannai?" Daniel and Emma both gave their names.

"Can I also have your ages and category," the woman added, to which they both said sixteen and novice. "Practice is at ten o'clock tomorrow and the heats begin the following day, thank you."

Trayan smiled at the pair and beckoned them to the side. "Well," he said, "the heats for the level two trainers begin in a couple of hours, how about a coffee then we can come back and watch from the hillside."

They left the arena and headed for the open-air market. It was still mid morning and yet the place was full of people. There were stalls selling all different foods and you could pick up hot potatoes, spicy chicken, pig's feet as well as fresh fruit and nuts. Trayan stopped at a stall called Elliott's, which was no more than a tent with a few les outside but was in a good spot to watch the People go by. After a cold tankard of beer for Trayan and fresh juice for Daniel and Emma, the three friends sat and enjoyed the sunshine.

An hour passed by and the crowds began to build so Trayan decided it would be best to head to the hill and get a good seat. They sat on the grassy hill and watched as the competitors warmed up, down in the arena. Most of the trainers appeared to be older than Daniel and Emma and they wondered how their tactics would differ from theirs.

The judges called the trainers to order using loud speakers and the crowd settled down for the first bout.

A young man, clearly from a different region by the way he was dressed and introduced to the crowd as Kadeir from Felatia. He was dark skinned and wore a silk shirt and trousers and when he summoned his Brannai a Taitu appeared. Emma looked in awe; for this Taitu was larger than hers was and had orange fur. Trayan explained that there are different varieties of the same breed just like the common dog. "Does that mean there are different types of Baer," asked Daniel. Trayan said, as with animals all over the world, there will be different types of the same breed, depending on the type of environment they live in.

Kadeir stood proud and faced his opponent a young man by the name of Simon, from the northern region of Arnorst.

Simon was a tall athletic looking man with black, sweptback hair and handsome features. When he summoned his Brannai, a large black cat appeared. The cat was like a panther but much bigger and had a long powerful tail, which had at its end a swollen section of bone.

Then the bout began and the crowd cheered.

Trayan looked to Daniel and Emma and said, "The inherent trait of the Taitu is intelligence and detection, were as the Panthrel relies on stealth and cunning let us see who shall come out on top."

Taitu stood, alert and wary as the Panthrel leapt from his trainer's side. The great cat took off and headed for the nearby trees as the ape looked on. Then the Panthrel appeared to disappear, or so it seemed to Emma and Daniel. What happened was, the cat camouflaged itself and as it ran, it blended with the shadows. When it ran through the grass, it mimicked the grass and when it passed a tree, it mimicked the tree. To all intents and purposes, it became invisible.

The crowd was silent as the Panthrel ran between trees and bushes. Then Kadeir whispered to his Taitu and the great ape prowled the area to the side of his master and in the open. Daniel could not see were the Panthrel was but he could detect the bushes as they moved and the grass weave as the beast passed them. Then there was a mighty roar as the Panthrel pounced high in the air.

At the same instant Taitu let out a loud howl and leapt high in the air, spinning as it did. Then it struck out with its mighty hand and caught the Panthrel on the head. The great cat suddenly became visible to the crowd, but only for a second as the Taitu pounced to finish it off, it bounced back off the grass as the cat rolled, disorientated after the blow to its head and the Taitu landed on the cat and rained down blow after blow upon it.

The cat disappeared in a shower of silver as the Taitu jumped up and down, howling loudly. Daniel and Emma leapt to their feet and clapped as hard as they could, Trayan, though, remained calm on the grass.

The sun shone down with all its intensity on the bustling market place. All over people were enjoying the weather and sales of wares were booming. The outdoor tavern run by an Elderly person and his good woman were doing particularly well, especially with the men of the town.

Three strangers wandered the streets, moving from stall to stall. They were all dressed in long gowns with their hoods up, totally out of place on the hot spring day. They stopped in the center of the market and the tallest of the three spoke, softly, to the others, after which they split up and went separate ways.

The tournament was going well and Daniel made mental notes of all the Brannai he saw. A huge bat like beast, the size of an eagle, that soared into the sky making loud clicking sounds as it flew and had long sharp claws on the joints of its wings. A huge hawk that flew so fast, it was hard to follow, even with the naked eye.

Daniel also recognized a Kedra; the wolf he and Braer had met in Brien, only this one was pure silver in color and was the size of a cow with beautiful ice blue eyes sparkling in the sun.

The end of the day's bouts finally arrived and Trayan, Daniel and Emma returned to the inn.

They enjoyed a summer supper of fresh salad and the finest cut of ham, accompanied with freshly baked loaves. All the guests talked about how well the town had prepared for festival.
"Of course, in Bedding, the preparations are on a greater scale," added Colin, to which all the guests ignored the remark and carried on talking amongst themselves.

Supper passed off quickly and quietly especially since Daniel and Emma wanted to go to bed early, in anticipation of their day's competition.

The following morning Daniel was up with Trayan and the pair headed downstairs to the dining room. Emma greeted them, already enjoying breakfast, she looked up at the pair who had stopped and were looking at her in amazement.
"What? She said, with a mouthful of toast. "I only want to see our competitors." Trayan and Daniel both laughed aloud, it had been the first time Emma had beaten them anywhere, for breakfast.

After breakfast and a thank you to Arthur and Bessie, they set off for the arena. They passed by the shops and the market place until the main stand came into view. "Remember you only have today to practice, use it wisely," Said Trayan.

When they reached the judges table, only the two brothers sat in attendance. Daniel and Emma gave their names then made their way out into the arena. As they passed through the roped off border, they both felt a small pain in their stomach and they smiled in anticipation.

Once again, Emma slipped into a dream like state as she wandered around looking at the marvelous animals that were on show. Daniel on the other hand, summoned his Braer straight away.

"Walk with me," he said, then took Braer into a clearing amongst the trees were he spoke again to the beast. "Yesterday I witnessed some magnificent animals; they were powerful and beautiful too. Tomorrow we enter our competition and I want to share something with you."

Then he stood in front of Braer, raised himself, proudly to his full height, and spoke with a tone of certainty, "There are many types of Braer, many types of Taitu, but you, are one of a kind. You are the most powerful, the fastest and most beautiful of all Brannai and you are mine and tomorrow we will win this tournament."

Braer looked into the heart of the boy and found it true and honest and he loved him. The training went well, with Daniel, for he and Braer ran through the arena side by side filling their lungs with the summer air. For Emma, the session was almost over before it began. She limited training with Taitu, even then, it was only to walk and discuss the other Brannai.

At two o'clock, the training was over and they all went to the market place for some lunch. The crowds all had the same idea and congregated in the open-air market. Trayan sat them at a wooden stall that was selling fresh sandwiches and once they sat, he spoke of their chances in the coming heats. "Never under estimate your opponent and have confidence in your own abilities. Remember that whoever you face is just as nervous or scared as you are and that to do your best is all that is required." Just as he finished speaking a woman came over and took their orders.

The three strangers had gathered in an inn and had ordered a round of ale. They sat in the corner away from prying eyes and ears. The representative lowered his hood revealing a face scarred by battle and thick jet-black hair, matted and unwashed. He took a long drink from the tankard then wiped his lips with the sleeve of his tunic. The other two mimicked the spokesperson by lowering their hoods and taking a drink of ale. "There has been no sign of the boy, are we to spend all our time in this pathetic town."

It was one of the other two who spoke, a short, fat man, with a balding head and yellowing teeth. "We stay until the end of the tournament; Lord Torek has given his orders, "said the spokesman, the last of the trio now spoke up. "There are many tournaments around the land, how do we know he will be at this one." "It does not matter, if he is here, we will catch him, if not we move on," and his words were final.

The following day brought the day of the novice finals and everyone at the Crooked Frog was up early. There was a full le laid out at breakfast, bacon, eggs and fresh bread. Bessie had seen the importance of the tournament to the guest has and had done them all proud with the early morning meal.

All the guests enjoyed the setting and the conversation was all about the morning's bouts. Colin turned up late on the pretence of making a big entrance and once seated he introduced himself to everyone as the future Doran champion.

"As I have said before me and my Brannai are quite unbeatable, "he said confidently and then left early to prepare.
Trayan spoke to Daniel and Emma, insisting that they sit and eat, as they would perform better on a full stomach and with a calm mind.

Arthur and his wife met the trio at the door as they left and wished them well in the upcoming tournament. They made their way straight to the arena and booked in at the judges le. Trayan took his place in the stand after wishing Emma and Daniel well. "Remember to trust your judgment," he said to the two young trainers.

Daniel and Emma separated once again in two different waiting areas. Daniel with another boy in a tent to the back of the arena and from there they could hear the shouts of the crowd clearly.
Emma in a tent with Colin, an experience she was not looking forward to.

Colin spoke up first. "Emma, it is a good thing they put you in here with me, it gives you a chance to progress, at least until you face me." Emma just smiled at the boy's attitude and then smiled to herself as her name rang out.

She made her way to the starting position in the arena. The stand was full of people and all around others had taken up vantage points on the hills to make the scene quite intimidating. One of the brothers called the crowd to order and introduced the two trainers.

"Ladies and gentlemen may I introduce you to the first of our eight competitors in the novice category. From the village of Tork, I give you Emma and her Taitu."The crowd all clapped loudly, which gave the nervous young girl some confidence. The judge waved down the applause as he then introduced Emma's opponent.

"From Atlan in the country of Baleria I give you Jonas and his Braer."

Jonas was a small stocky looking lad with mousy hair and wore dirty peasant type clothes. His Braer was small and squat with matted black fur over its body. Its head was dark brown and had spectacles of black fur patches around its pale blue eyes.
The judge called them both to order and then gave the countdown for the contest to begin. The Braer was first off the mark; it had an ungainly run, and would constantly roll on the floor as it closed down the distance between itself and the Taitu. Emma made the mistake of telling Taitu to meet the charge of the Braer with a charge of its own. When the two met in the center, Braer gained the upper hand. Taitu jumped and spun out of the Braer's swipes but eventually it caught Taitu across the midriff with

one of its front paws and from then on the contest was over, culminating in a swipe from Braer at Taitu, which caught it across the head sending it disappearing into a shower of silver.

Daniel heard the roars of the crowd and grew excited at the prospect of battle. Finally, he heard his name and straight away took in the atmosphere created by the packed crowd. He reveled in the cauldron of the natural amphitheatre, and stood proudly to face the crowd. Opposite Daniel, stood Colin Parkes, with his Bransar, donkey like with smooth black hair over its body and a mat of dark brown hair on top of its head as though someone had just placed it there. The Bransar stood on all fours with its head tilted up slightly, as though it smelled the aroma of a nearby meal.

Colin looked across at Braer then turned to speak to his Bransar. However, his Bransar spoke first. "I know, I know, Braer's are cumbersome creatures with too much aggression, it will attack and I shall simply bring it down." It spoke with an uppity self-confidence that reflected its trainer's attitude.

When the countdown arrived, Braer did just as the Bransar had said, he charged. However, far from being cumbersome, Braer attacked with speed, a speed the Bransar had not foreseen and when it shot out its roots The great beast simply dodged past them, until, when it was just ten paces away it vanished and re-appeared at the side of the Bransar. The small donkey like animal looked up at the towering Braer and fear gripped it. Braer took just one mighty swipe with its great claw to seal the victory, then stood on its hind legs and roared to the crowds.

"Foul! Foul! His Braer disappeared," cried Colin, "that is not possible for a novice," but his shouts were waved away by the judges and he sank to his knees, humiliated.

Braer was unstoppable, beating his next opponent easily and reaching the final once again.

There he faced a powerful animal from the eastern land of Chinst, called a Mushtu and his owner, a small boy dressed in black by the name of Chin. The Mushtu was a large animal, with all the characteristics of a Tiger, although this one was black with red stripes and had a main of black fur on the top of its head running down to the shoulders. The two advisories faced each other from opposite ends of the arena and the anticipation grew as the starter called them to order. "On my mark," he said and then with a canvass flag on the end of a short pole he started the bout.

The roar of Mushtu was powerful as it set off after the great Braer, but Braer stood on his hind legs and directed a roar straight at his opponent who had to lock his legs to the ground to prevent being blown backwards. Both Braer and Mushtu fought well, the charge of one was met with the charge of the other and both animals received cuts to the body from slashes received from flailing claws. After an attack, the two would separate and circle each other, gracefully looking for an opening until finally, in a grapple in the middle of the arena Braer managed to deal a fatal bite to the neck of the cat that sent it disappearing in a shower of silver.

The crowd were on their feet cheering loudly, along with Trayan and Emma, who had got over her disappointment of an early exit and had supported Daniel all the way. Daniel held gold cup and a bag of silver at the ceremony for the champions. The noise of the roars were loud in their ears as the two young men stood on the podium surrounded by flags and banners and they threw streamers down from the stand, covering the podium in a mass of color.

To the side, stood a man, dressed in a long cape with the hood raised around his head and underneath the cape hung a sword with a hilt of leather. He looked over at the podium and then moved off before the ceremony was over to meet up with his two travelers to discuss the next phase or their plan.

Trayan, Emma and Daniel made their way back to the Crooked Frog and received a tumultuous welcome from Arthur, Bessie and the rest of the guests. Colin however, was nowhere and missed the celebratory meal presented by the owners.

Bessie set the gold cup on the mantelpiece over the fire and then set a party out on the living room le. There were pies, chicken legs, sandwiches and ale. The entire crowd sang for he is a jolly good fellow several times and the celebrations went on for hours. Daniel felt on top of the world and Trayan and Emma were proud of him.

Colin approached the stranger in the long gown who stood at the signpost that marked the entrance to Doran. "I have heard you have been asking questions about a boy and two other travelers, I may be able to help you out, for a small price."

The stranger did not answer Colin he simply beckoned for the boy to follow him and the two walked to a nearby inn were they were met by two other strangers.

"Sit and tell us what you know," said the tall stranger who then lowered his hood, revealing his rough battle torn face.

The following day the whole town awoke to an overcast sky and the threat of rain. Trayan had talked to Daniel and Emma and told them they would head south for a little rest and maybe a spot of fishing.

After some long farewells to Arthur and Bessie and the rest of the guests, they headed out; however, Trayan decided to take the less busy east exit out of town. They looked up at the sky and decided to put on their coats expecting a downpour at any time.

BRIGANDS

The rain fell fast and heavy and was soon followed by a strong wind that drove the rain into their faces. The path soon became muddy and they bent their bodies to face the storm as they sought some area of the land that would act as shelter from the sudden downpour.

It had only been a couple of hours out from the town when they came to a rise in the land. There were trees and woodland all around and in the distance on the rise in the path, standing in the pouring rain was a single lone soldier atop his horse.

He waited in the middle of the path; his hood raised and attached to his saddle was a crossbow on one side and a sword with a leather hilt on the other. Trayan stopped and held out his arm to halt the others, then took out his sword and looked at the rain soaked traveler.

The soldier on the horse now raised his head for the first time and Trayan could detect a faint smile on his face.

"I want no trouble here," said Trayan who battled to keep his gaze on the soldier with the rain belting into his face.

"There is not going to be any, old man, just hand over the boy and you and the girl can be on your way."

Trayan knew this to be a lie, for although Emma was with him, in this heavy rain and with her cape up around her neck and its hood over her head you could not tell whether she was a girl or not, but somehow this man did.

Trayan shouted loudly in the storm. "Run!" Head for the trees," and then he charged at the soldier with his sword held high and a scream in his voice.

Daniel grabbed Emma by the arm and headed for the nearest group of trees, just as another rider emerged out of them. The young couple sank in their tracks and slipped in the mud. Daniel changed his tack and ran to the right, clutching Emma's arm, pulling her along as fast as he could. They ran but Emma could not match the boy for speed, or strength and she slipped and finally stumbled to the floor.

Daniel looked across at the new threat and quickly decided that they would not make the safety of the trees before this new rider was upon them. He stopped and helped Emma to her feet, then, quite calmly, he looked straight into her eyes. He filled with a calmness that swept over him. "Run!" Moreover, he pushed her gently towards the nearest trees.

Emma knew he was trying to protect her but she also knew it was the right thing to do and so she ran. She ran with all her strength and just once she looked back to see the young man with his sword, raised in defense, facing a charging man on horseback and she felt a pain swell in her heart.

Daniel raised his sword in a defensive pose just as Thomas had taught him. The rider saw the boy raise his sword and now slowed to a stop and dismounted. He was a small, squat man, heavy set and he drew his own sword and lowered his rain soaked hood, revealing a baldhead and scarred face. "Put the sword down boy and I will make this as painless as I can."

Daniel did not lower his sword; instead, he became more steadfast as the thought of Emma running for cover filled his mind. The rain hammered into the young boy's face as he faced his attacker.

The man came at Daniel fast with a blow to the head, but Daniel parried the blow, then he parried the next and lashed out with his own, sending the man on the defense. "You have been trained well, but you will need more than that to outwit me." Then he rained blow after blow on the boy, who weakened under the weight of the heavy sword.

Slowly he moved back until he slipped in the muddy field. The opening was just what his attacker needed and he landed a kick to the midriff of the boy, driving the wind out of his lungs. Daniel keeled over, and then felt a heavy blow to the back of his head and the surrounding landscape drifted away into darkness.

Daniel slowly came round and his head was swimming with pain. His eyes focused on his new surroundings, he found himself in a wood surrounded by trees and bushes; sitting down with his back tied to a fir tree and his hands bound tightly behind him. Daniel could feel a trickle of cool liquid going down his neck and along his spine, then, slowly he heard the sound of voices nearby. He raised his head and took in the scene in front of him.

There was a camp with a fire in the middle and three soldiers sitting and laughing around its flames. The rain seemed to have stopped and all that remained was the water soaked leaves on the trees and bushes around him.

"Look here," said one of the soldiers, "it looks like our little rabbit is back with us, gave our Fudge here a right run for his money, and nearly had him beat."

Then two of them started laughing at the third. Fudge grew angry at the jests thrown his way and stood up. He went to Daniel and looked down at the lad then kicked his feet in disgust and spat at him. Daniel briefly looked up and recognized the man as his assailant when he had made his stand in the field. Fudge then went back and took his seat by the fire. Another of the soldiers, a thin scrawny person with long shaggy hair then spoke. "What does Torek want with the lad anyway?" The other tall soldier answered.

"I am not privileged to that information; however he did not say we could have some fun with him on the way." Once again they all laughed.

Then Fudge spoke again. "What happened to the old man?" Daniels ears pricked up at the mention of Trayan. The leader of the group, the one they called Aaron answered.
"Nearly a gonna I was, the old man was a dab hand with that sword of his, would have had me too if it was not for Jake here, put an arrow in his

back he did." Then he went to Jake and patted him hard on the back. Fudge then asked the provocative question as Daniel leant forward to hear, "what then." "Left him lying face down in the mud, then we went off to search for the girl but she must have found a good hiding place."

Daniels heart sank and the loss of his friend and the searing pain in his head once more sent him into blackness.

When he regained consciousness, he found he buffeted, up and down and his head thrown around, causing him pain. He lifted the lids on his eyes and realized they tied his hands; face down on the back of a horse. Suddenly, a great thirst took hold of him and he cried out for water.

Jake rode just behind Daniel's mount and now he pulled alongside and cuffed the boy around the head. "Quiet you little maggot, you will get water when we stop and not before."

The soldiers did not set a great pace, there was no need to, they had the boy and there was no one on their trail to worry about. They talked amongst themselves as they passed through the woodland. By midday, the sun was high in the sky, the heat began to tell on young Daniel, and he cried out for water once more.

They ignored his cries; however, Aaron called out and said it was time to rest the horses. He picked a spot near a small stream and once stopped; Fudge dismounted, then went to the back of the horse and threw Daniel to the floor. Daniel managed to arch his back as he fell and so avoided any more damage to his already sore head.

The soldiers watered their horses in the stream, then filled their own casks and drank. Daniel had managed to sit himself upright against a log and now Jake went over and lifted the lad by his hair. He emptied a water cask into the boy's mouth from a height and laughed as Daniel tried to take in all the liquid he could.

Aaron then called over to Jake. "Enough, we still have hours of daylight." Jake grabbed the boy and dragged him to his feet, then threw him onto the back of Fudge's horse.

They travelled on for a few more hours and Daniel drifted in and out of consciousness until finally he awoke and found to his surprise that the soldiers had stopped and had made camp for the night. The weather had warmed under the early summer sun and there would be no need for tents. Fudge tended the fire and watched over Daniel, whilst Aaron and Jake went hunting for the evening meal. As Fudge stoked the flames, he looked across at Daniel, who limited, once again, to a tree. In a rough unfeeling voice, he spoke to the boy. "Led us quite a merry dance you have, been searching all spring. Lord Torek said you would turn up at one of the tournaments eventually. He must want you pretty bad; I don't envy you when he finally gets his hands on you."

Daniel looked up, "I'm hungry." The truth was he could not remember the last time food had passed his lips. Fudge gave Daniel a stern look and then carried on stoking the fire in silence.

It did not take long for Aaron and Jake to return and when they did, they had a brace of rabbits tied to Jakes belt. They may be ruffians but they knew how to live off the land and they soon had a fine stew cooking over the blazing flames.

Daniel had never known such hunger and the smell of the cooking was almost unbearable. Aaron filled a small plate with the stew and took it over to where Daniel was sitting. He stood over the boy and straight away noticed a problem. Daniels hands felt tight behind his back and his legs bound. He freed the boy then dragged him around the tree and knelt him face first up against the wood. Then he pulled his hands around a tree and tied them again. He then placed the food on the floor and left without saying a word.

It took Daniel no time at all to pick up the plate and then hastily and clumsily, devour the lot. Daniel remained tied to the tree all evening and soon his knees began to hurt as they pressed into the floor by his own weight. He managed to scrape himself a smooth area of ground in which to lie down, a feat he managed by lying on his side with his knees curled up. Aaron and the other soldiers finished their meal and then Fudge went to his horse and retrieved a skin of ale.

He took a long drink then returned and passed it around. The three soldiers continued to drink for another hour and their high spirits got the better of them. They sang songs, louder, louder, and more rowdily until Fudge stood and started to dance around the flames. The others clapped loudly drinking from the skin all the time until the final drops drained. Jake held the empty skin high in the air and tried to get the last dregs out, Fudge spotted the dilemma and danced his way over to Jakes horse and held up another skin of ale. Jake and Aaron both cheered as Fudge danced all the way back.

Daniel stirred on the floor and it was enough to get him noticed. Fudge went over to where the boy lay, his face was red with all the ale and he looked in a mischievous mood. He kicked Daniel in the back and when he turned over Fudge bent over him and poured ale into his mouth. "This will put hairs on your chest, if you had any." However, Daniel kept his lips tight, a sight that annoyed Fudge immensely. He only saw a great waste of the precious ale and a temper rose inside him. He bent down closer to Daniel and tried unsuccessfully to prise his lips apart. The ale poured down the side of Daniel's mouth, onto his neck and down onto the floor around him.

Fudge stood, "you don't know what's good for you, ungrateful little wretch." Then he kicked Daniel in the back and head, one kick for each bad tempered word that he spoke. Finally, out of breath he looked down at the boy as he lay, still on the floor. Without another word, he returned to the fire to rejoin the others who had not even batted an eye at his outburst. Daniel lay battered and weak and his body in pain, he drifted off to sleep.

He dreamt of his mother and the songs she would sing to him when he was little, then of Emma and the look of fear on her face as he let go of her arm and told her to run. He dreamt of Trayan, his friend. The man who had shown him the Brannai and then his thoughts turned to Braer, he could see the bright blue eyes staring down at him and his kindly face with a look of sincerity on it.

Then the look changed and a great anger took hold of the animal. His body arched and the fur rose on his back. In his dream, Daniel stepped back in fright. Then the animal lashed out with his great claws and gave a roar like the thunder in the sky. Repeatedly the great beast struck, but at what Daniel could not tell, there were crashing and roaring and the sound of distant voices, terrified voices. Daniel pulled his hands over his ears and cringed. Finally Braer calmed, his body returning to the animal he knew, Then Braer turned and looked at Daniel and calmness came over the boy and he woke up.

HEALING

Emma crawled out from the bush were she had hid, her clothes were dirty, full of mud and leaves were she had lain, clutched to the floor. The rain had eased and she wiped the tears from her eyes as she stood. It had been some time since the soldiers had stopped their search and left and yet, she still felt wary of their presence. Cautiously she made her way through the trees, slipping in the wet ground as she went. Somehow, she found herself in a clearing and stopped to look around.

A vision came to her, of Daniel standing, with his sword held high facing a lone soldier and she cried out his name. Her voice echoed around the wood and bounced from tree to tree. Then she noticed the path were the soldier on horseback had first stopped them and as she looked over she saw a figure lying down, motionless on the floor just where he had been. "Trayan!" she shouted and a great dread came over her as she ran to him. She stopped a few paces from the body and held her hands to her mouth as she looked at the arrow in his back. Slowly she approached, then knelt down beside him and cried.

Emma lifted herself up and looked around for help and as she did so she heard a faint murmur from the body on the floor. Frantically she shook Trayan, all the while looking around and shouting for someone, anyone to come to her aid.

She stood and screamed at the top of her voice and then in the distance she saw it, a shape approaching through a path etched through the trees. Closer it came, until she could make out a cart with a single driver in its seat. She waved her arms in the air and cried, but this time they were tears of joy, for help had arrived.

Joseph had seen the girl waving in the distance and sped his horse on as fast as it would go. When he was near enough, he could see the body of a man laying face down on the path. His body was old but he got down from his cart as quick as he could and went over. The arrow was sticking out of the man's back and there was blood all around, lots of blood.

Emma was frantic and Joseph's first job was to calm her as best he could. Then he bent down and snapped the shaft of the arrow off, an inch or so above the wound. Next, he tore off some cloth from his shirt and pressed it around the broken arrow to stem the flow of blood.

Together he and Emma managed to lift Trayan onto the back of the cart where Emma stayed, next to her friend. Joseph had told Emma not to worry, he said he did not live far and that his wife had the healing touch and would be able to tend to the wound with a bit more skill.

He was true to his word, for it did not take long before they reached his farm. It was at the end of the wood were the land opened up to fields and hills. Joseph's house was fenced off in the middle of a field and when they reached it the old man called out to his wife, Laura.

A late middle-aged woman came to the door with a towel in her hands and a pinafore around her waist. She was small and plump with a very kind and gentle face and when she saw her husband, she called out. "What is all the fuss about," then she noticed Emma in the back of the cart, resting beside the body of a man and she ran over.

"What happened," said Laura as they struggled with Trayan.

"Looks like brigands ambushed them were the old path meets the road to Doran," replied Joseph. "Is he your father dear?" Laura asked. Emma cried as she answered. "No, he is just a very dear friend."

Laura asked Joseph to boil up some water and bring some clean linen, then she cut away Trayan's shirt and looked at the wound. The arrow embedded deep into the shoulder and needed removing. She went to Emma and clasped her on the shoulders with both hands. Then in a kindly and steady voice told her that it would all be fine. They managed to take Trayan into the house and once there they laid him down on a bed. Then she went to a drawer, took out a small blade, and doused it in some of Joseph's whiskey. Joseph turned up with a basin of hot water and some fresh linen draped over his arm. Laura pulled up a chair and sat beside the bed, then asked Joe to go in front and hold down on Trayan's shoulders. "I do not want any sudden movements dear," she said. She held the blade in the boiling water for a few minutes and then with a steady hand she began to cut around the arrowhead. Slowly but surely she cut away until, with a gentle pull the arrow came out.

Laura expertly stitched the wound and covered it with some ointment and a clean bandage. She then stood and washed her hands in the basin. She then turned to Emma and spoke. "The wound was clean, I have seen this type many times and in my opinion he should recover fully," and she placed a reassuring hand on Emma's shoulder.

Laura then took Emma through to another room and sat her down at the le. She looked across to her husband and nodded in the direction of the stove. Joseph understood his wife perfectly and poured some water into a kettle to make some tea.

Laura pulled up a chair, sat next to Emma, and put a motherly arm around her shoulder. "Would you like to talk about what happened?" Joseph brought two cups of hot sweet tea and placed them on the le, then smiled at his wife and sat at the end of the table.

Emma told of the stranger who Trayan had bravely charged at with his sword held high. Then she paused and picked up her tea and told of the brave young man who had looked her in the eyes and told her to run. Then the cup in her hand began to shake slightly as the nerves in her body rose to the fear she now felt as she recalled the moments when she had hid, low down in a bush.

The two soldiers were calling her, teasing and thrashing the bushes with their swords. Closer and closer, they came until they seemed they were right on top of her and there would be no way they would not find her. Laura sensed the girl's tension and eased her with a gentle squeeze on her shoulder.

"You're here now dear, the soldiers are all gone and you are safe."

For the rest of that day and all of the next Emma sat by the bedside, nursing Trayan whenever he murmured or became hot, she slept very little and when she did, it was to flop down her head and rest it on the covers by his legs.

Sometimes Trayan would call out and fight off imaginary foes in dark dreams and other times he was calm and cool. Through all his fight with his recovery, Emma was there, by his side and Laura noticed the love she held for this man.

There was a loud clatter on the roof of the cottage as a sudden downpour passed over the region. The noise was enough to make Trayan stir and wake. With his hands, he felt the warm touch of the bed linen, and then slowly he opened his eyes and looked around at the room where he lay. The room was bright with curtains on the window and gentle colours painted on the dry walls. He tilted his head to the side and saw Emma asleep in a chair by his bed with a quilt, draped over her shoulders.

Slowly he reached out with his hand and touched her on the knee and she woke with a sudden start. Emma looked at Trayan, quickly bent over, and gently hugged him.

The rain passed as quickly as it came and soon the sun burst its way through the clouds and brought with it a new day.

Trayan was soon sitting up and being spooned homemade broth, by the caring hands of Emma. He looked over at Joseph and Laura and then raised a hand to stop Emma from feeding him.

"I must thank you both, for saving my life and showing unbelievable kindness to me and to Emma."

Joseph simply stood at the side of his wife, put his arm around her shoulder, and smiled. Trayan turned a little too sharply in his bed as he looked at Emma and the pain shot through his body, making him wince. He placed his hand on his weak shoulder and spoke to the girl. "Daniel."

Emma took her gaze away and looked down at the floor. "The soldiers took him." Slowly she brought her gaze back to Trayan, "he stood alone in the field with his sword held high, it was the last I saw of him." Trayan fell back on his pillow and looked up at the ceiling.

It took Trayan another full day to recover enough strength to dress and leave the bed. There, he sat and enjoyed the meal Laura had provided. "I must thank you, but our time here is over and we must be moving on, I have a very brave young man to find, we will leave tomorrow."

Laura new the man was not yet strong enough to leave, but she also knew she would not be able to stop him.

The following day the clouds gathered in the sky as Trayan and Emma prepared to leave the farm. Trayan struggled putting on his coat but he tried to hide it as Laura came over to help him. She gave him some fresh bandages and more of her special ointment and then looked up at the darkening sky.

"Be careful you are not fully healed," she said. Trayan looked at the woman and hugged her and then he held her by the shoulders and kissed her gently on the forehead. He looked over at Joseph, "If you could do me one last favour my friend and drop me off were you found me."

Emma went over to Laura, hugged her like a mother, and then jumped on the back of the cart. Once again, it did not take long until they reached the point where the attack had took place. All three climbed down from the cart and then made their way to the trail that led from Doran. Joseph stepped back as Trayan looked around and Emma went to him and stood by him. Trayan returned and stopped in front of the old man. "Thank you and thank Laura, you give without taking and have a kindness that does you proud, I will not forget you my friend."

He then held out his hand and shook it, patting Josephs arm with his other and then he turned and walked slowly away. Emma went to Joseph and gave him the biggest of hugs. "Thank you." She said and then she turned and followed Trayan.

THE WILDERNESS

Daniel slowly opened his eyes; his head was swimming with dreams and the pain from the beating he took the night before. He looked up and could not believe the carnage before him.

There were no soldiers and the only sounds were the birds and the running water coming from the nearby stream. He felt for his hands and noticed that his bonds were gone and so, slowly he got to his feet. The camp resembled one that had been devastated by a terrible storm. The debris from the fire spread everywhere and there were clothes, pots, and pans everywhere. As he looked around in disbelief, he even noticed branches on some trees hanging or laying down on the ground where they remained, ripped away by some unknown force.

Daniel tried to clear his head and he went over to the stream and dipped his head under the cold refreshing water. Hazily he drifted around the wreckage looking for anything he might need. He picked up a piece of cloth and dried himself, until slowly he became himself.

Daniel kicked at the ashes on the floor as he wandered around, then out of the corner of his eye he spotted a glint in the grass. He went over and bent down and there on the floor was a stone flint, he picked it up and inspected it, he turned it over in his hand then placed it in a pocket.

Daniel also found a soldiers dagger and a water skin, which he filled from the stream. Then he stood and looked around at his surroundings, it was a beautiful early summer's day and the warm rays of the sun sparkled through the branches and lit up the land. There were birds singing through the wood and the devastation from the camp looked out of place.

 It was then he remembered his dream and the way Braer had appeared and had gone wild with temper. Had Braer saved him, how could he? The animal could only appear in an arena. Then his thoughts turned to Trayan and he pictured him face down in the mud with an arrow in his back, alone in the wilderness. His heart sank, he lost his grip on the water skin and his eyes flooded as he let it slip to the floor.

Brannai

Daniel sat down on the warm grass with his arms draped at his side, Trayan was gone and Emma could be wandering the wood alone, or worse. He thought of Braer, and with tears in his eyes, he looked to the sky and shouted out his name. His voice echoed around him but no one came, the boy was alone.

It was then that he spotted a small wren, perched on a little branch. It sat there with its tail propped up and it had a beak full of down. Daniel looked at the tiny animal alone in the wood; he wiped the tears from his eyes with the back of his hand and stood. "Braer would not want me to be weak and Trayan has taught me better than to sit around and cry. Thank you my little friend for showing me the way." Then he gathered up what possessions he had and looked around. He took a deep breath and set off for the only person who could help him, Thomas Sheridan.

Daniel did not know where he was and so he made for open ground, a hill or something, were he could get his bearings. At first, he followed the small stream hoping it would lead him out of the woodland, however after several miles the terrain did not change and so he decided to climb a tree.

He picked a clearing in the land and then found a tall fir tree with branches that began low enough for him to reach. Daniel was an excellent climber, a trait he had learned back home in Barrow wood when he would go looking for the hawk that had made its nest near his home. Soon he was high enough to see around him and there off to the left, far in the distance were the Regal Mountains.

Daniel was still hurting and not only from the beating, His thoughts would often stray to his lost friend or to Emma, but he was a strong young man and one with a purpose, to find Thomas.

Daniel worked out that by following the stream it may turn into a river and lead him to the mountains and so he kept the flow of water by him as he walked.

His journey took him through a region of the land with the most picturesque landscape. An area of bright green fir trees with a mountain fresh stream running lazily through it, lit up by the bright blue sky on a warm early summers day.

As the boy walked along he suddenly realised he was becoming hungry, he looked up through the trees and saw that the sun was high in the sky. It must be around midday, he thought, and so he began to search for a meal.

The river had plenty of fish, but he had neither line nor hook and the last time he tried fishing he caught nothing. Then he remembered his early days with Trayan and how he had shown him how to read animal tracks. He set about setting traps with only the use of the wilderness for tools.

Daniel collected some wood and set up a fire by the water's edge, then set his water skin down and went hunting with his knife. Daniel looked around for signs of rabbits, once he found a run; he set about making a trap.

With his knife, he cut a small branch from a tree, then trimmed it and cut a notch near the top. This he hammered into the floor with the butt of the dagger, next he found a smaller twig that had branched off into a v-shape. He removed both laces from his shoes and tied one around the twig. Then using a low branch of a nearby bush, he tied the other end of his lace. By pulling the branch down, he could lodge the twig into the notch he had cut in the branch. This would be the trigger. Using his other lace, he made a loop, tied a slipknot in it, and then tied the other end to the trigger. The loop hung in the rabbit run supported by two smaller twigs and then he lay down in the Grass some paces away and waited.

The sun was warm on his face as he lay on his back looking up at the sky. The clouds rolled by and all the day's events caught up with the boy and he drifted off into a troubled sleep.

His mother was standing in a room, over the stove, holding a tray of freshly baked bread rolls. She looked over at Daniel and smiled, "come, tell me what you have been up to today." Then she beckoned him to come and sit at their table. Daniel sat down and told her all about Braer and his adventures with Trayan and Emma as they journeyed through the land. He was excited as he portrayed his new life to his mother, then suddenly she began to laugh.

He became confused, why was she laughing, "Mother," he called. She did not answer him, she just laughed louder still and then her face began to change. She stood and slowly took on a new form. Daniel pushed back his chair and stepped back as his mother took on the form of someone else.

A tall, late middle-aged man with thick jet-black hair dressed in fine clothes emerged before him. He drew his fine silver sword with its black leather hilt and held it out, pointing it straight at Daniel. The man walked towards him pushing aside chairs and laughing all the time, closer and closer, he came and his face contorted with rage until finally, he struck out with a killing blow.

Daniel screamed and then sat up in the grass. The sun was still shining and the air around was peaceful except for the noise of a rabbit squealing as it hung in the trap. The sweat dripped down off his head and onto the ground as Daniel looked around him. He felt the grass around him and saw the rabbit struggling in the trap, he knew it had been a bad dream, but who was the stranger who had come at him with the sword.

Now was not the time and so he went over to the trap and took his food and the trap back to the camp. Daniel skilfully skinned and cooked the rabbit and then split the parts up, eating some and placing the rest in a piece of cloth for later. He looked to the distant mountains and decided it would take at least three days to reach them and so he left his camp and set off again, although this time he had a full stomach.
 Keeping the water close by he travelled for a few more hours until the sun was low in the sky and he decided to make camp for the night.

Daniel had no bed, just the clothes he wore and so he picked a spot by the stream surrounded by trees and bushes for protection. The boy gathered plenty of wood, built a good fire, and then settled down for the night. Daniel had spent many days out in the wild, back home in Dantaal, but then he had a home to go to if he so needed. Here, he was all alone, Trayan was dead and there would be no help. The noises of the wild drew in around him and he pulled in his legs and moved closer to the fire.

WOLVES

Trayan and Emma travelled light and at a good pace as they followed the trail that the soldier's horses had left. "Do you think we will ever see him again?" Emma spoke as they walked but did not make eye contact with Trayan.

Trayan slowed and drew level with Emma. "I am sure we will, we must never give up hope. Hope is what defines us and if Daniel is out there, he needs our help." Then he paused and looked to the trees, "He is alive and well, we will find him and be together once more." Emma looked over and gave him an unconfident smile.

They travelled on for a short distance with Trayan checking for signs that the soldiers pace had slackened. He looked over at Emma and saw that she was struggling with the pace he had set and so he decided to stop for a rest. They sat and had a drink of water and a snack and Emma decided that they should move on.

They travelled for the rest of the day, always in the same direction and it was then that Trayan decided to change his tack. "We have followed them for a full day and there is no doubt that they are headed for Ballen castle. They are on horseback and we are walking, we can gain time on them if we head for the mountains and then cut straight through."

It was a chance, but he felt he had to change in order to give them hope of catching Daniel before they reached the castle. Trayan made camp for the night and set out beds and a warm fire. There they settled down and slept under the same stars as their friend ahead of them.

**

Daniel woke the following morning to a bright day ahead. The sun shone and the sky was a clear blue. He went over to the stream and washed in the cool water. The night had been peaceful, he had not been troubled with strange dreams, and so his mood was lighter as he set off. The land was changing, the trees were becoming thinner and the ground was starting to climb. Daniel noticed the stream had gained in strength the nearer he came to the mountains and his path sometimes took him away from its banks.

He encountered more rocky ground the further north he went and then at the end of his second day alone he found that he had come to a small waterfall. The land to the side of the stream was full of rocks and rose upwards to the top of the water's edge. There was still some time left before nightfall and so he decided to start the climb.

Up he went looking for footholds along the way, reaching out with his hands and pulling himself up. He looked up, he was nearly there and so he stretched out his right hand and took a hold.

Then he placed his foot on a rock and pushed off, but the rock gave way taking his leg with it. Daniel frantically reached out with his hands trying to grab a hold of anything, but he fell and tumbled to the floor at the bottom of the climb. He recovered his composure, sat upright on the floor, and looked up at the rocks above him. His arms and face badly scraped, but overall he felt ok. He dusted himself off and stood, however as soon as he put weight in his right foot a pain shot through his body causing him to drop to the floor. Daniel inspected his foot; slowly he moved it around in a circular motion and tried to wiggle his toes inside his shoe. Well it is not broke he thought then he looked up at the rocks above him.

Daniel then stood and carefully placed his weight on his injured foot. It hurt but he managed it and so he decided to try once more. As he went up he pulled with both hands and only pushed off with his left foot, protecting the injury as much as he could. Slowly but surely he reached the top and pulled himself over and there ahead of him in all their glory where the mountains.

During the end of the day, the clouds had gathered and it looked like rain was on its way. Daniel decided to look for some cover if the heavens decided to open. Gingerly he limped around looking for somewhere to spend the night.

Ahead, he came upon a rocky outcrop that rose slightly. Near its peak, it looked like there might be some sort of opening and so he made his way up the slight gradient.

He was right; near the top was an opening in the rocks. It was not a cave but it had a rocky roof and a small entrance and would provide ideal cover for the night. Daniel limped down the hill and looked around for anything he could use for a fire. He gathered up what he could and set them down at the back or the rocky hollow. Just in time, he managed to light a fire as the heavens opened up. He sat and looked out at the rain soaked land and then took a drink of water and a piece of the cooked rabbit. Daniel sat back against the wall of his den and for the first time began to think of his father.

What was he like, what type of man was he, did he have the same looks as him. Suddenly it dawned on him, Philip must have loved someone, and his real mother was out there somewhere. Why had she abandoned him and had him taken away. He loved his own mother dearly; Kate was everything to him, his strength and his passion, but was there someone else, someone who loved his father? Just then, his ankle began to hurt and he rubbed it and then stoked the fire and added more wood.

**

Trayan and Emma awoke to a change in the weather, the clouds had drifted over and it looked like rain was on the way. The gloomy conditions brought with it a chill breeze, as they set off in pursuit. Everything seemed dowdy and uninterested. Still, they wrapped up and pressed on in the hope of finding their friend.

The rain finally fell, drenching the trees and the grass. The two had some protection as they walked through the wood; the thick branches of the fir trees took most of the pounding from the weather. Trayan did not speak much as he pressed on through trails etched on his mind and Emma, although she loved the man could not help but feel alone without Daniel there to talk to and her spirits dropped like the weather around her.

Emma walked hurriedly behind Trayan and as she did, she noticed various animals around her. Squirrels, darting up the tree trunks and doves perched together, high in the branches. From her position in the wood, they overlooked a stream that ran some distance away and it was there that she thought she saw movement near its banks.

At first, it looked like a dog, but then it vanished among the trees and shrubs. She kept on looking back for further signs until the trail took the stream out of view. By the end of the day, Emma was soaked to the skin and very tired, Trayan had pushed her hard but he knew he had to. Finally, as the light began to fade Trayan stopped and made camp.

Trayan would have slept lightly out in the open but the conditions and the look on Emma's face told him to put up the tents. Even in the wet, it always amazed Emma how he could find dry tinder for the fire and once she had changed into some dry clothes she sat with him around the flames. A hot mug of tea and some freshly cooked pigeon cheered the girl up, "its funny how, even in the hardest of weather, life in the wild goes on. Whilst we have been walking, I have seen all sorts of animals. There was a stream back there and I even saw what looked like a dog playing by its edge." As she said the last words, Trayan looked over at the girl.

"These woods are alive with all sorts of wild animals. But dogs, I think what you saw would have been a wolf, they are known to hunt in these parts." Emma curled herself up and cuddled the hot mug as she moved an inch or two nearer to the fire.

**

Daniel decided to settle in the break in the rocks, but when he looked over at his stash of firewood, he knew he would require some more for the night ahead. He limped down the hillside and wandered around in the fading light, looking for branches or twigs, but everything was wet. Still he gathered what he could and headed back to his camp, unaware something watched him. The fire was bright and looked fierce in the moonlight and Daniel felt safe behind its flames. Before he settled down he stripped some of the branches to reveal the dry wood underneath should he need it through the night.

When he awoke the next morning he found that the rain had gone but the land around was still very wet. He had himself a drink of water from his skin and the last of the rabbit that he had saved. Daniel stood and tested his ankle, it was still sore although not as bad as the previous day and so he set off down the hillside. His plan was to spend another day here and give his ankle time to heal and so he looked around for anything to eat.

Wild berries or nuts would be fine he thought or maybe I can set up my trap again. As he looked around, he became aware of a feeling deep within him, a feeling he had felt before. He stopped and slowly turned and made his way back toward the hillside. The boy turned his head and looked around him and as he did and his heartbeat rose inside his small body.

Ganash was the leader of the trio of brothers, he was powerful and strong and the most fearless of the three wolves. Large paws and pure black fur, together with black eyes gave him a fierce some appearance. Pinder and Bane were slightly smaller but no less formidable, with their dark brown fur and yellow eyes, in fact the only way to tell them apart was that Pinder had a white end to its bushy tail.

Ganash hid in the darkness of the trees, sending his brothers to the other end of the clearing. Daniel knew something was out there and he searched the darkness with his keen eyes. Then he caught a glimpse of movement to his left, he turned his head and looked. There, hiding like vipers in the darkness were two large wolves and they were looking at him.

He felt a fear rise inside him and he stumbled on a loose branch and went down on the wet grass. It was all Ganash had been waiting for and he sped out of the shadow. Daniel stumbled along the floor trying to get a grip with his feet as he watched his nemesis in the distance, just then he turned and to his right was another, but this one was large, fierce, and charging straight at him.

Quickly he managed to get to his feet and then he turned and ran, pulling out his Dagger as he went. The boy stumbled and slipped as he climbed up the rocky hillside, not once looking back at the beast that was hunting him down.

Ganash chased hard, he could sense a kill and his chest heaved with the effort. Saliva poured from his open jaws and he growled loudly as he closed in.

With one final effort, Daniel pulled himself up and jumped into his rocky home. There he turned in an instant and faced the entrance with the dagger held out in front of him. Ganash was at full pace when he suddenly saw the flames of the fire and had to turn sharply to avoid them, but he saw a gap between the rocks and the fire and he dived straight for it. Daniel was waiting for the beast and as it charged in, the boy thrust his dagger forward with all his strength.

Ganash was not expecting such a sting and he howled in pain as he thrust against the rocks. Instantly he scrambled to his feet and fled back down the hill. Daniel screamed aloud and the fear that was present inside him, suddenly left and he stood breathing heavily and looking down on his foes.

Ganash limped back to the trees with blood dripping from the wound in his right shoulder and immediately the other two cowered around him trying to lick the cut clean. Nevertheless, Ganash was angry and he lashed out at his brothers with snarling teeth and claws, sending them whimpering to the floor with their tails between their legs. Daniel quickly threw more wood on the fire trying to send the flames higher in the opening and then he stepped back, panting hard and waited.

Ganash turned on his brothers, the animal he hunted had hurt him, he wanted revenge, and so he growled furiously at Pinder and Bane and sent them on the kill.

Together they ran, growling and sweating as they charged up the hill. The gap at the top of the hill was narrow and just like Ganash, the flames of Daniels fire suddenly confronted them and they bumped and barged into one another in an effort to get to the boy and avoid the deadly heat. Bane forced himself ahead of his brother and with his teeth bearing, he ran at Daniel.

Daniel was ready this time and he had picked a burning branch out of the fire, which he now thrust into the face of the wolf. The pain was unbearable, and howling, Bane turned and bumped into Pinder sending them both hurtling down the hill.

Now the night had closed in and the flames from the fire burned bright in the moonlight. Daniel was no longer shaking; he had faced his fear and had come through a braver person for it. He looked at his stock of wood, he was not sure if it would last the night and in any case even if it did not, he would have to get more tomorrow.

For now, the wolves were hurt and their pride dented but there was a long night ahead of them and so they filtered into the darkness and waited, for their chance would come again.

**

Emma and Trayan both settled down for the night, Trayan had put extra logs on the fire and so it burned fierce and bright as they both went to sleep.

Trayan was walking through trees and bushes and there were glimpses of sunlight as the rays trickled through openings between the leaves. He felt the warmth of the summer air all around him as he pushed past overhanging branches. There were animals nearby, he could sense them, but there was something else.

Ahead, in the shadow, out of the sun lurked a creature. It would not show itself and yet, somehow, Trayan did not feel afraid, instead, he was compelled to seek it out. The man walked on until the wood opened out into a small clearing and there he stopped. There was a rustle of leaves and the great trees shook ahead as the creature he sought came into the open. There in front of him appeared Braer and he walked slowly toward Trayan. The beast stopped a pace short of the man and looked at him through his bright blue eyes, then in a clear voice he spoke, "you must head west, the boy is in trouble and he needs your help, you have no time to lose." Then Braer vanished and Trayan turned and ran.

Emma woke in her bed and she opened her eyes and looked up. Trayan was standing over her; he looked her hard in the face and said, "Hurry, Daniel is alive but he is in danger."

**

Daniel settled, he knew he had dealt a serious blow to the wolves' hopes of defeating him and he knew that they would return if the fire went out and so he kept one eye on his supply of firewood and the other on the land below him. With his dagger held tightly in his hand he sat down with his back to the rocks, then slowly his heartbeat returned to normal and he began to relax.

The three brothers huddled together in the shade of the fir trees licking their wounds and then suddenly Ganash lifted his head to the sky and let out an eerie howl. Pinder and Bane responded to their leader and joined in and so the noise echoed through land for miles around. Daniel listened to the song of the wolves but did not move, he knew he was in for a long night. The brothers did not attempt another attack that night but every now and then, they would let out a howl, just to let their prey know that they were still there.

The sun slowly rose over the land and tried to break through the mist that had formed in the early morning.

Daniel was still sitting by the fire; however, it was now only a smoulder and the last of the firewood used up some time ago. The boy's eyes were heavy and his head began to droop under its own weight, then slowly the dagger slipped out of his hand and fell to the floor.

Ganash and the brothers were pacing the ground, the light from the fire was becoming duller and their excitement was growing. They could sense that their prey was failing and as the sun finally broke through and shone its power on the land, the light on the hill went out completely. Ganash ripped up the ground as he took off, Bane and Pinder followed, however, the uninjured Pinder reached the bottom of the hill first. In addition, he scrambled up its rocky slope.

The wolf ran wildly, hoping to be the first to the kill, but as it did so, it dislodged loose rocks and sent them hurtling downward. It was just enough to wake Daniel who rose quickly to his feet, only to see the fierce some beast running up the hill at him.

There were no flames left to protect him, but he was not going to go down without one last fight. He stood at the entrance to the camp with his knife held out in front and bellowed out a roar to greet his advisory.

Pinder could not contain his fury and he roared as he leapt at the small boy.

The arrow came from nowhere and took Pinder in the throat in mid leap. Daniel had stepped to the side of the wolf and plunged his dagger into its side and the two of them jumped backwards. Daniel landed on the floor with the great wolf at his side; he stood, and was ready to face the others when he noticed the arrow sticking out of the side of the beast.

Daniel ran to the entrance and looked down, there at the bottom of the slope, lay Bane, dead on the floor. Ganash had seen his brother's fall and had fled into the trees. Trayan pulled out another arrow as he ran toward the base of the hill, however, Emma spotted Daniel at the top and she ran to him with all the speed in her tired legs.

The two met halfway and Emma flung herself around him almost knocking him to the floor. Daniel hugged her with all his remaining strength and then over her shoulder he saw the tall figure of Trayan with a bow, ready in his hands. He looked in astonishment at the ghost that approached him and then with a huge smile on his face he let go of Emma with one hand and embraced his lost friend.

The joy was overwhelming as they hugged, laughed and cried. Daniel could not believe it, "you should be dead, the soldiers told me that they put an arrow in you and left you face down in the mud." He was laughing loudly as he spoke the words to Trayan. "How did you find me?"

"Now that is a story I will tell when I have checked you are alright and we have built a strong fire," and Trayan looked at the boy with blood on his chest and a dagger in his hand.

Trayan erected two tents and started a blazing fire and then went to the wolf at the bottom of the hill and skinned it, then cut it up and cooked it on the fire. Emma tended to Daniel, she sat him down and took off his shoe and strapped his sore ankle with some cloth.

"I never thanked you, I thought I never would. Back there, when the soldiers came for us, you were very brave." She looked deep into his eyes and gently kissed him on the lips. Then she stood back, smiled and turned to help Trayan with the chores. Daniel blushed, but inside he felt on top of the world.

Trayan decided to keep camp where they were, to give Daniels foot time to heal properly and so he cooked up the meat and brewed some fresh tea.

PEACE

"How did you find me, here in the wilderness?"Said Daniel, and he chewed on a piece of meat as he spoke. Trayan told of his dream and the meeting with Braer, "It was your beast that told us of your plight and where to find you, he is a magnificent creature."

Daniel then told Trayan of the dream he had when he was being held by the soldiers, "I have never seen him like that before, I could not tell who was there in the dream but I knew Braer was in a fury. He lashed out with his claws and the hair on his back was spiked up in temper."

Daniel asked Trayan if he thought Braer had rescued him that night. "I do not know." replied the old man, "There have been strange forces at work, but one thing is clear and that is Lord Torek is fearful of what you will become. He does not want you to become as powerful as your father."

Then Trayan looked directly at Daniel. "I will make you a promise my friend, I will not stop until you have become exactly what he fears most."

The trio stayed at the camp for another day and then they packed up their belongings and headed north. They travelled in beautiful sunshine and all around the land filled with life.

The glorious mountains came closer and their peaks reached up to the sky as they neared the foothills, Trayan then took them east around the base of the mountains, through a land filled with trees and rolling hills.

"Just a half days travel and we should come upon an arena, it is to the east side of the mountains and it will give you some time together with your Brannai."

It was just as Trayan had said, they travelled along until midday and then they came to an area of land were the hills dropped away into a small valley and the trees surrounded a small lake. Daniel and Emma both felt a small pain in their stomachs as they rose over the last hill and the lake came into view.

Braer and Taitu appeared before them and immediately engulfed with hugs from Daniel and Emma.

Daniel hugged the mighty beast with all his strength and then stood back a little and spoke. "It was you who saved me from the soldiers, wasn't it."

Braer looked down at the boy with his bright blue eyes and then answered him. "I cannot always appear for you, but that does not mean I am not with you. I see what you see and feel what you feel." Braer did not answer Daniels question and he loved him even more for it.

Emma greeted Taitu with a great hug and the pair walked together by the side of the lake. Emma told Taitu of the attack on the road from Doran, were Daniel had fended off the soldiers with his sword before they took him. She also told how Trayan nearly died if it had not been for the intersession of Laura and Joseph. Taitu stopped and looked back at the boy, "he has a good heart." Moreover, Emma agreed.

Trayan set up the tents and made camp while the two teenagers spent time with their animals.

Daniel walked through the grass and then sat down next to Braer. Braer lay down in the grass beside the boy and stretched his back legs behind him and put his head down on his outstretched front legs, and let Daniel cuddle into his side.

Daniel picked a long stalk of grass and began to chew on it, then said. "Thank you for sending Trayan to me, if he had not come when he did the wolves would have killed me. I was tired and weak, you see, I am not like you, I do not have your strength."

Braer lifted his head off his paws and turned it to the side and his eyes sparkled in the bright sunshine.

Then in a calm and powerful voice, he spoke. "You have been attacked by mighty wolves and survived alone in the wilderness. You have been beaten to within an inch of your life and I tell you this, you are as tall as a mountain and as strong as the great oak, your size belittles the Inner strength that lies within you and I am proud to be your Brannai and even prouder to be your friend." Daniel fell into the warm fur on the side of Braer. "You and I will be friends forever."

That night they all sat around a great fire and feasted on freshly caught fish and exchanged stories of the past weeks adventures. Trayan went to his pack and brought out a flask of wine that Laura had given him when they left her farm. He poured a little into cups and gave one each to Daniel and Emma; he then stood and made a toast.

"To honour and victory, but most of all to friendships, may they last forever." Daniel and Emma both stood and raised their cups, Braer, and Taitu who stood and roared to the heavens joined them.

Trayan sat back down and when the others too had settled he spoke again. "I think tomorrow we should set out for a town I know, it is on the northern border of the land, it is called Narat."

Emma quickly changed her tone. "Do you not think the soldiers will be watching every tournament in the land and all the approaches in and out?" She was very worried and rightly so, after all they were young and a Lord and his men were trying to kill them.

Trayan raised his hands to gently calm Emma and then he spoke, but with calmness in his voice. "At this time of year there are tournaments held all over the land, lord Torek cannot watch all of them, and anyhow I have friends in Narat who will watch out for us."

He also pointed out to Daniel and Emma that Narat sat geographically cut off from Ballen by virtue of the mountain range.
Trayan hoped he had eased Emma and Daniel but he too could not help but worry for their safety and prayed he had made the right decision.

The following morning was lit up by a wonderful sunrise and soon the trio were on the road to Narat. The land was beautiful with open plains, heavy with grass and summer blooms and hills that gently rose and fell. The pace was a gentle one, as if to go along with the lazy summer air and as they strolled along Daniel spoke. "How long did you know my father?" The words were quietly spoken, but very deliberate.

Trayan did not break step and seemed pleased to answer the boy.

"All my life, Philip and I grew up together, near a town called Bagdale. It is a small place close to where the river Godwen meets the sea." He appeared happy to recount the memories of his friend and he continued in a friendly state of mind.

"Philip, your father, and I, we went to the same school. He loved to fish did Philip and he always hated the fact that I could see Brannai, even from an early age. My father took us both to Brien one summer, for the tournament there; I suppose it was then that we started on the road to what we were to become."

Trayan then paused and slowed his step. "I remember it like it was yesterday. It was Philips sixteenth birthday only a few days before and we had gone fishing. The day was not unlike this one and we had taken a bottle of wine from father's cellar. We had just opened the bottle when suddenly out of nowhere appeared a monkey and sat on the bank next to your father."

Emma looked across at Daniel and then back to Trayan. "He was a magnificent beast, jet black and large with shiny fur and powerful arms, he would become unbeatable."

Then he looked at Daniel. "Your father was the finest trainer I have ever seen and such a passion; you have a lot of work ahead of you if you are to become as good as him."

Trayan then smiled and continued along the summer fields. Daniel paused before following, suddenly his father was no longer a memory, he was a real person and in Trayan, he had a direct link.

Torek paced the great hall, he had not heard from any of the mercenaries he had sent out into the land. How he would love to gather up all his resources and send them to all the four corners of Arnorst, but that would show the world, how afraid he was of this boy. No, he must be subtle, the fewer people who knew of his obsession the better. Torek would bide his time, if all went to plan, the boy would come to him and then he would defeat him and humiliate his beast, then he could enter and win the tournament at Kingdale and once again be known as the Lord of the Brannai.

NARAT

Narat was a beautiful little town, set in open grassland with a small river winding through its centre. There was a small town square with a picturesque stone built clock in the middle. The river ran just to the side of the square and spanned by a beautiful white curved stone bridge. All the dwellings painted white and the gardens well kept.

Narat had a splendid town hall set in the town square. It was three storeys high, painted white with a beautiful blue roof and matching blue shutters at the sides of each window and to add to all this, there were flowers at every corner.

The town's mayor had organised a flower festival to coincide with the tournament that was to take place and all the townsfolk played their parts with enthusiasm, dressing in their finest clothes and decorating the shops and streets with fine colours and banners. The arena for the tournament was just outside of the town perimeter and it too stood decorated with flowers and banners.

Trayan and his party arrived at the border of the town were Trayan asked Daniel and Emma to wait. It was a small copse of trees, enough to hide their presence whilst Trayan went ahead to the town to look things over.

Daniel and Emma both sat against the base of trees and took in the beautiful summer air. The sky was a clear blue and the rays of the sun flickered through gaps in the leaves.

Emma removed her pack and looked over at Daniel as though something troubled her. "This tournament, well I have decided not to enter."

Emma did not look worried as she spoke the words; in fact, she looked relaxed and quite certain. Daniel was relaxing with his back to the tree and now he sat up and looked over at Emma.

"You seem sure." He said and then he picked himself up, went, and sat by his friend.

Emma looked deep into Daniels eyes as she continued. "I have been giving it some thought for quite a while now, battle is not for me and I do my Taitu no justice." Emma leaned forward and took hold of Daniels hands.

"I have seen the dedication in you and the pride you have when Braer fights. You are your father's son and you will go on to become as great a trainer as he was, there is no doubt of that."

Daniel blushed slightly not only at the words but also by the fact that Emma had a hold of his hands and they felt warm to the touch, and suddenly from deep within his chest, he felt his heart race.

"You are a great trainer," said Daniel, "you just need to put a little more," but Emma smiled at him and shushed him with a finger pressed lightly to his lips. To Daniel's dismay Emma then backed away and sat with her back, once again to the tree.

"When I left my home I did so because I sought adventure and excitement and I have certainly found that. I always believed that my Taitu came to me for a reason and now I understand that reason. He came to show me his world and all the wondrous creatures that reside there." Then she appeared to sigh, and a great sadness came over her and tears welled in her eyes as the next words came to her lips.

"I have to let him go, there is too much pride in him, too much fight." however, she could not finish, instead she just broke down. Daniel reached forward and put his arms around her to shield her from the world, and then he placed her head on his shoulder and let her cry for she had done something he could never do, she had said goodbye to her friend.

Trayan returned soon after and beckoned Daniel and Emma from the trees. "The way is clear he shouted." Then he just turned and headed for the town unaware of the decision the young girl had just made.

Trayan did not take them to an inn; instead, he stopped outside a small white cottage and knocked on the door. The door opened and there stood a huge man, he must have been at least six foot five, with a mass of black wavy hair and enormous hands. The man had to stoop to come outside and greet the three travellers.

"This is Norman and he has been kind enough to let us stay at his home for the tournament," said Trayan, and then he introduced Daniel and Emma to him.

Norman very politely bowed and shook Daniel's hand, then he bowed and did the same to Emma, and then he showed them to the inside of his home.

The inside was quite spacious, however when Norman walked around he made the room look tiny. There where beams from wall to wall propping up the ceiling and Norman instinctively ducked as he moved under one. There were two rooms downstairs, a living room and a dining area and the whole house was spotless.

"Betty's out at the moment, she's gone shopping but she said she can't wait to meet you all." Norman spoke with a deep and powerful, yet gentle voice. "I'll show you to your rooms shall I."

There were two bedrooms and a small attic, Trayan, Daniel would share one room, and Emma the attic.

The tournament itself was only small, although very select as the mayor was careful on the type of people who visited his village. The flower festival had been in full swing for several days and the tournament was about to begin the very next day and Trayan had only been given a late invitation because of his apparent reputation. Trayan spoke to Emma and Daniel up in the bedroom; he sat them on the bed and explained. "When we arrived I did not know whether or not the tournament was still on, as it happens it is tomorrow, but you are both ready and should do very well." Emma immediately spoke up, saying that she did not feel too well and would like to sit out. Trayan looked at her quizzically and then nodded politely but inside he suspected something more.

Trayan told Daniel that there are only a few competitors and that it was more for how they present themselves rather than how they perform in an arena that decided who competed.

He said that the whole town likes to put on a show and that they are very conscious of how the world perceives them. "That is why all the houses are painted the same colour and all the people take part in the presentation of the village."

Emma then added, "But you must admit the place is very beautiful."
Just then, there was the sound of a door shutting from downstairs and Trayan said that it must be Betty, so he ushered them all down to meet her.

Betty was a surprisingly small woman, very petite and very pretty. She had dark short hair and a tanned complexion and when she spoke, she did so with a strange accent.

"Oh, you must be Trayan; my Norm has told me all about you." Then she went to Trayan and kissed him on both cheeks. Then she looked towards Daniel and Emma. Firstly, she went to Daniel and after introductions, she kissed him across both cheeks too.

She then went to Emma, took hold of both her hands, and held them out, "this pretty thing must be Emma," she said. "You do yourself proud being in the company of such men." In addition, she looked Emma up and down agreeably.

Betty insisted that they must all be hungry and so she set herself to work in the kitchen and it was not long before she emerged with three plates full of ham, eggs and fresh bread. Norman sat at the table with the others and poured out two tankards of ale for himself and Trayan.

From the conversation that followed it appeared that Trayan and Norman originally came from the same village, Bagdale, Although Norman left when he was young. After their lunch, Norman said he would show them around the village and later he would take them to the arena.

Norman had a long slow stride and when he spoke, it was with a huge booming voice. He took them along the river's edge and made a point of showing all the different flower arrangements that were on show at different houses, to which Daniel found most amusing. Norman also stopped at the town square and pointed out the beautiful town hall with its blue roof and matching shutters before strolling to the outskirts were he showed them the arena.

Even from a distance, you could make out the small stand with its white seats and blue barriers and all around the perimeter were white posts linked together with blue rope. The grass was in pristine condition and the only things visible within its boundary were two tents at both ends, and a small bush situated at the far side. As Norman was showing Daniel and Trayan around, Emma slipped away and stole onto the grass. She felt a pain in her stomach as she crossed the threshold but it was nothing compared to the one she now felt in her heart.

Trayan and Norman were deep in conversation, when Daniel looked around and spotted Emma at the far end of the arena. He looked on with a great sadness as he saw Taitu appear by Emma. The young girl appeared to talk for a little while and then she sank to her knees, but to Daniel's surprise Taitu went over and raised her back to her feet and then he gently hugged her. Daniel smiled to himself as he watched the two of them walking together, then slowly they stopped and Taitu appeared to look over at him before disappearing.

When Emma returned she had wiped away the tears and appeared happier within herself and she came and stood next to Daniel who gently put his arm around her waist for comfort. The walk back was subdued and was in sharp contrast to the bright early summer's day and the wonderful scenery.

The townsfolk were all busy tending to their own individual flower arrangements but always had time to say hello and exchange idle gossip with Norman and Trayan. They reached the house in the late afternoon and Norman asked Daniel if he would help him with a window box that he was going to erect on the sidewall. As the two went away to prepare, Trayan seized the moment and ushered Emma into the garden. When they were alone Emma looked sadly at Trayan and was about to speak when he raised a hand to quiet her. "For some time now I have watched you, what you did today was very brave." Emma thought that Trayan had not even noticed when she had slipped away at the arena.

Trayan sat Emma down on a garden bench and sat next to her before he continued with his comments. "There is not much that misses my attention, today on the arena, you said goodbye to your beast."

Emma's eyes welled with tears and she found it hard to speak. Trayan spoke for her, "it is always best to be open with your feelings, perhaps you would like to tell me why."

Emma nervously looked up at him, "When I left home I wanted some excitement and I certainly found that, but I always thought my Taitu came to me for a reason, I now know that reason was for me to become a trainer like yourself," and she looked at the old man with hopeful eyes. Trayan paused and sat back against the back of the chair, he did not smile nor did he frown at the proposal.

After a short while, he looked to Emma and spoke. "It would be a pleasure for me to pass my knowledge on to someone such as yourself. You shall become my apprentice Emma." Then he lent forward and kissed her on the forehead.

The following morning there was great expectation in the air, Daniel was looking forward to the tournament and Emma was beginning a new career as Trayan's apprentice. They met at the le for breakfast with Norman and Betty. The hosts had prepared bacon, eggs and fresh bread and at either end of the le was a jug of fresh orange. Trayan explained to Daniel that originally, there were six people entered and that due to

Emma being, unwell, one of the participants had kindly dropped out, leaving just four. "The tournament is small, though none the less important to your training."

Betty looked over at Emma, "I hope you are feeling much better, the country air will do you a power of good."

Trayan asked if Norman and Betty were coming to the arena, to which they both answered enthusiastically that they were. "I have packed us all some lunch for the day's events," She added.

Therefore, they all set out for the edge of town. The weather was warm and the sun was shining brightly lighting up all the whitewash on the houses and causing all the blooms in the town to glow with colour. The townsfolk headed in the same direction although there was no great hurry in their progress.

The stand was slowly filling with people when they arrived and Daniel went straight over to the judges table to give his name in. There was only one person at the table and he stood as Daniel approached. The man was a jovial soul, portly and small in height. He had a crop of tight blonde curly hair and a suit that was a tad too small. His face was bright red and he wore a long gold chain around his neck." There will be no need for names my lad; we are all friends here today," and he beckoned Daniel to the tent to the right of the field.

The small man was the Mayor of the town and he now stood on top of a box to introduce the day's event.

"Welcome my friends to the Narat Brannai tournament in conjunction with the annual flower show. This year's tournament is a very special one as we have with us Daniel the champion from the tournaments at Brien and Doran, an up and coming young man from the town of Dantaal. He will be joined by Thomas the champion of Dantome, Gregory the champion of Parkhurst and finally, Jared the champion of Monkskaat."
All the people gave a friendly clap with each name, and then they settled down for the start.

Daniel went out first to gentle applause from the crowd; shown a position just to the right of the main stand next to a white post. Opposite Daniel on the far side of the arena stood a young man who introduced as Jared and next to him stood a large Braer. The beast was slightly smaller in height than Daniel is Braer and was a deep brown in colour. It had a large rounder shaped head with fury ears on the top but it appeared every bit as powerful as Daniels did. Jared was of medium height and very stocky, with thick brown hair and brown eyes.

The Mayor turned to the crowd and spoke in a loud and clear voice. "Let the tournament of champions begin."

Then he took hold of a blue flag and raised it in the air.

Daniel looked to his own animal and said, "You are the best, the strongest, the fastest and you are unbeatable." Then the Mayor lowered his flag and the two animals set off.

Daniel's Braer tore up the grass as he leapt from his side and headed straight for his advisory. The brown Braer had started in just the same way and the two met in the middle with a huge clash of fur and claws. They pushed and swiped at each other looking for an opening until they fell apart and circled each other breathing heavily. Daniels Braer then roared and set upon the other beast in a wild frenzy swiping with its claws and catching it across the head, sending it reeling backward. Jared recalled his Braer just in time as Daniel's Braer was gaining the upper hand.

Daniel too recalled his Braer who had a slash across his back and was breathing heavily.

"That animal is strong, but I am stronger and I will defeat him on my next encounter." Said Braer. Daniel looked over at Jared and then he turned to Braer and spoke softly in his ear.

The other Braer had regained his composure and once again set off, roaring as he did so, however Daniels Braer stood and let the beast come on. When the other Braer was about ten paces, away it vanished and Daniel cried out, "now."

His Braer vanished and when the other Baer reappeared, it swiped out with its claw into fresh air. Daniel's Braer had reappeared just to the side of the other Braer and now it sent down blow after blow upon its advisory knocking it to the floor until it vanished in a shower of silver.
The previously restrained crowd now applauded loudly at such a piece of skill and they all stood in their seats and cheered. Daniel went and congratulated Braer, but Braer acknowledged Daniel for his insight.

Daniel was then led away back to the tent, the Mayor had said that it would be an unfair advantage if Daniel watched the next bout as the other two competitors had not watched his.

The next half hour passed slowly for Daniel interrupted only by the crowd as they whooped and cheered. Inside the tent, he was alone and so he summoned his Braer and they talked over the tactics of the fight ahead.

"We cannot always rush in my friend; we must give respect to the opposition until I can work out their weakness." Daniel was sincere with his words and Braer acknowledged the boy's growing talents.

The cheering began to die down and so Daniel asked Braer to disappear. Soon after a man came into the tent with refreshments and told Daniel that the next match would take place in fifteen minutes.

Precisely fifteen minutes later Daniel moved out onto the open grass, to stand by the white pole. Opposite Daniel stood a very tall and thin looking boy with short black hair and a fair complexion.

Next to the boy an enormous snake sat, the biggest Daniel had ever seen. It must have been at least thirty feet long and had a girth the size of Daniel's body. The snake curled up in its coils next to the boy, it

Brannai

flickered its tongue out in the direction of Braer trying to get a taste of his scent. Daniel looked at the snake and could not believe his eyes as it changed colour from yellow to green to match the grass on which it stood. He also noticed that it had some sort of rattle on the end of its tail and he began to wonder.

The Mayor once again stood on his podium and settled the crowd with a wave of his hands. "My friends, we have been treated to an excellent show so far, but now comes the final two. On my left, I give you Daniel with his Braer, and on the right, I give you Gregory and his Phythian.

The sun had just gone behind a cloud as the Mayor was speaking and now it reappeared and Daniel noticed a shiny wet sheen coming from the great snake's skin. He looked up at Braer, be wary my friend but remember it is just another Brannai.

The Mayor had finished addressing the crowd and he now turned and raised a blue flag above his head, then quickly in one sharp movement, he whipped it down.

Braer moved off cautiously on all fours and he barked out warnings as he went. The Phythian set off through the grass, winding its way slowly towards Braer. They met right in front of the stand and circled one another. The great snake tasted the air with its tongue and Braer barked out warnings to its enemy, then without warning Braer pounced on the reptile and grabbed it with its claws. However he could not hang on to the beast, its slippery skin made it impossible to hold and it simply slipped through his grasp.

Then the snake stopped and raised its tail high above the ground. The rattle on the end of its tail was not a rattle at all, but a kind of lure and it waved it gently back and forth in front of Braer.

The movements were mesmerising to Braer and he found himself swaying rhythmically with its beat. He had not realised that he had stopped moving and was now standing still in front of the crowd.

Daniel was shouting at his friend but his words were not getting through and so, breathless, he composed himself and closed his eyes.

Daniel concentrated on Braer so hard that he began to sway were he stood then in his mind he roared out to his friend.

Braer came out of the trance he was in and not a minute too soon for the snake had begun to wrap itself around his body, becoming tighter and tighter.

Every time the great Braer tried to catch a breath, the snake would squeeze a little more. Daniel called to his friend, "look for the head." And as the snake lifted up it brought its head alongside Braer's and hissed loudly at him poking its tongue out tasting the beast it was about to devour. However, Braer was ready for him and in one last enormous effort he reached out, grasped the snakes head between his jaws, and crushed it. The snake dropped to the floor and disappeared in a shower of silver.

The crowd initially appeared dumbstruck; the Phythian seemed to have the upper hand until Braer had turned the contest on its head, and now they all stood and cheered and any that had hats, now threw them into the air.

Daniel was proud of his animal but he knew it had been a narrow escape and he also knew he would not make the same mistake again should he ever come across another Phythian.

For now, Daniel took the plaudits and under the summer sun, he stood on the podium and waved to the crowd as champion of Narat. The Mayor presented Daniel with a bag of silver and the champions pendant, which had the towns emblem of a shield crossed with two yellow lilies and he received a huge bouquet of flowers.

The Mayor then stood back and ushered Daniel to the front of the podium and the crowd settled down in their seats and went quiet.

The boy may be becoming a fine trainer but he was not prepared to make a speech and suddenly he became very nervous.

"Well, err I think I would, err." The Mayor stepped close to Daniel, "Don't be afraid, you are the tournament champion, now nice and loud if you please." Daniel pulled himself together and started again.

"Firstly I would like to thank the other trainers they were marvellous and they proved that they are true champions."

The crowd clapped at the boy's generosity, and then Daniel cleared his throat and continued. "I would also like to thank my friends Trayan and Emma for their support; I could not have done it without them."

Daniel then stepped back from the Front of the podium and made his way down the small set of steps to applause from everyone.

The crowd began to disperse and he met Trayan and Emma at the edge of the stands.

Emma walked toward the young boy and said, "Nice speech Daniel."
"Thanks, I found that a bit scary, you know in front of all those people. Oh! By the way these are for you." he handed Emma the bouquet of flowers.

"Why thank you kindly," she said and she gave a light courtesy, to which Daniel and Emma both laughed.

"Well done lad, I thought the reptile had you for a while but you kept your senses about you and I was most impressed with the contact you have with your beast."

Trayan truly was proud of the lad.

Enticement

Lord Torek looked out from a narrow window, high in the upper floors of Ballen Castle as the rain covered the land. Even after all these years that fight with Philip still ate away at his soul, how clever he had been in keeping it private for no one had been witness to it, his only defeat.

There was a clamour from down below in the courtyard but Torek paid no heed to it, he simply lifted his head slightly, then turned, and went to his chambers. He sat in his favourite chair facing the blazing fire, with a glass of the finest wine in his hand. There was a knock on the large oak door and Torek called out in a quiet but firm voice. "Enter."

A small man entered the room; it was Torek's personal servant Sebastian. The man had been faithful to his lordship for many years but age was getting the better of him and now he walked bent over with a crook in his back and on frail, aged legs.

"What is it Sebastian," but Torek did not take his gaze away from the flames in front of him as he spoke.

"My lord, you have a visitor it is one of the mercenaries you sent out." Sebastian did not add anymore, he knew his master well and now he simply turned and left.

Torek stood and with the wine still in his hand, he turned and faced the door. Two soldiers entered the room; one of them appeared badly injured as was being carried by the other. Lord Torek looked at the injured soldier and with no emotion on his face; he waved the other out of the room.

Aaron fell to the floor, he was exhausted, his clothes torn to shreds and he had deep cuts to his face and body. Torek took another sip of wine and then simply said, "Well."

Aaron could not recall what had happened in the wood, only that a terrible beast had rampaged through the camp tearing up everything in its rage. He had been lucky to escape with his life. Torek paced in front of the fire before he spoke again. "The boy, what do you know of the boy?"

"Aaron was disgusted at the man's lack of sincerity but he answered all the same. "The boy was unharmed, the last I saw of him he was still tied to a tree."

Torek called the guards and had Aaron taken away. "Feed him well and see to his wounds."

Before Aaron left, he looked back to Torek and spoke. "As you said my lord the boy was travelling with two companions an old man and a girl, the man is dead but the girl is missing," and then he was carried away.
Torek called Sebastian. The old man entered the room and he now bowed slightly. "My lord," He said.

"Sebastian I want you to find Trayell," Sebastian nodded slightly and was about to leave when Torek added. "Be Discreet my friend."

Torek paced the floor of his private chamber contemplating what the mercenary had told him, if what he said was the truth then the boy is protected. What he needed was a plan to bring the boy to him, the girl, if she travelled with him would most certainly have become close friends.
Torek stood intrigued, when there was a knock on the door. Torek calmly spoke the words enter and in walked Trayell.

Trayell was a small man, thin with pale skin and high cheekbones. His hair was thinning and his hands were very long for his size with very long fingernails blackened at the ends.

Torek hated the sight of the man but over the years, he had proved very useful to him especially when it had come to the darker side of the Brannai.

"I wish to make you a proposition." As Torek spoke he turned and faced the warmth of the fire

"The boy lives, however he is on his own, somewhere to the south of the mountains but for now he is not my main concern. There is a girl, she travelled with him and is also alone, and I would like you to bring her to me."

Torek then appeared to smirk as he spoke the next words, "It would also appear that Trayan is dead, slain with an arrow in his back." Slowly he turned and looked at Trayell and then he sipped wine from the glass in his hand.

Trayell had not shown any emotion and his bland face remained blank as he clasped his long fingers together and looked down onto the stone floor. "My lord, Trayan lives, this I know for sure."

Torek's smirk faded, he finished the wine and threw the glass into the fire before he spoke again. "That is unfortunate; your powers still astound me. It seems the bond between brothers is still strong. It changes nothing. Bring me the girl."

Trayell turned and left closing the large oak door slowly behind him. He made his way down the stone steps that led from the tower to the courtyard always keeping his hands clasped together in front of him as he went. Trayell passed servants and soldiers along the way and they all bowed to him, but kept a distance. The man's presence and reputation preceded him were ever he went and he could feel the hate on the people he passed, but he did not care because eventually it would be him who would be high Lord of Ballen.

He reached the courtyard and called to the stable master. "Ready my horse and pack provisions, I shall be gone for several weeks."

The sky was heavy and dark as Trayell left the castle gates and it started to rain, he stopped and pulled up his hood and then glanced up at the tower. There was a lonely figure staring out from the narrow window but Trayell paid no heed, he just turned up his collar, then whipped his horse around, and sped off.

The soldier had mentioned the town of Doran and so it was there that Trayell would head to and try to pick up the trail.

Betty had lain on a party to celebrate Daniel's victory; she had moved the table outside into the garden and had set it with all manner of party food. There were also casks of ale for Trayan, Norman, and wine for herself and Emma. Daniel was expected to join in with the men; however, the boy baulked at the taste and chose a glass of wine instead.

Norman and Betty were very proud for they had the champion of the whole village staying at their house and over time they would let them all know about it. They celebrated until the early evening, until the law of the village prevented them from carrying on, the peace was always kept after dark and in any case Daniel and Emma had both had quite enough.
The following morning Daniel awoke with a terrible headache and the sight of the bacon and eggs which Betty had prepared for breakfast, turned his stomach and he vowed there and then never to drink again. Trayan and Norman tucked into the food and laughed at how many times they had said those very words. It was mid morning on the other hand before Emma turned out of bed and when she did make an appearance she looked the worse for wear. Betty gave the girl a homemade remedy and said she would feel much better in an hour or so. However, it did not curtail Emma's appetite and she tucked in to breakfast.

Trayan decided they would stay for one more night before heading off in the morning to give the younger generation time to recover; it was a decision that pleased Emma and Daniel.

TRAINING

Dark clouds loomed over the bright town of Narat, it held the promise of some rain, and so Daniel, Emma and Trayan wrapped up well as they headed out. They took a southerly heading, Trayan wanted to return to the arena by the lake, just north of the mountains, his intention was to help Emma with her new career and to give Daniel some practice. Narat was still in view when the heavens opened, but for all that, the downpour could throw at them it could not dampen their spirits.

"Another tournament and another victory, you are learning fast but you must keep your feet on the ground, even if the path is full of mud," and Trayan went over and clasped the boy around the shoulder and all three laughed.

The countryside was a beautiful place even in the drab rain, there were trees with branches that were leaning down under the weight of water and the greenness of their leaves stood out against the grey sky. Even the grass fields had a sheen that would sparkle when the sun broke through a gap in the clouds.

For two days, they travelled until they reached the arena by the mountains, with its lake sunk in the middle of bright green hills and surrounded by white bark fir trees and bushes. They approached the top of the final hill and looked down onto the arena and the beauty and peacefulness of the place reached out and filled their hearts with calmness and a feeling of good.

Trayan and Emma set up camp near the water's edge whilst Daniel went in search of wood for a fire. They set two tents with a fire set in the middle and straight away Trayan set a pan of water over its flames, ready for the evening stew. He and Daniel then went out hunting with their bows and left Emma alone to prepare the pot.

The old man and the boy had not travelled far when Trayan spotted a small wild deer grazing in the shadow of the trees. Trayan left the hunt to the boy and only insisted on one thing. "When you shoot your arrow you must be sure of its intent, aim only for the heart, for the kill must be swift and as painless as possible."

Trayan was a good hunter but he loved all animals and did not take any joy in taking a life unless it was very necessary.

Daniel gauged the wind and its direction and then slowly and surely he moved closer to the beast keeping himself downwind all the time. Carefully he stepped through the grass keeping low as he went. Trayan stayed a few paces behind watching patiently. Daniel then took up a position behind a tree and raised his bow. Slowly he took aim and then drew in a long and deep breath. The deer looked up and just for a moment, it appeared to sense some danger, its ears twisted around searching for sounds in the wood and its large dark brown eyes hunted the trees and bushes. Daniel pulled back on the bowstring and let fly. The arrow went swiftly and found its mark with precision, felling the deer in an instant.

Daniel and Trayan ran over to the kill and as they arrived Trayan clasped Daniel on the shoulder in approval, then went, and knelt down by the dead beast. He then laid a hand on the deer's side and closed his eyes in reverence. Daniel watched and felt a pride for the man and the love he had for all life.

They arrived back at the camp were Emma had prepared the vegetables to add to the stew once the meat was nearly cooked. They sat in the evening sun, ate, and talked through the night.

The following morning Trayan set off early with Emma and Daniel for the far side of the lake, away from the camp. To begin with, he said he would like to be alone with Emma and so Daniel happily set off to a quieter section of the arena.

Trayan took Emma to a clearing between the trees. "Look around you, what you see is the heartbeat of the land, the trees, and the birds. Close your eyes and feel their presence, feel the gentle breeze on your face and hear the rustle of the leaves as they blow in the wind."

Brannai

Emma did as ordered and as she stood there, calmness filled her body.

Even with her eyes closed, she could still picture the scene around her and could clearly hear Trayan's voice in the background seemingly drifting through her mind.

"Now, picture a brannai, just one and concentrate on it. See it standing before you, here in the clearing and at the same time let the life force of all the living things around you flow through you body. Hold your arms above your head and concentrate all your energy into them. Now slowly open them and when you are ready I want you to clap and at the very instant of contact with your hands you must think of the Brannai."

Trayan stood back and watched as the girl stood amidst the trees and the wild and slowly raised her hands above her head. She lowered them slightly and then in one swift movement she clapped them hard above her head. When Emma opened her eyes Trayan was standing before her, alone in the wood and Emma's heart sank.

"There is no need to feel disappointed, you have done very well it is just a matter of practice and perseverance." Then Trayan went over and consoled her with a gentle pat on the back.

Emma practiced all morning until a rumble in her stomach told her it was time for something to eat. They headed back to the camp and found that Daniel had not yet arrived and so they set to making some early tea. The pair was halfway through their meal when Daniel arrived.

"You have been some time, your dedication does you proud, and there is food in the pot, you can help yourself."

Daniel helped himself to a bowl and hungrily ate and spoke at the same time. "How did our new Trainer of Brannai perform?" Emma looked disappointed, but Trayan answered for her.

"She has done exceptionally well and has the makings of a fine trainer." Daniel smiled at Emma and then finished his meal and stood. "Well, that's it for me I must get back," and he left in a hurry and set off for the far side of the lake."

That lad does not rest, he sometimes borders on the obsessive, a trait left to him by his father." Emma looked at the old man and smiled politely for she knew Daniel was making his plans.

After dinner, Trayan and Emma once again set off to the clearing for more practice. This time Trayan tried a different approach. He rolled up his travelling cloak and tied it around his waist so that it looked like a round pillow and then he stood facing Emma in the centre of the clearing. He made the girl stand square in front of him and then he spoke. "I want you to punch me, but not just any way. You must focus your energy, let your hand and arm relax and then snap out using your reach and only at the very end, the point of final contact must you clench your fist. Do you understand Emma?" Emma nodded but could not see the reason Trayan wanted her to punch him.

She struck out with her fist repeatedly, each time Trayan would say good, well done. He continued with the exercise for at least an hour resting every couple of minutes to give her time to recover.

When the hour was up, he removed the coat from around his waist and waited for Emma to catch her breath. Emma was on the floor completely worn out, sweat was dripping down her face, and running onto the grass were she lay. As she recovered, breathing heavily on the floor Trayan came over and knelt by her.

"As you struck out with your fist you learnt to concentrate all your energy into the point when your hand struck me, so it is with the Brannai. You must relax your body, take in the air around you, listen to the trees, the breeze as it blows through your hair, and then you must picture the Brannai that you wish to see. Only then can you control your mind and as you raise your hands above your head concentrate all your emotion into the clap."

Emma now understood the reason for the exhausting training and she now stood. She was still breathing heavily from the punching and she had

Brannai

to take deep breaths to collect herself. Then she closed her eyes and took in all the sounds around her.

Trayan watched as the girl very slowly raised her hands above her head. Emma lowered her hands and then in one swift movement she clapped. There was a loud crack, as her hands met and then slowly and confidently she opened her eyes.

She took in a deep gasp as standing before her was a beautiful blue bird. It was about the size of a large swan with a long slender neck and graceful head. It had long slender tail feathers that split into two and on the end of each were beautiful white flowers.

The huge bird spread its wings and flapped them as though stretching before taking flight and then it folded its wings and very gently bowed before the girl, and then it spoke to her in a wondrous feminine voice. "My young mistress, what can I do for you?"

Emma had a huge smile on her face and she looked over at Trayan. The old man looked back and beckoned her to return the bow. Emma faced the bird and bowed gracefully back and then she spoke. "Thank you for appearing for me, I am graced by your presence, you are the most beautiful flowertail I have ever seen. For now I do not require anything of you and you may return to your world." Then she raised her hands and clapped them above her head, and the bird disappeared.

Emma ran over to Trayan, jumped into the air, and hugged him with all her might. "Thank you that was the most amazing thing I have ever done." Trayan smiled at Emma and then he said. "It is just the beginning of your new life." He then put an arm around her shoulder and led her back to camp.

The sun was just beginning to set when Daniel returned and they all settled down by the lake and under a clear and starry sky.

DEATH

For several days Trayell travelled, heading south at first and then turning east as the great mountain range came into view. He did not stop at any towns or villages, not even a local farm took his interest. Trayell did not care much for people and he believed that they did not care much for him either.

He was on the main track that led into Doran when his horse began to waver under his weight and so the man pulled over and dismounted. He went and stood in front of the horse and looked deep into its eyes, and then he went to the back and lifted its left hoof. There was a stone lodged in the hoof, Trayell pulled out a knife and was about to remove it when a lone man appeared, travelling on a cart.

The stranger pulled over when he came near to Trayell. "Can I be of any assistance my friend?" Trayell looked up at the man and smiled and slowly and out of sight, he put away his knife. In a cold and monotone voice, he spoke to the man. "My horse is lame, it cannot take my weight, I fear for his leg if it is not seen to." The man gave his name as Joseph and he led Trayell back to his farm to meet his wife Laura. Trayell rode on the cart next to Joseph with his horse tethered behind.

Joseph was completely unsuspecting as to the evil passenger he had just picked up and now he spoke to Trayell. "How strange that I should find another traveller right here at these very crossroads."

Trayell looked at Joseph and what colour that filled in his pale face now drained away. However, he kept his gaze on the path as he answered, "another traveller you say,"

"Attacked by brigands he was, had an arrow in his back. The young girl was most upset. I don't know what the world is coming to, these parts used to be so quiet and peaceful." Trayell did not say another word until they came to Joseph's farmhouse where Laura who was tending a hanging basket near the front gatepost met them.

She greeted her husband with a bright smile and approached the cart. Joe climbed down and went over and laid a kiss on her cheek, and pointed to the cart at his passenger. Trayell was on the far side of the cart and he had climbed down out of view, but now he appeared from rear.

Laura looked at the thin man standing before her and suddenly her heart became cold and empty and all hope seemed to leave her body.

Joseph introduced Trayell and said that the man's horse was lame. Laura though, kept her distance and nervously, but politely she managed to raise a smile. "I am very sorry but I know nothing of horses, my talents as little as they may be, restricts me to my humble farm and my aged husband."

Joseph looked strangely at his wife, he had known her for nearly forty years and she had never refused a stranger in need, but he could also tell when his wife was scared and he had the quick wits to back her up.

" I told our friend here of the other travellers I found not more than a few weeks ago, you know, the ones I dropped off at the town. I was about to take him and his horse there but I thought he May need some provisions." Laura looked from her husband to Trayell and added, "Perhaps you would like to come in and have something to eat."

Trayell hated the way people lied openly to him, he could smell their deceit and their hate for his physical form, but he had learned to hide his distaste and for now, he politely refused their false hospitality.

 "You have done far too much already and despite your kindness I must be on my way." He then gave the couple a low bow, turned, and went to the back of the cart to unhitch his horse and then he simply turned and began to walk.

Laura ran to her husband and squeezed him, placing her head on his shoulder as she did.

"Joe, Joe, there is something evil living inside that man; I can feel it, why did you bring him here?" Joseph patted her on the head and watched as Trayell walked slowly away and then he led Laura into the house.

Laura ran to the window to obtain a view of the path that led from her home, but there was no sign of Trayell. Her breathing became heavy and she suffered with panic and fear as she raced to the other window. She looked out and then she clasped her hands to her mouth and then took a step backwards. Joe grabbed his wife and shielded her from the view. There in the field stood Trayell, all alone with his head looking down to the furrowed ground below.

Slowly Trayell raised his gaze and looked at the house. Laura could feel his evil eyes piercing her heart and she quickly buried her head in her husband's shoulder and wept. Trayell looked up to the sky and raised his hands above his head, the once blue heavens now clouded over, and the area around the farm became suddenly dark and cold.

At the house, a strong wind suddenly blew in through gaps in the door and down the fireplace and Joe could see the breath in the air as his wife struggled to breathe. Then it came, the sound of powerful wing beats echoing all around the room and bouncing off the walls. Joseph clung tightly to his wife and the pair stood petrified in the middle of the room looking upwards to the ceiling.

Then came a mighty hammering on the roof of their home and Laura screamed aloud. Time and time again came the pounding on the roof until dust and debris hurtled down onto the innocent old couple, their furniture was shaken and fell to the floor as though an earthquake had hit the land. Laura and Joseph then squeezed their hands over their ears as the room filled with the piercing shriek of an animal born from the depths of hell itself.

Finally, the roof caved in and the screams suddenly ceased. The dust settled on the torn and smashed property but no life stirred within its broken walls. Trayell looked on the scene with an evil passion but did not smile nor show any other human emotion, he simply turned and walked back towards the crossroads were Joseph had found him.

Brannai

At the crossroads Trayell stopped and dismounted from his horse, He tied the horse to a nearby tree and then walked around. He studied the clearing and attempted to picture the scene in his mind and every now and then, he would bend down and feel the soil between his fingers. He untied his horse and walked for a few hundred yards before he decided to stop and make camp.

Trayell had built himself a warm fire and he now sat on a fallen log with a hot cup of tea, warmed himself in front of the flames, and contemplated his next move. The mercenaries would have taken off through the wood and would have headed in a straight line for Ballen Castle. My dear brother and the girl would certainly have followed; his ability for being self-righteous would have compelled him to do so. If he did find the boy and I am sure he did, then where would he go?

CAPTURE

The morning sun rose above the distant hills and spread its light and warmth over the lake and the beautiful countryside that surrounded the arena. Daniel was up early and was already helping Trayan with the breakfast, when Emma emerged from her tent. "Good morning," said Trayan," how is our fine new trainer of Brannai this day."Emma smiled and her skin bloomed in the sunshine.

Trayan smiled and was in good spirits and thought that the two children deserved a long break and so he asked them if they would like to spend a few days at the side of the lake. Daniel and Emma agreed both and looked forward to the few days' rest. After breakfast, Emma and Daniel both went their separate ways, Emma to train on her own at the far side of the lake and Daniel to continue his training with Braer on the other side. Trayan looked at the two as they set off and decided a break was a good idea for him and so he fashioned himself a rod and went fishing.

**

Trayell had followed the path through the woods as though he was heading for Ballen and all the time he looked around at the trees and ground for signs that the soldiers had passed that way. Although any signs that would be left would now be gone or barely visible Trayell new that his powers of tracking were the best, anyway he only needed a sniff to find the general direction until some harder evidence came along.

After two more days, that evidence came into view. Trayell had found a small stream that flowed through the wood and appeared to head north toward the mountains. He walked into a small clearing and instantly knew he was in the right place. It had been a campsite and although the land and its wild had engulfed most of the evidence animals, there were still signs that he could read. The remnants of a fire partially hidden by the grass that had begun to recover over the scorched earth, but more than any other sign, Trayell spotted something that was present all around the area.

On the trees and bushes around, he found deep cuts into the bark as though made by a wild animal, branch snapped, depriving them of the lifeblood of the bush or tree, and so they had lost their colour.

"So, your animal came and rescued you from your torment, how quaint." Trayell spoke aloud and then continued to search the area. He looked at the stream and thought aloud, "if I were young and frightened the stream would provide me with hope," and so he followed the path of the water with his eyes as it headed north. There in the distance were the mountains, his next destination.

For another day and a half, Trayell kept the stream near to him as he drove his horse northwards. By midday he came to a rise in the land were the stream veered up through a waterfall. Rocks filled the sides of the waterfall and there would be no way through for a man and his horse.

Trayell veered inland and took a path through the trees winding in and out of the rays of sun as they managed to find a way between the branches and leaves. The land rose all the time and then suddenly it opened out into more open ground. The stream was visible to the left and Trayell noticed an outcrop of rocks to the side.

Trayell lifted his nose in the air; there it was, faint but there all the same, fear.

It was a close companion of the man and he could detect one drop in a million drops of water, for it was what drove him on. He walked his horse gently over to the outcrop of rocks and then at the base he stopped and dismounted.

On the ground just were the land rose he found the remnants of a dead animal. Mere bones now, they had been there for some time but he could still make out the form of a wolf and his eyes lifted from the marks on the floor to the outcrop of rocks above him.

Trayell paced up the small rise and at the top, he found a small crag in the rocks and on the floor was the burnt marks of a campfire. He looked around the enclosed space and then went out to the opening and stared at the landscape below. "You have faced the demon and you have come through, but where will you go now my friend."

Trayell had also found an arrow head buried in the remains of the wolf and realised that his brother must have found the boy and the three of them were now together. All he had to do now was discover where they went.

Trayell placed his hands in front of him and clasped them together as he sat in front of a warm fire. The flames danced on the sharp contours of his face putting him in shadow and then light as it flickered in the bright moonlight. They had already been to Doran; the mercenary confirmed that, they must have been heading west when they left that town. He put the chain of events into his mind and with reason; he concluded that they can only head north.

"Yes, the town of Narat, it makes sense, for that town is protected from the prying eyes of Ballen by the mountains." His deduction made perfect sense to him and so the following morning he set off.

**

Trayan lay down in the grass with his head propped up on a rolled up coat and the warmth of the sun beat down onto his face. He was content and totally at peace with the land around him, Daniel and Emma were both training hard and it was time for him to relax a little and so that is exactly what he did. The old man took out his pipe and then caressed the tobacco into the bowl, before lighting it and taking in a long and deep breath.

Trayan exhaled smoke circles as he lay in the grass and enjoyed the scenery. Suddenly he sat up with a start, in his mind came a premonition, a feeling of foreboding. He was not sure what it was but the feeling niggled at the back of his brain and it filled his soul with loss. Trayan put his pipe on the grass and stood up, he turned and faced the waters of the lake and then he closed his eyes and tried to open his mind to the beat of the land. Slowly he lowered his breathing and tried to concentrate on the feeling that had taken hold of him, but something blocked his thoughts and put a veil over that which he now sought. As hard as he might he could not pinpoint the feeling and so he opened his eyes and looked around at the beautiful scene. Everything around him was still the same as it had been just a moment ago and he could feel the warmth of the sun and the gentle breeze on his face once more.

Whatever the feeling had been it was now gone, but it left a question mark with him for the rest of the day.

That evening he sat with Daniel and Emma and enjoyed a meal of cooked venison roasted over the flames of the campfire. Emma was excited and she told both Daniel and Trayan how she enticed the flowertail another two times and how they had spoken to each other. Daniel asked if she had attempted to summon a Taitu, but Emma's smile faded and she said she was not sure whether she was ready to confront her friend so close to losing him. Trayan looked at Emma and then he spoke in a quiet voice. "The animals you summon into your presence are not yours, they are," and he paused to look for the right words, "sort of wild, yet to be picked up."

Emma looked sad and yet relieved. "So if I were to attempt to summon a Taitu it would not be my Taitu." "That is quite correct my dear," said Trayan, and at his words Emma turned her face to the floor and tears began to fill her pretty eyes. "Then my friend is indeed lost to me forever."

Daniel was about to go over to his friend to comfort her but Trayan raised his hand and gestured for him to sit down. Trayan knew that it was a decision Emma would have to learn to deal with in her own way.

Trayan called the two trainers together the following morning and asked if they would like to travel down to his own town of Bagdale and both Daniel and Emma agreed that would be a fine idea. Daniel grew excited at the prospect of seeing the place where his father had been born and wondered whether his real mother might be there also. Something Daniel had thought of putting to Trayan, it had felt somewhat inappropriate in the past.

As the fates would have it Trayan and the two young trainers set off south keeping the mountains to the right and Trayell set off north keeping the mountains to his left.

After a day's travel the land around the three travellers changed and the open plains and sparsely populated trees transformed into a land filled densely with white bark fir trees and rolling hills. It was also a land teeming with life in the height of a warm summer. Buzzards, pigeon and all manner of birds, together with deer and squirrel were all busy making the best of the sun and the warmth. In one such wood Trayan stopped and in a clearing he set up the tents and made camp for the night. The sun was low in the sky, it cast a red glow on the few clouds that were still present and the moon, and a few of the brighter stars in the heavens had come out to join in the evening dance.

Daniel brought in some wood from around the clearing and began to build the fire whilst Trayan set off into the wood to hunt for the evening meal.

Emma helped Daniel with the collecting of the firewood and she placed what she had found in a pile near to the fire. Daniel looked around for some branches to make a stand for the pots to sit on and as he did so Emma picked up a pile of the firewood and placed them on the flames. She must have picked up some debris from the floor as she did for not long after she put them on the fire, thick smoke rose into the air. She shouted Daniel who said that it was nothing to worry about; the smoke would die away soon.

Unknowingly in the near distance, a lone rider on horseback stopped on the crest of a hill and looked over at the smoke as it rose into the red night sky.
Trayan returned and was carrying two small wood pigeons in his hands, there was a pot of hot water beginning to boil on the fire and he went over and sat near the flames.

Emma and Daniel sat with him and Trayan looked over at Emma and asked if she would do the honours with the pigeon. Emma had always hated that side of living in the open and she politely refused with a sour look on her face. Trayan smiled and threw one of the dead birds over to Daniel who immediately started the process of removing the feathers and de gutting the body. The birds hung on wooden skewers over the flames and while they cooked, Trayan made a pot of hot tea.

"Such a beautiful evening I think I will sleep in the open tonight and look up at the night sky." Daniel agreed with Trayan but Emma said that she would still like to sleep in the tent. Daniel knew that she was still, after all this time, not quite at home unless she had walls around her to make her feel safe and he smiled to himself.

After eating, the three friends sat and chatted as they drank hot tea warmed by the flames of the campfire. Emma asked Trayan if she needed to be able to have seen the Brannai that she would summon or could she do so from memory. Trayan's face lit up orange by the flames of the fire as he looked over at the girl and answered. "To begin with it would be best to only try to summon animals that you have met; however as you progress and your capabilities increase you will probably find that they will start to appear in your dreams. From there you can start to build a sort of library in your mind." Trayan looked over at Daniel and asked how the training was going with Braer, "you certainly have shown some dedication over the past weeks."

Daniel felt a hot flush at the simple question but his blushes went unnoticed by the evening and by the flames of the fire and he answered. "Braer is the finest animal I have ever met; training with him is always a pleasure."
The evening drew on and the three friends called it a night and then settled down to a good night's sleep.

The following morning brought a mist to the woods; however, it was not so thick that the summer sun would burn it away in an hour or so. Trayan awoke and once up he soaked his head in cool fresh water from a skin in his pack and the noise of it stirred Daniel from his slumber. "Where did this mist come from?" asked Daniel.

"Have no fear boy, the sun will be out shortly, it promises to be another fine day." Trayan stoked the fire and once lit, he boiled up some hot water to make tea. There were still some dried bacon in the rucksack and Daniel smiled and then brought it over and gave it to Trayan to cook.
The smell of the bacon was always guaranteed to bring Emma out of dreamland and over to the fire. Daniel and Trayan finished their breakfast and most of their tea but there was still no sign of their friend.

The early morning mist was beginning to clear when Trayan looked over at Daniel, "You had better go and wake her, we need to be on our way soon, that girl would sleep through a storm if you let her." Daniel went over to the front of her tent and politely called her name. There was no answer and so he tried again only a little louder. Again, there was no reply, anxiety took a hold of the boy, and so he peered around the entrance in case she was indisposed.

Trayan finished off his tea and began to gather the tin plates used for breakfast when there was a shout from the tent. EMMA!
Trayan dropped the plates, ran over to the tent, and went straight in. There was no sign of the girl and there was a large cut in the rear of the canvass.

Daniel was in a panic and he looked to Trayan for help, the old man raised his hand to quieten him and then he noticed something on Emma's bed that made his heart turn cold.

There on the bed were the girl had slept were three twigs placed in the shape of a triangle on the pillow. Daniel looked at Trayan and his heart beat rose as the old man went down on his knees.

"What is it, what's wrong?" said Daniel, but Trayan could not answer, he simply starred at the sticks on the bed and as he slowly picked them up a tear formed in his eye.

Brannai

Trayan did not look at Daniel as he stayed on his knees and spoke. "When we were very young we used to play games around the village, your dad, me and my brother Trayell. The three of us were always in trouble with something or another and so we devised a signal to help us. Whenever one was in trouble we would meet in an old barn near to the village and the signal we gave was always three twigs in the form of a triangle."

Daniel went over to the bed and looked down at Trayan, "What does all this have to do with Emma,"

Trayan listened to Daniel's voice, gathered his senses, and stood up. He turned and looked at the young boy standing in front of him. "Your father is gone; this could only have been left by my brother Trayell." He threw the twigs to the floor and went outside and Daniel followed him.

Trayan asked Daniel to sit by the fire whilst he poured himself a hot cup of tea and then he sat opposite him.

"Trayell has no good in him; he is a void and a plague upon this land. I do not know exactly when he started on the road that he chose; perhaps it was always in him right from his birth. What is important is Emma and we must get her back at all costs. The old barn were we used to meet is just outside Bagdale, I believe he has taken her there."

Daniel did not know what to say or do, he looked deep into the eyes of his friend, and he thought he saw something he had never seen in him before, dread.

"Does this brother of yours work for Torek?"

Trayan looked over at Daniel and answered, "Yes, they go together like the vipers they are. I have not heard of nor seen him in a long time and I hoped he had passed on from this world." Daniel thought for a moment and then he spoke again. "If he works for Torek then surely he will try to take her there, to his castle." In addition, he stood and hurried over to his things and started to pack.

Trayan sat still, on the log by the fire and watched as the young lad panicked to gather all his things. "If we go to the castle Torek will kill you, it is what he wants."

Daniel though could not hear his words, he was in a panic, and he had to rescue her, she could not go through what he had to.

Trayan then stood up and went over to the boy and grabbed him around both shoulders then spun him around and looked him deep in the eyes.

"Torek will kill you if you go to him now, what is best for Emma right now is for us to remain calm."

Daniel was breathing heavily and as he looked up at his old friend, he let out a scream born out of frustration for his lost friend and then he dropped to the floor with his hands tearing through his hair.

Trayan consoled him with a hand on his shoulder and then he went and sat back on the log by the fire.

"We must head to Bagdale and play the game out, remember it is you that he really wants, Emma is just the bait in his evil game."

Trayan and Daniel gathered up their things and started on the road to Bagdale, to what they did not know, but what they did know is that they must face their destiny whatever it was.

**

Trayell headed west, south of the Regal mountains and along the spine of the land to Ballen. He had Emma tied to his horse in front of him as he rode hard along the paths, through woods and fields. After a day's travel, he pulled over and made a rough camp in a small copse near to a village. He set up a small fire and tied the girl to a tree with her hands behind her back.

"You will be quite safe here; I have some business in the village." Emma looked up at the man standing before her and the distaste for him was present on her face as she spoke. "You will not get away with this, my friends will come and when they do," but Trayell interrupted her, "my dear I am counting on it." Then he turned and mounted his horse and left the girl alone in the wood.

The road to the village was clear and it only took Trayell an hour find the village. He tied his horse to a tree on the outskirts and headed in on foot. He found the blacksmiths he sought and walked straight in without knocking or announcing himself. Samuel was busy hammering on the anvil and sweat was pouring down his face under the heat of the furnace when he noticed a figure standing in the doorway. He looked over and wiped the sweat from his eyes before he spoke. "Trayell, you are far from your master's castle, what are you doing here."

"I have an errand for you my friend." he walked over to the blacksmith and placed a bag of silver coins on the anvil.

**

The journey south was arduous for Trayan and Daniel, the summer was in full bloom and the land was at its peak but the pair could not afford to enjoy the scenery, there was far too much on their troubled minds. They kept up a fair pace as they walked through the woodland and the conversation was limited to just a few words.

They pulled up after the first day next to a stream with sparsely populated trees nearby. Trayan built a fire but did not erect any tents; it would be less time in the morning. The pair sat opposite each other at the fire as they enjoyed a brew of hot tea and some cold meat and until Daniel spoke.

"I am sorry for the way I reacted earlier, at the camp. Emma means a lot to me and I cannot bear to think what she is going through." Trayan gave a glint of a smile as he returned the conversation the boy had bravely started.

"Emma means a great deal to both of us my friend, and do not apologise, it is I who has brought this down on you. I did not foresee my brother's intervention." Daniel looked over and saw the genuine concern on the face of his friend. If they were to beat this, he thought then they would have to be strong together.

"Tell me about this Trayell," said Daniel. Trayan did not mind the question; in fact, he had been expecting it.

"There is not much to tell, I have not seen nor heard from him for many years, as sad as it is to say I was hoping he had met with an ill fate." The man then took a long drink of tea and continued. "There was a time when we were children that I loved him, I do not know exactly when, but his heart turned cold and black and as we grew so did his desire for power and control and then he met Torek." He paused at the mention of the name and a strong determination came over him.

"That is enough about that, for now all our attention must be on Emma and her safety, now finish up we have a long road ahead of us."

Daniel and Trayan settled down for the night and whilst Trayan worried over the appearance of his lost brother, Daniel could only dream of Emma and the plight she was in.

BALLEN

Trayell returned to the wood to find Emma just where he had left her. It was evident that she had struggled with her bonds for her wrists were marked and bleeding. "My dear you should not have tried to escape, I have been in this game for many years, and you only harm yourself." Then he lifted her to her feet and sat her by the fire.

He brewed up some hot tea and then offered the girl some bread and cold meat. Emma would have refused but they had travelled all day and Trayell had not stopped once. Emma had feared that the man never ate at all. For now, she accepted the food and ate it hungrily.

Trayell finished the small dinner he had set out for himself and then over the flames of the fire he stared at Emma.

"You and the boy are close, yes? That is a good thing for if you were not, you would not be alive right now." Emma looked at him and did not answer but in his eyes, something frightened her and she was wary.

Trayell laid out a bed for the girl but tied her feet and wrists together. "For your own good," he told her. "The wood is filled with all kinds of wild animal and I would not wish any harm to befall you, at least not until lord Torek has, shall we say, spoken to you."

Trayell and Emma headed west to Ballen castle whilst Trayan and the boy headed south for the town of Bagdale.

It was with an overcast sky and the threat of a heavy downpour that Trayell approached the gates of Ballen castle. High on a hilltop overlooking the town of Kingdale the castle was a magnificent sight. It had a moat surrounding the outer walls and a large drawbridge with a strong black iron gate protecting the main courtyard. Ramparts and narrow loops overlooked the entrance. Off the courtyard was the great hall with its tall high lookout tower rising into the sky. There was a stable for the lord's cavalry and several outbuildings designed to house the guards and staff, including a barracks that sat on raised ground against the east wall.

Emma was sitting upright on the horse with her hands tied in front and Trayell sat on the saddle behind her, something he had let her do if she would promise to co-operate with him, this she thought was better than being thrown sideways on the beast for the whole journey.

The noise of the horse's hooves echoed loudly as they crossed the wooden drawbridge and entered into the main courtyard. A small friendly looking man raced over, took a hold of the rains at the front of the horse, and steadied it ready for his master to dismount.

Emma looked down at the man and gave him a smile and she thought he was about to reciprocate it until he glanced up at Trayell and thought better. Trayell dismounted and then held out a hand to guide Emma down, once she was on the floor he turned and faced the man holding the rains and spoke sternly to him. "See to the horse and then have the girl cleaned and washed and brought to my chambers. You have one hour, and have the cook prepare something to eat."

The man simply nodded and then turned and called over to a nearby guard. When the guard approached, the man looked at where Trayell had gone and then he spoke in a soft and kindly voice," take her to the matron and ask her to clean the young mistress then have her presented to Tyrell's chambers."

Emma was taken to a building that was just off the great hall and as she entered, she began to smell the aroma of freshly baked bread. She was led down a small stone staircase and into a large kitchen where she was met by a small stout woman dressed in an apron and cooks hat.

The woman came over, looked at the girl, then turned, and spoke to the guard, "well, what am I to do with her?" The guard explained that Emma was to be washed, cleaned and then presented to Trayell in his chambers in one hour.

"What am I," she said," a chamber maid and cook?" The woman complained but it was in her nature to moan and she continued to do so as she led Emma to another room just off the main kitchen. The room was small but it did have a tin bath for the female staff, the cook told Emma to undress while she went and heated up some water. "There is a dressing gown on the back of the door, I'll be back shortly."

Trayell sat on a large chair facing an open fire and sipped a glass of wine, he had not yet reported to lord Torek, however he knew him well and it would be more acceptable if the girl was presented in the proper fashion. Behind Trayell, a long wooden table had candelabra set in its centre and on the le were plates of freshly roast venison and vegetables. There was also a large bowl of apples and peaches, all of which were Tyrell's favourite foods.

There was a knock on the door and Trayell quietly spoke, "enter." The guard who had tended to his horse now walked in and bowed lowly, and then introduced Emma.

Emma walked in and Tyrell's attention immediately drew to the girl. Emma had washed and dried her hair and it shone under the light of the blazing fire. She had a long peach gown that hung beautifully on her slender body and Trayell was captivated.

He held his hands out in front and clasped them together and his dark eyes sparkled as he walked toward her. "My dear it would seem that the dress was a fine idea, it fits you most elegantly. Will you not join me for some dinner?" He beckoned her over to the le and Emma looked down at the fine food on offer, but she felt uncomfortable under the man's gaze.

She smiled politely as Trayell pulled a chair out for her to sit on and as she sat down, he let himself draw near to her neck. He pushed the chair gently forward as she sat down and then he took in the aroma of her perfect flesh. Emma felt a cold breath flow through her body as Trayell was near to her and she shivered.

"My dear girl you are cold, let me stoke up the fire a little."

He then clapped his hands together loudly, giving Emma a fright in the process and the man from the courtyard hurried in.

Trayell did not speak to the man he just nodded toward the fire and the servant went over and placed extra logs onto the already large blaze. The servant then turned and looked over at Trayell and glanced at the girl who sat at the le. Trayell caught the act and walked slowly over to the man and then without a thought, cuffed him with the back of his hand across his face."Get out!" He said. The servant bowed low and hurried out of the room.

Emma immediately filled up with rage, threw back the chair, and then rushed over to the servant to see if he was all right. The servant saw the girl approaching and quickly diverted his exit to avoid any contact.
Emma turned quickly and Faced Trayell. "That was the most inhuman act I have ever witnessed, you are nothing but a bully and I will not put up with this charade any longer." She then turned and went to the exit to leave but she stopped in her tracks as a dagger flew past her and embedded itself in the wooden door in front of her.

Trayell stood and his face had changed from that of a few minutes ago and now it had filled with a cold rage.

"I have tried to show you a little kindness and this is the way you respond, you are just like all the others."

He then called out loudly to the guard, who was standing just outside the door and who now came into the room. "Tie the girl's hands in front, and make sure the bonds cannot come undone." Trayell then watched as Emma struggled against the powerful guard and then he ushered the two of them to follow him, it was time to introduce the girl to his master.

Torek's chamber was the largest room in the castle with its high stone ceiling and spacious living area. The walls were decorated with a variety of swords and shields, all with the crests of past lords depicted upon them. The centrepiece was the huge open stone fireplace and above it, hung his crested shield of a silver eagle crossed with two black daggers.

Torek paced the hard cold stone floor, dressed in his favourite black trousers and silk shirt. He held a glass of the highest quality red wine from the castle cellars and he felt content as he went over the plans he had for Philips son.

There was a knock on the solid oak door and his servant Sebastian walked in. "My lord, Trayell has arrived and he is on his way up to see you, he has the girl."

Torek nodded and then took another sip of wine; the web to trap the spider had arrived.

Trayell entered the room with Emma in front and as soon as he saw Torek he gave a low bow, then walked over to the fire, stood with his hands held together, and out in front. Torek went over to Emma and paced slowly around her, as he looked over her every bone. He stopped in front of the girl and reached out with his hand and gently placed the tip of his forefinger under her chin and pushed back her head. Emma shook him away with distaste, which made him smile and then he quickly turned on the spot, went back to the fire, and took another drink of his fine wine.

He looked at the girl and spoke. "So my dear you are the flower for my young bee." Emma answered back in a sharp tone. "If you are referring to Daniel, we are just good friends."

"Come now," replied Torek," a young boy fends off; single headedly, one of my soldiers so his friend can simply run away. I must be reading more into the situation than is present."

Emma looked at Torek, the hate swelled inside her body, and she could feel her blood boil. Torek's cold eyes stared at Emma as he continued in a calm and soft voice, "you are the web that will catch my little spider." Emma snapped inside and ran at him with all her fury, but before she was even two paces away Torek had drew his sword and had stopped the girl in her tracks with its sharp edge pointed straight at her throat.

"Do not take me for a fool; it would be a shame to end the life of such a pretty young thing as yourself; however you are part of my plans for the boy."

Emma suddenly became quite frightened, not only for her but also for Daniel, for as she held her head back against the point of the silver sword, she looked into the man's eyes and saw nothing but hate. Torek slowly lowered his sword and then threw the remainder of the wine into the fire. He then ordered Emma placed in a room in a high part of the castle, under constant guard.

Torek looked over at Trayell, "You have done well my friend I take it you have prepared the way for our meeting." Trayell held his hands in front and warmed himself by the fire as he answered. "Indeed my lord, as we speak Samuel the blacksmith is delivering a letter to my dear brother; if all goes to plan then they should reach the Hollow in two days." Torek smiled and took a deep breath, "finally, now go and make preparations, we leave tomorrow."

CHANGELINGS

It had taken Trayan and Daniel three days of hard travel to reach the outskirts of Bagdale and as they stood on the top of a hill that overlooked the town, the pair could only wonder what lay in store for them.

Bagdale was only a small village, but very picturesque. It lay on the banks of the river Godwen about a mile from the open sea. The houses congregated together around a central lawn and were small and constructed from wooden beams. A stretch of river branched off from the main river and moved inland. On that stretch was an old mill with a waterwheel and to its rear, an old storage barn. The land around was green and fertile with a scattering of woods, overall quaint, plain and very beautiful.

It had been a lifetime since Trayan had last visited the town of his birth and he wondered with some trepidation what it would be like. He thought it best that they set up camp outside of the main village, by the old mill and on the banks of the subsidiary. Once they had set up their tent, Trayan took Daniel to the old barn at the rear of the main mill for a look around.

It was, as it always had been, old and run down. Trayan had entered through the broken main door, slowly at first not knowing what to expect, but once inside all fears were set aside as there was nothing but broken wooden walls were the rays of the sun shone through and straw on the dried muddy floor lay idle as though it had been left there many years before.

"So this is where you and my father would hang out, I must say it makes a great place to get away from everyone." Daniel spoke aloud as he explored around the open expanse of the old barn.

Trayan did not answer he just looked around and reminisced until a barn owl took flight from one of the eaves and brought him back to the present. After several minutes, Trayan called over to Daniel and beckoned them to leave. He took Daniel to the old mill by the water, derelict now, but once it must have looked a beautiful sight with its huge wheel driving all the wooden gears inside.

"We used to come here quite a lot when we were young, it was not in use then and you could play games as you ran through the gears and rooms." Daniel listened as he walked around the floor space of the run down old mill and in his mind 's eye, he could picture two boys playing hide and go seek or soldiers as they ran in the summer warmth through the empty building.

After several minutes they left the mill and went back outside into the sunshine and once there they both turned and stared at the run down old building.

Daniel spoke without taking his gaze away. "Do you think Emma will be alright?" then he paused because Trayan did not answer him and so he drifted his gaze over to the old man and spoke directly at him "Will they bring her here to your old town?"

Trayan turned his head slowly to the boy and smiled down at him and then he placed an arm on his shoulder and answered, "I do not think so, I believe that here we will receive directions to our ultimate fate. For now though we must eat and prepare ourselves for whatever comes our way." Trayan then took Daniel back to the camp and they both settled down to a meal and some hot tea. After the small lunch they both decided to wander along the banks of the river, the sun was bright and low in the sky but there was still plenty of time before she would drop below the skyline. They walked along looking around at nature's greatest gift, the beautiful land around them. Flies hovered over the water and Swallows and Martins chased them through the air, Ducks and Moorhens paddled through the glistening waves and there was silence all around except for the noise of the birds in the trees. Trayan watched Daniel as he walked ahead of him and he pictured Philip doing exactly the same thing all those years ago. He was not sad, he just missed his friend.

They walked away from the town for at least an hour before the sun began to sink and they decided to head back and settle down for the night. Trayan promised Daniel he would take him to the town the following day and show him where he and his father lived.

The following morning they both woke early and enjoyed some hot tea by the river's edge, Daniel said he would like to go for an early morning walk on his own to which Trayan agreed to so long as he did not stray to far.

Daniel walked for a few minutes and without knowing he ended up at the old barn, there he stood for a moment then pushed past the broken door and went inside. He walked slowly, kicking his feet through the dry dusty ground as he went. He looked up at the wooden beams in the roof and was startled as dust and debris dropped to the ground in front of him. The boy took a step back and his heart raced slightly before he realised that it was the barn owl with a vole in its beak enjoying an early morning meal, suddenly Daniel felt a presence in the barn with him, he turned quickly on the spot, there in front of him was a man, standing just inside the doorway. He was tall, had dark hair and a thick bushy beard but also the most powerfully built arms that Daniel had ever seen. Daniel did not speak he just stood and looked over until the man began to walk slowly toward him.

"That will be far enough my friend," and a sword pressed at the man's back, which made him halt his step. Trayan stood at the door with the daylight behind him and with the sword held out in front he walked around the man, went, and stood next to Daniel.

"My friend there is no need for the weapon, I mean you no harm. My name is Samuel and I am a blacksmith from a town some days travel north from here," he then reached into his coat at which point Trayan raised the point of the sword a little higher.

"There is nothing to be afraid of, I take it that you are Trayan, I was told I would find you here. I have a message for you, from a man called Trayell."

Trayan lowered his sword and saw the honesty in the face of the huge blacksmith. Samuel then took a step toward them and handed over a piece of parchment rolled and tied with black silk. When Trayan took hold of the scroll Samuel bowed politely and then turned and walked out of the building. Trayan and Daniel followed him outside and watched as he walked away and then they looked down at the piece of rolled up paper and went and sat on the grass on the bank of the river.

Trayan took a hold of the silk and pulled at the bow letting it fall to the floor and then he rolled out the parchment and read the words,

My dear brother how wicked the fates are to have dealt us such different hands. I trust you are well and in good health. As you know I have the girl and have taken her to Ballen castle. She is well and unharmed and she will remain that way so long as you follow my instructions to the letter.

Take the road north to the town of Tarsdale; there you are to head for the arena at Bereks Holllow. You may accompany the boy as far as the wood at templedown, there you will leave him. The boy is then to travel on his own to the hollow.

We shall meet again brother   *T*

Trayan folded the parchment, placed it on the grass near to his feet, and then looked over at Daniel, "I cannot allow you to go through with this on your own, it would be madness." Daniel turned his head and looked out over the gleam of the sun as it shone on the river. He thought for a moment and then he turned back to his friend and spoke, "Torek has Emma and he will kill her if I do not go, this I believe to be true, if you think otherwise then now is the time to let me know."

Trayan knew the boy was right but he also knew he would never leave his side and so he simply nodded over at the brave young man sitting on the grass opposite him.

They returned to the camp and gathered up their belongings and once they had packed, the two friends stopped and faced each other. Trayan went over to the young man and placed two hands on the boy's shoulders. "You are every bit like your father, you put everyone else first before yourself no matter what the danger, I am proud to be your friend." Then he smacked Daniel across the shoulder and said, "Now, let us go and save our friend together."

Once again they set off, this time they headed north across the southern land of Arnorst. After two days, travel they reached the town of Tarsdale, but only viewed from a distant hilltop as the travellers then turned east. The weather had been warm and sunny but on this second day the clouds loomed in the distance and the threat of a storm was in the air.

The wind began to pick up and it blew in the branches of the trees making whirring sounds. The leaves began to thrash against one another and the animals of the wood sought refuge anywhere they could. The sky became overcast as the dark, rain filled clouds drew nearer. The two companions had reached Templedown wood and Trayan pulled up his collar, for he knew that an evil wind was approaching.

The rain suddenly came down hard as Trayan and Daniel entered the wood, they walked on through dense bushes and the sodden clothes began to weigh heavily on the boy's small frame.

They reached a small break in the landscape where the trees and bushes thinned making way for a small open expanse of now sodden grass and there at the far end of the clearing stood a single lone figure dressed in a black raincoat.

Trayan put a hand on the boys shoulder and gently beckoned him to a halt and then he took a step forward, putting himself between Daniel and the figure at the far end of the clearing.
Trayell looked over at the two companions and then he raised his voice above the noise of the wind and the rain.

"Welcome brother, do you like what I have done with the weather. I thought it most appropriate, don't you agree?"

Trayan had to shout above the noise of the wind, as he answered, "I will not let the boy go to his doom on his own just to satisfy the evil cravings of a twisted mind."

Trayell laughed loudly and even in the darkened sky, you could make out the hate on his face.

"You have no choice my brother, if you wish to see the girl alive, and besides your answer was all I expected of you. That is why I am here."

Trayell then raised his gaze to the rain soaked heavens and let out a terrible scream. Trayan put an arm out and had Daniel stand behind him as the rain pelted into his face.

Lightening struck out across the tree line followed by a crack of deafening thunder as a huge dark beast appeared next to Trayell. The beast stood twelve feet from the ground from hideous head to feet. It looked like it had come from the very innards of the earth itself as it looked up and screamed at the sky. The beast had a wretchedly thin body and its ribcage stood out against its reptilian skin and on its shoulders sat the head of a demon, purely bald with two small pointed horns. It looked over with its deep red eyes, flapped enormous bat like wings violently in the air, then shook its long scrawny arms and talons, and beat them down onto the wet grass.

Daniel had not seen anything like it and he moved closer to Trayan so that he could make himself heard above the noise of the wind and the rain, "What in god's name is that animal."

Trayan did not take his eyes off the beast as he answered the boy, "That is not an animal, it is a creation born out of the mind."
Trayell now shouted over at Trayan, "now is the time for the boy to leave, as you can see, you and I have business to conclude, brother."

Trayan turned and looked down at Daniel. The rain-washed over the young boys face and Trayan thought he looked every inch a fine young man. Under the thrashing of the trees and the noise of the beast on the far side of the clearing he placed a hand on Daniels right cheek and said, "Go, I will follow as soon as I can" and he smiled at him.

Daniel looked up at Trayan and could see the conviction on his face and so with fear and determination he turned and began to walk out of the wood.

Daniel had reached the side of the clearing when he stopped and looked back at the two brothers as they faced each other and under the downpour, you could not see the tears as they fell down his face and onto the floor. He watched as the beast on one side screeched and flapped its wings in temper and on the other Trayan simply drew his sword and waited, Daniel then turned and walked through the trees to meet his destiny.

The wind and rain came down even stronger and the branches of the trees twisted and strained under power of Mother Nature. Trayell laughed at Trayan standing there with his sword held high and he shouted over to him. "If you think that a puny weapon like that will be enough to fend off my beautiful beast you are badly mistaken my friend."

Trayan answered back in his own strong and powerful voice. "The sword is not for your creation, you seem to forget brother, I am a master myself," and with that came a golden flash of light that lit up the entire area, temporarily blinding Trayell and his beast, and then suddenly next to Trayan appeared a large and majestic eagle.

She was as tall as two men were and even under the darkened sky her golden brown feathers shone with a regal beauty. She then looked down at Trayan with her pale blue eyes and in a sweet and powerful voice spoke to him. "I am at your command my lord."
Trayan smiled at the great bird, bowed gently and then he turned and raised his head to the sky and let out a mighty war cry, then he raised himself to his full height and ran at his brother. The eagle took flight under mighty beats from her powerful wings and headed straight for the beast on the far side of the clearing, screeching as she went.

There were about fifty paces between the two brothers and Trayan sought to close the distance as quickly as he could, but he had to dodge between the two creatures as they fought in the centre of the storm ridden clearing. The demon rose to meet the challenge of the eagle but the bird was so swift in her attack that she managed to plunge her enormous talons straight into the body of the demon causing it to let out a hideous howl. The great bird squeezed her talons tightly, piercing the leather like skin of the demon and it immediately began to pour with black blood.

Trayan moved to the side as the great beasts clashed but he did not take his eyes off the figure at the other end of the clearing. Trayell witnessed the fight in the middle and he now raged with anger as he let out a loud roar. The rain lashed against his face drenching his hair to his head, he looked slowly up as Trayan ran at him and then he lifted his hands to the sky and his face appeared to contort under an immense strain. There was another flash of lightening and the follow up call of thunder as another beast appeared next to Trayell.

The animal was wolf like in appearance but it stood a foot taller than its master. Dense black fur covered its body and the front half of its body was grossly oversized compared to the back half. It bore a large head that topped by two pointed ears and saliva drooled from ugly mouth. Now it scraped the floor with its huge claws and took off after Trayan churning up the sodden grass and sending mud and debris flying into the air.

Trayan did not falter in his attack; he simply smiled at the beast that raged toward him. The beast growled and snarled as it ran and it could taste the scent of its victim as it now took off with a mighty leap into the air, to be wrapped in a tangle of vines and roots that now shot out from the lord of all Bransars as it appeared from the edge of the trees. The roots entangled themselves around the legs of the great wolf and held it as struggled to free itself. Trayan ran to the left around the snarling beast and closed in on Trayell.

Trayell took a step back and looked from one fight to the other and then he saw that his brother was almost upon him and so at the last minute he drew his sword and steadied himself for the clash of steel.

Trayan brought his sword down with a fury and it rang as it bounced off Trayell's blade, but such was the force of the attack that it sent the evil brother reeling backwards. Trayan rained down blow after blow driving his brother to the floor, until tired and beaten Trayell yielded with the sword of his brother held at his throat. Trayan stood over him breathing heavily, and the rain dripped from his thick hair onto the floor as he looked down at the sorry figure that lay before him.

"I should kill you right here were you lay, for you are nothing but a plague on this land."

Then as he pressed the point of the blade against the skin he took in a long and deep breath and backed off. "Even vermin like you have a life force and I cannot take away that which I do not own."

Trayan then stood up and as the battle raged on behind him, he turned and slowly walked away. Lightening tore across the sky and the heavens erupted with a mighty clash of thunder as he walked through the battlefield, just then there was a loud shriek from the eagle and the noise made Trayan turn on the spot. He had just enough time to fall to his right as a dagger shot past his head. Trayan rolled on the wet grass and in one swift movement he stood and threw his sword through the air. It ran straight and true and plunged itself into the heart of his brother who now stood in shock as he looked down at the blade sticking out of his chest.

The two beasts disappeared from the arena leaving the eagle and the Bransar alone on the battlefield. Trayan looked over and ran to his brother, there he bent down and held him in his arms. Trayell appeared to speak but no words passed his lips and then his eyes glazed over and became vacant.

**

Daniel walked for about a half hour through the thick forest of trees and bushes. The further that the boy travelled away from the battle at the clearing the more the rain eased and the more that the sky began to clear.

Daniel wiped his rain sodden hair with the back of his hand and trudged on, the pack he was carrying had become heavy under the downpour and he had to re-adjust the straps as they began to slip from his shoulders and every now and then, he would pause as a crack of thunder sounded in the distance.

Quite without warning, Daniel felt a sharp pain in his stomach as he passed into another open clearing, and the nerves and the tension rose inside him. He looked around as he walked forward into the open expanse of wet grass and mud and then to his right came a loud cry from his friend Emma, "Daniel! Go back it's a trap."

Daniel turned his head and saw Emma tied to a tree about half way down the tree line and he threw off his backpack and ran toward her, but almost instantly, he stopped in his tracks as Aaron came from behind the tree and held a knife to the girl's throat. Then came a loud and clear voice from the far end of the clearing and Daniel turned to face it.

"So Daniel my dear boy, at last I have the pleasure of your company, although I do say it took some time to achieve it." Daniel was breathing hard and was unsure where to look, and a fear was growing inside him.

Torek was wearing a long raincoat but the storm appeared to be passing by and he now unclipped the buckle from around his neck, went, and hung it on a nearby branch. Dressed in fine dark breeches and a black silk shirt, he walked toward the boy and unsheathed a long slender silver sword.

"As you can see, I hold all the aces; oh the girl will remain unharmed as long as you do exactly as I say." Then he swiped the blade several times through the air. Daniel watched as Torek walked toward him and then he turned and looked over at Emma tied to the tree with a knife poised at her throat and suddenly all nerves left him and he filled with a powerful anger.

Daniel closed his eyes and took in a slow deep breath and when he re-opened them his friend the mighty Braer was standing next to him. Braer looked down at Daniel and then over to Torek who was still walking slowly toward them and then Braer raised his head to the cloudy night sky and roared a great battle cry.

Torek stopped about fifty paces from the boy and his beast and then he smiled, for this was what he was waiting for.

He stood resting gently against his sword with the point in the ground and then spoke aloud to Daniel. "You have a fine animal there, perhaps you would like to meet mine and we could duel. The winner gets to keep the prize of the young maiden and the loser, shall end up in OBLIVION."

He shouted the last words aloud and then he raised his sword to the sky and a lightning bolt shot out of the clouds and struck the floor next to where he stood. There was a cloud of smoke thrown up from the earth and when it cleared, there was a huge beast standing next to him.

It had the body and lower half of a man, with a powerful torso and strong legs, accompanied by two enormously sculpted arms one of which held a huge wooden club. The head of the beast appeared to be that of a bull with a main of heavy black fur and two slightly curled horns   And as it let out a breath it looked like it was on fire and the smoke had found an escape through its nostrils.

However, the most impressive and intimidating thing about the animal was that it stood at least five feet taller than Braer even as he stood up on his hind legs.
Daniel looked at the beast and then up at his friend and he spoke to him in a confident and steady voice. "No matter what is put before us we must remember that they are just Brannai like you, except that you are stronger, faster and unbeatable and nothing will ever stand up to your power."

Braer took in a deep breath, looked over at his advisory, and answered the boy with a loud and mighty growl and then he took off after the huge beast. Braer ran with all the speed he could muster and the bull too, charged straight for him. They met in the middle of the arena and as

Braer readied himself to strike with his claw, the bull ducked his head, buried his horns into the body of the beast, and sent him reeling backwards. Daniel could feel the pain of his friend and he winced and held his side.

Braer recovered and stood facing the bull on all fours, he was breathing heavily from the blow and now he stalked in front of him. Braer growled in a low and powerful voice and then charged at the beast once again. The bull swiped out with the club but Braer ducked underneath and landed a mighty blow with his claw across the midriff of the beast, but the bull did not falter he simply shook off the blow and on the return stroke he struck Braer across the head sending him reeling to the floor once again.

Daniel could not bear to watch and he recalled his friend back to him. Torek called out to the Bull who returned to his master and then Torek shouted over at Daniel. "Surely that is not all you have, I thought that the son of Philip would put up a better fight than this."

Daniel raged inside but he could do nothing for his friend the Braer. Braer was breathing heavily, blood was now pouring from a wound on the side of its head, and yet he stood and faced the beast again letting his anger show in the form of a mighty roar. Daniel tried to look confidently up at Braer and they both nodded to one another before the animal set off again, charging at the bull.

The bull met the charge with one of his own and once again readied himself by lowering his head. Braer waited until he was ten paces away and then he disappeared. The bull was surprised and its head lowered ready to attack, Braer reappeared at the back of the bull that had now stopped and Braer savaged the huge beast with bites to its midriff. The bull roared with the pain but the bites were just not deep enough to make a difference and the bull swung out with the club catching Braer across the side.

Blood wept from the bite marks on the bull's side, but now it struck out with the club repeatedly and again sending Braer into a spin as once again it hit the ground in pain.

Braer lay defiantly on the wet grass and roared up at the beast that now stood over him. Daniel could not take any more and he roared out Braer's name as he ran to his side.

Torek could not believe what was happening, this had gone even better than he had ever hoped for, the beast beaten to a pulp and the boy wept at its side. He stood and laughed, with his head raised to the dark overcast sky he laughed.

The bull was breathing heavily and steam pumped from its nostrils as it readied the club one last time, but Torek recalled him, he wanted to saver the moment just a little longer.

Emma screamed for Braer as it lay beaten on the floor and she fought hopelessly against the restraints that bound her to the tree.

Braer ushered the boy away as he stood and faced the bull again, he stood on his hind legs and held a paw against a wound on his side and tried to stem the flow of blood. Daniel watched and wept, for he knew his friend would never give in and against the flow of tears, he went over and stood next to his friend and faced the beast and waited.

It was then that something extraordinary happened.

The air around the arena suddenly became quite still and even Torek stopped laughing and looked around. A mist began to form in the air just above where Braer and Daniel stood and now it descended and covered the two warriors. The mist became a fog until you could not make out any forms under its shade, then suddenly there was a huge crack and the arena was lit up by a golden glow that came straight out of the centre of the mist sending it spreading into the air around.

Torek and his beast hid their eyes from the golden spark and when it all settled down and the glow and the mist had gone Lord Torek laughed no more.

For there standing before him was Braer, his hazel fur had turned a silvery colour with patches of hazel still around the claws and the nape of his neck and his paws and his teeth had developed into killing machines. But most of all he now stood fifteen feet from his foot to the top of his head and that was not all that had happened.

Braer looked down at Daniel and smiled for the boy too had changed, he was no longer the small boy with the brave heart, there was now a young man standing in his place, six foot tall with strong arms and legs and the heart of a lion. They both looked each other up and down and then Daniel spoke. He looked over at Torek standing on the other side of the arena then he raised his hand above his head and roared, "for Philip!" and he was accompanied by a thunderous roar from his friend that shook the trees around them.

Daniel did not take his eyes off Torek as he said, "Round one was theirs, but round two will be ours my friend," and then he looked up at Braer and added, "Now, go and show that beast what a real Brannai can do."

Braer ran at the Bull and his fur gleamed as the muscles in his body moved gracefully, powering the animal up to a blistering speed. The bull charged and once again lowered his head ready for the clash, this time Braer took the hit full on and instead of being thrown to the floor he now thundered into the bull and with all his newfound power, he drove it backwards. His legs pumped as he pushed the beast back, until with one great effort he threw the bull to the floor. Braer stood and roared at Torek who watched on helplessly and then he looked to the bull again and charged once more.

The bull tried to fend off the Braer with swipes from his club and one or two even made contact with Braer's arms, but such was the animal's new strength that Braer fended them off and ducked inside its guard until he was close enough to send a devastating bite to the animals shoulder. The huge teeth penetrated deep into the skin and bone and blood immediately poured from the wound sending the bull reeling back in pain.

The bite had damaged the nerves on the bull's right arm, he now lost the strength to keep hold of the club, and it dropped to the floor.

Daniel watched with joy as his friend now took the fight to the bull but there were other things on his mind as well as the battle in front of him. He noticed that Torek and Aaron were consumed with the fight in the centre of the arena and so he seized his chance and ran to the pack that he had dropped earlier.

There he drew his sword and ran down the tree line to Emma. Daniel ran swiftly in and out of branches until he was but a few paces away and then as he closed down the distance he trod on a withered branch and the crack rang out all around. Aaron turned on the spot and then drew his sword as he saw Daniel standing in front of him. Daniel was breathing heavily from the exertion of the run and now he stood and looked over at Emma. The girl had not seen him in the transformation because the light had blinded her and so now she looked on him with quizzical eyes.

Emma screwed up her face as it dawned on her who was standing before her and the word came out softly from her mouth. "Daniel?" The young man smiled over at her and then bowed giving a low salute with his sword.

Aaron did not have the intelligence to understand what had taken place and it was only when Emma called out Daniel's name that he now understood who stood before him. The anger boiled up inside and Aaron ran at Daniel with his sword raised high. Daniel parried the first blow easily and countered with an attack of his own, one two three swipes, he moved freely and gracefully and the sword became an extension of his arm driving Aaron back against a tree and all the pain of his time in the wood when he was beaten came back to him and fuelled his anger.

Aaron defended desperately but he could not keep his attacker at bay. His wounds were still deep, he had not yet fully recovered his strength, and so with one final effort he lunged at the young man. Daniel parried the lunge, ducked skilfully to the right, and then drove his blade through Aaron's guard and into his side. Aaron's face grimaced with pain and he dropped his sword and fell to the floor.

Daniel was breathing hard and he now turned and went over to Emma, he stood in front her and bent over her shoulder to cut the bonds with his sword and their faces stood only inches apart. He reached down and as the bonds were cut Emma looked deep into his eyes and then she threw her arms around his strong shoulders and kissed him longingly on the lips.

There was a loud roar from the centre of the arena and it caused Daniel and Emma to break apart.

"Braer!" said Daniel in a low voice and he took Emma's hand and led her onto the grass. Braer was standing proudly on his hind legs but there was no sign of the bull or of Torek for that matter and when Emma saw the new beast, she ran over and hugged him around his legs.

Just then there came a shout from behind them and Trayan appeared from the trees. Daniel and Emma's faces beamed as they saw their friend approaching and they ran over to greet him.

Trayan saw the two youngsters running toward him but he only recognised Emma and he paused with a quizzical look on his face when Daniel came near. Daniel stopped just in front of his friend and as he was still holding his sword, he now sheathed it in its holder on his back. Trayan immediately recognised the sword that Thomas had given the boy and he looked hard into Daniel's eyes. From over the young man's shoulder strolled the mighty Braer and he now stood proudly behind Daniel and Emma.

"Well, it would seem you have been quite busy in my absence." He then threw his arms open and the three companions embraced.

LITLE DALE

Trayan had set up a camp within the boundaries of the arena and that evening they sat around a warm fire and enjoyed a hot meal, together. Braer sat under the glow of the burning wood and the light flickered off his silvery fur silhouetting his huge bulk against the nearby trees.

Daniel explained to Trayan and Emma of the transformation. How a golden light that had set his whole body a glow had engulfed him. Trayan listened to the story and then added, "What happened to Braer was a natural phenomenon amongst Brannai, he has quite simply evolved, but in a human, now that is something I have never heard of before."

Trayan continued to eat as he added, "What happened to Torek?" Braer who answered in a now low and mellow voice.

"When I defeated his beast I looked up to the heavens and roared out my victory, it was then that I saw the coward flee."

Daniel looked up from the hot drink that he was holding and his face, lit by the flames of the fire was stern and determined. "I agree with Braer, this Torek is a coward and it is about time he and I met face to face, but this time I want it to be in front of the whole world."

"That can be arranged," said Trayan. "There is a tournament held at the end of the season it is open to all comers, the winner has the honour of facing Torek in single combat."

Daniel stood and cried out in excitement, "I will humiliate him in front of everyone." Trayan held out a hand to quell the young man's vigour. "It is not that easy my friend.

The tournament is open to everyone, but only the champion of Arnorst and the champions of neighbouring countries are eligible, and that is not all. The bouts consist of a best of three and trainers usually have at least two Brannai, you my friend only have Braer and he will have to fight at least twice on the run to advance."

Daniel looked over to his Braer and the Braer looked back, "We will defeat anything that is put in front of us," said Daniel, "for I have the finest beast in all the land."

Trayan then added that the tournament to decide the champion of Arnorst held at a town called Little Dale and the final open tournament of the season was at Kingdale in a month's time. "Then what are we waiting for" said Emma and she quickly stood up as if to leave there and then.

Daniel and Trayan both looked up at Emma and Daniel said, "can we at least finish our dinner," to which both Daniel and Trayan laughed causing Emma to blush and sit back down.

The following morning brought a ray of hope and determination to the three companions; they now had a direction, albeit a dangerous one. The tents were packed away and the remnants of the fire cleaned up and then they set off, they headed north at first and the sun shone down brightly upon their backs as they left.

Summer was now in full bloom and there were green fields and colours all around. The sky was clear and the sun warm as they moved through the southern lands of Arnorst.

Little Dale was not such a small town as the name suggests; it was situated on the coast and about one day's travel down from its sister Kingdale. You approached the town from up high, surrounded by a range of hills and once you reached the peak of any of the hills you could look down and see the wonderful views that lay below.

The town's houses were stone built with thatched roofs and were congregated around a village green, but the most impressive sight of all was the arena that was situated on the edge of the East side of the town.

The natural shape of the surrounding hills had been used in the ancient architecture, so much so that stone steps embedded into the natural curve of the hillside providing a sort of amphitheatre. This alone was a wonderful site and from the top of the hills, it passed off as a creation from a far-gone age. The arena itself was a large expanse of open ground centred with a pristine area of green grass and surrounded on three sides by large oak trees.

Trayan led Emma and Daniel down a dry path that wound its way from the top of a hill, down to the town below.

The town itself decked out with canvass banners that stretched across the streets from house to house and there were canvass flags tied to wooden poles at various places around the town.

The companions decided to stay at an inn called the Kepegest, which situated, on the outskirts of the town away from the arena. The building was of modest construction and used the same stone as other houses in the town; it too had a thatched roof and so matched all the other buildings for looks the only difference being that it was three stories high and had a wooden sign hanging from wooden beams from over the front door.

Trayan and Daniel booked into one room whilst Emma given a separate one of her own on the upper floor and overlooking the dry dusty street below.

The town bustled with life and the innkeeper himself, a stoutly man by the name of Jeremiah Johnson, had said that they were lucky to find rooms this late on with the tournament just around the corner.

He was right of course for the town heaved with people from all over the land who had travelled with the sole promise of a place in the grand final at Kingdale.

Brannai was the word on every ones lips; from shopkeeper to citizen. The only theme in a town that had come together for this sole purpose. Once the three had settled in and gathered themselves Trayan took them across the town to the arena to book Daniel in the tournament.

The judges sat at long wooden les on the edge of the stone stand with a wooden board behind them and on the board there was a pattern drawn out depicting the all the entries and their eventual route to the final, were two blank names were stacked opposite each other.

Daniel gave his name to one of the judges who in turn passed it on to another. This judge then wrote down Daniel's name in fine writing on a piece of parchment and placed with the other entrants on the wooden board. Overall there were some sixteen names and it did not take Daniel any time to work out he would have to fight at least four times to win it. Daniel looked over at Trayan and Emma and he smiled because he believed that any other Beast could not defeat his Braer even if he had to fight twice to do it.

Daniel and the others made their way to the arena to get a feel for place and to get their first chance to see the other competitors. On entering the place through a gap in the roped fence, Daniel turned to the others and then he bowed slightly to Trayan and asked politely but firmly if he could be allowed to practice and train alone with his animal.

Trayan looked a little put out but somehow he trusted the young man and so he bowed back and agreed. Emma how ever looked over at Daniel and smiled to herself for she knew the plans that were in Daniel's mind and what the young handsome man had in store.

Trayan and Emma walked around the picturesque arena and see all the animals that were on show, but they kept a respectful distance from them as they went. The stands, even on this practice day were beginning to fill as people wanted to get their first sight of the competitors and their animals.

Daniel however was nowhere; he had chosen a quiet place away from prying eyes, beyond the oak trees where the arena stretched out into the wood.

Emma was once again amazed at the animals on show but more over she impressed by their size, for this was a tournament for experienced trainers and all the Brannai had evolved to their full potential.

She spotted a Braer but he was dark brown in colour and had a large more rounded head than Daniel's Braer and he appeared to be very aggressive roaring and turning on any other animal, that came too close. Next there was a Bransar but unlike the ungainly one that Emma knew, this was covered in black fur and was powerfully built standing the same size as a shire horse, all in all the animals were intimidating and far more threatening than she was used to.

Eventually the day passed and the three companions returned to the Kepegest. Trayan, Emma and Daniel sat down to their evening meal. Jeremiah had prepared a fine rabbit stew and served in a large wooden bowl in the centre of the table. "So, how did the training go?" Trayan spoke the words as he tucked in to the bowl of hot stew." You were away for many hours; your dedication to the task ahead is commendable."

Daniel did not answer at first as he too had a mouthful of the stew, but Trayan saw the young man glance over at Emma before he answered back. "It went well; Braer is so strong now there is nothing that can stand up to him."

Trayan liked the young man's confidence but he added a word of warning, "Beware my friend, power and strength do not always win the battle, sometimes a little guile does not go amiss."

Daniel thanked Trayan for the advice; he would never turn away anything the old master had to say especially when it came to Brannai.

The next two days were spent in glorious sunshine; Daniel practiced hard spending long hours at the arena training with his Braer and Trayan used the time to educate Emma on the various Brannai that were on show.

The day of the tournament arrived and the people of the town flocked to the stands early to get the best seats. The grass was in excellent condition and the tall oak trees stood proud against the blue sky. Although the arena stretched beyond the trees, for the tournament, the oaks marked the boundary of the fighting area. In between each oak tree, there was a long wooden pole with a white canvass flag mounted on the top. Two decorative canvass tents stood at each end of the grassy area, to house the combatants; one was red and the other blue.

Trayan and Emma wished Daniel good luck, Trayan patted him hard on the shoulder whilst Emma went over and kissed him on the cheek and then they set off and took up their seats in the stone stand.

Daniel went to the red canvass tent on the west side of the area, a judge walked him over and once inside he found himself one of eight other people in there. The tent was large and there was plenty of room for all eight to walk around and stretch their nerves off should they so wish. Daniel found himself a chair and sat down and then he composed himself ready for the task ahead.

A small wooden stage had been set up in the middle of the arena just in front of the stand and now an elderly but well dressed man climbed up the steps and stood there waiting for the crowd to come to order. Once the crowd had settled down, the man, known as Bartholomew stepped to the front and addressed his audience.

"Fine people of Little Dale, welcome to this, the end of season qualifier to find the champion of Arnorst."

The crowd clapped loudly at the initial speech and the noise sent nerves soaring through the contestants in the two tents. However, the cheering of the crowd did not unsettle Daniel, or by the event itself, he had gone through far too much over the past months and in fact, those events had steeled his resolve and strengthened his character.

Therefore, whilst other members in the tent were becoming nervous or agitated Daniel sat quietly and confidently on his chair.

Bartholomew raised his hands to bring order to the proceedings, and once the crowd had settled down, he continued.

"The tournament will consist of eight first round matches and will then continue in a knockout format until one winner emerges victorious. For

your pleasure you can follow the progression of your favourite trainer on the scoreboard at the judges le if you so wish. Each bout will contain a best of three with a five-minute break in between. A toss of a coin will decide the tie break should it so arise and the winner of that toss will decide which of his or her Brannai he or she shall use in the final match."
 Bartholomew then gently bowed to the crowd and stepped back from the front of the podium. Just then, three men dressed in long blue gowns stepped forward from the side of the stand, walked to the front of the podium, once there they held up long trumpets, and preceded to blast out a fanfare that officially marked the start of the games.

A man dressed in a long red gown entered Daniels tent and called out his name as the first contestant of the day. Daniel stood and confidently walked out into the strong sunshine and the cheering crowds and then took his place at a pre-marked place on the grass.

Opposite Daniel, a man dressed in a long blue gown to his position ready for the starter's flag was leading another man this time.

Daniel's opponent was tall and went by the name of David, who straight away held his hand up to his eyes to protect them from the glare of the sun, a feature Daniel noticed immediately.
The trumpeters had departed, the podium removed, leaving just the starter in the centre with a flag in his hand. The starter raised the flag in the air and shouted out, "gentlemen summon your Brannai."

The noise levels and expectation rose in the crowd and then there was a loud whoa, as the two animals appeared next to their trainers.

Braer stood proud and tall and his silver fur shone majestically in the warm sunshine. He raised his head to the sky and roared out a warning, his bright white teeth bared and they looked menacing.

Opposite, David summoned his Brannai and it now appeared next to him, a huge Kedra. The wolf stood a little taller than Daniel did who himself was over six foot, It had bright silver fur and white paws. The animal looked over at Braer and bared its impressive fangs and then it raised its head to the sky and let out a howl.

Daniel immediately looked up to his Braer and whispered something in his ear.

The starter readied his flag and the two animals snarled and faced each other. The flag dropped to the floor in one swift movement and the two animals took off with the noise of the cheering crowd in the background.

At first Braer made straight for the wolf as it charged at him, but after just a few strides, something happened to the wolf. A mist began to appear around the animal as it ran and its form became translucent as though it was not there.

Daniel called out loudly to his Braer, "

Now!" and the great beast disappeared.

The wolf's transparency grew and the mist descended so that it covered the animal as it ran, suddenly there was a flash of bright light and out of the mist, two wolves shot free. One ran down the left, right in front of the stone stand, and the other ran right and headed for the cover of the shade, forded by the great oaks.

Daniel had already foreseen what was about to happen and his Braer was ready. It reappeared on the right just in front of the stand and was already running at an impressive pace toward the wolf.

David saw what had happened and in a panic, he shouted over to the wolf near the oak trees and tried to redirect its attack.

Braer was just too quick for the animal and it was soon upon it. The wolf was fearless, it leapt in the air with its teeth bared, and it snarled loudly as it did so. Braer met the challenge with a mighty swipe from its giant claw and it caught the wolf as it was in mid air. Such was the power of the strike that it sent the animal flying backwards until it disappeared in a shower of silver.

Braer had turned ready to face the twin with such speed that David took a step back from where he stood. The other wolf too, was fearless and after witnessing the demise of its brother, it roared loudly and charged at Braer.

Braer now ran at the wolf and its long fangs appeared to lengthen as it did. The two met in the centre of the arena and there was a mighty clash of fur and teeth. The wolf clamped its teeth around Braer's right arm and although it drew blood, the wound was not deep. Braer on the other hand brought his mighty jaws down on the neck of the wolf and crushed the bones in its neck and back killing it instantly.

The Braer turned to David and roared out a warning sending him reeling backward and the crowd cowered under the noise of the mighty beast.

Daniel recalled his friend and the beast returned to stand once again by his side, breathing heavily from the excursion.

The starter re-appeared and shouted out a five-minute warning to the two trainers. Daniel reached up, patted Braer on the side, and then took a quick look at the cut on his right arm. "How do you feel?" said Daniel. Braer looked down with his pale blue eyes and then in a clear voice he answered his friend. "I am fine; do not worry for there is nothing here that I cannot overcome." Daniel smiled and then turned to face David.

Trayan and Emma watched from the stand Emma stood and cheered loudly when Braer eventually won the first bout. Trayan simply nodded at Daniel's tactics and he filled with a confidence for the young man.
After the five minutes were up the starter re-appeared and took his place in the centre of the arena. He raised the flag to signal to the two trainers that they are to summon their next Brannai, David did so and a Taitu appeared next to him.
The monkey stood ten feet tall and was black in colour; it had a long thick tail and powerful hands and feet. The head of the beast was large,

its bright blue eyes shone in the sunlight, and when it saw Braer, it bared its powerful white teeth.

Daniel did not take his eyes off his opponent but he spoke out a whisper intended for his friend. Braer looked down and then returned his gaze to the Taitu opposite him.

The starter steadied his hand and then in one swift movement he lowered the flag.

Braer took off after the Taitu, however as he ran he appeared to limp on the arm that had been bitten by the wolf earlier. David kept his Taitu by him and watched as the great beast finally came to a stop about twenty paces away. Braer stalked in front of the two but he held his wounded paw off the ground to protect it and then he roared out in defiance at his advisory, which now, began to become agitated.

David could see his chance, he now ordered the Taitu to attack, and it took off from his side in a wild frenzy.

Braer was still dangerous and the monkey thought it best to get in and out quickly using its superior agility to hit and run. The Taitu paused just out of reach of the Braer and waited for the animal to turn in such a way that it could not launch itself from its weakened paw.

The Taitu then leapt high in the air and readied his hand for a swipe at the Braer's head. Braer however had deceived the Taitu and now it pushed off from the ground on its supposedly weakened paw and met it in mid air.

Braer lashed out with a swipe from the claw on the injured paw and caught the beast across the head sending it reeling back where it rolled onto the floor, Braer then hit it with two powerful strikes from his front paws. The Taitu disappeared in a shower of silver.

The crowd all stood and cheered wildly for the deception and David sank to the ground in despair.

David moved to a section in the stands to the side but at the front, roped off for the beaten contestants. Daniel was taken back to the red tent were refreshments had now been prepared on a wooden le to the rear. At the judges, table Daniel's name was placed in the section for the next round of matches.

As the next matches took place, the heat became quite stifling inside the tent and so Daniel managed to sneak under the canvass and escape into the fresh summer air. The eight bouts went on for some time amid the cheering and screaming from the excited crowd. Daniel walked around amid the shelter of the great oak trees and collected his thoughts in the cool shadows and was surprised when met Emma.
"What are you doing here," he said although inside he was glad to see her.

"I knew you would not let yourself be cooped up inside a hot tent and so I told Trayan I had to go to the rest room."

Daniel smiled and then walked slowly toward her, Emma let the young man approach until he was just a pace away and then she lowered her eyes to the floor in a shy manner. Daniel did just as she had hoped and he reached out with his hand and lifted her head by placing his hand gently under her chin.

Then he moved close, took her in his arms, and kissed her sweetly on the lips. Emma did not fight back any of the feelings that now raced through her body and she gave in to him, completely.

After a short while there came a trumpet call from behind the tent and the two broke apart, Emma looked up into his eyes and spoke to him. "You had better get back, the next round is about to begin and I do not want your mind wandering."

With that, she moved away but he did not let go of her hand until at full stretch their hands let go and dropped to their sides. Emma turned and then quickly walked away leaving Daniel to return to the tent, where he sneaked back under the canvass.

The man in the long red coat then came back into the tent and called out Daniel's name once more, and the other three trainers looked over at the confident young man as he walked proudly out into the open air.

Daniel once again moved to his spot to the left of the stand, the man in the long blue coat led out where he now stood and watched as his opponent from the far side of the arena.

Daniel's opponent this time was a young girl who from the distance Daniel thought was small and yet pretty and his mind shot back to when Emma first stood in front of him and challenged him with her Taitu.

The starter then walked out into the middle of the arena with his flag at his side, stopped, and faced the stone stand. Daniel summoned Braer who stood magnificent at his side.

The girl at the far end, whose name was Frances now summoned her Brannai and out of the bright summer air, a Bransar appeared next to her. Frances's Bransar was a mighty beast and not the small donkey that Daniel had fought against at the beginning of his training.

This animal stood eight feet off the floor at the shoulders and had a powerfully built body. It still had a mat of hair on the top of its head but Frances had combed it back into a long main that stretched down its back.

The starter now raised his flag high in the air and the crowd began to cheer with excitement.

Daniel looked over at the Bransar and thought to himself, he became unsettled and wary. What would the Bransar have that he did not already know about; Daniel quickly looked up at his friend and spoke to him. "The roots of that beast will be as thick branches and if they get hold of you, even you will not be able to break free."

Daniel continued to speak to the Braer until he saw that the starter was about to lower his flag and so he turned and told Braer to ready himself.

The flag dropped quickly and a great cheer went up from the crowd. Braer took off at a phenomenal pace and almost at once strong heavy roots shot out from the hair on the top of the Bransars head. Braer did not even try to avoid them he simply vanished and re-appeared on the right hand side of the arena still running toward his foe. The roots shot out again with amazing speed but just in time Braer vanished again, this time he re-appeared in the centre and continued his attack. The Bransar now gave out a huge roar as it became increasingly frustrated and now it charged at the great beast shooting out its roots as it ran. Braer disappeared once more and the Bransar now stopped, breathing heavily from the excursion. The animal looked around in all directions not knowing where the Braer would appear next and panic took a hold of it. It lashed out with the roots in a wild frenzy until suddenly Braer loomed menacingly by his side and the Bransar was swallowed in a huge shadow as its nemesis swiped out with its huge claws once, twice, sending it to oblivion.

The crowd now all stood on their feet, cheering wildly for Daniel and his mighty Braer.

The starter now returned to the centre of the arena and once again shouted out the five-minute warning.

Daniel was relieved when his Braer dealt the final blow to the Bransar and now when the great beast came and stood by his side once more he stood proudly by his side and then turned to face the next opponent.

The crowd began to settle in their seats after the excitement of the battle with the Bransar and it seemed too soon to Daniel that the starter now returned to the arena with his flag at his side.

After just a few more seconds, the starter raised his flag as a signal for the two trainers to summon their next Brannai. Braer remained at

Daniel's side. Frances was surprised not to be facing a different opponent and she looked quizzically at Daniel, before she summoned her next animal.

Appearing next to her was a creature Daniel had not seen nor encountered before and he looked hard at the creature trying to see any indications as to what it could do.

The animal that appeared next to Frances was for all intensive purposes an insect.

This insect though stood ten feet tall. It was bright green in colour with a small head and large bulbous eyes. It had a long slender neck and a body similar to a grasshopper, with two enormously powerful rear legs. The front legs curled up in front so that it stood only on the rear ones and it had hands on the front legs with three elongated fingers on the ends.

The flag dropped to the floor, and in an instant Braer set off after the beast, he ran with great speed toward the insect and Daniel looked on intently. Braer drove straight at the animal appearing as though he just wanted to run the creature over, it was what Daniel wanted because he wanted to see the animal's reaction. Its reaction was explosive, for when Braer reached a striking distance the insect sprung high in the air leaving Braer standing alone.

The creature landed twenty feet away and turned to face Braer once more. This time Braer approached cautiously and now stalked in front of the insect snarling at it. The Braer moved from side to side looking for an opening but as he did so he moved, just a little too close to the insect and the animal shot out its fore legs with incredible speed. The attack was so swift that Braer did not react until clubbed on the side of the head and knocked back. Daniel recalled his friend after watching the last attack and the crowd grew silent.

Daniel looked over at the huge insect standing next to its trainer and saw a smirk on the face of Frances and his anger and determination boiled up inside. Daniel looked up to Braer and spoke in his ear.

Braer took off once more, this time he ran at such a speed that it made Frances look over to her insect and shout something to it. Braer ran so fast that when it was only ten feet away the insect took off and leapt high in the air.

Daniel had noticed that the insect's feet had developed for forward motion and now his Braer disappeared. However Braer did not re-appear at the spot where the insect stood, instead Daniel had foreseen the leap and directed Braer to re-appear back ten feet and so as the insect landed on the ground Braer appeared right behind it and now it lashed out with its claws and decapitated the rear legs.

The insect cried out in agony in a high-pitched squeal, which deafened the ears of Daniel and most of the crowd.

The insect now stood in the centre of the arena and blood poured from the wounds that the Braer had inflicted on it. Daniel recalled his Braer and then he started to walk toward Frances.

He had Braer remain back in the field as he stopped near to the injured animal and he now bowed in front of it, then turned, and bowed to Frances, and then he turned and walked back to his friend. Frances with tears in her eyes now called for her friend to leave, which it did in an instant.

The crowd did not cheer but out of respect for the way Daniel reacted, they now stood and clapped loudly, filling the air with generous applause.

With the bout over Trayan sat back down with Emma and then he turned to her and asked if she would like to go to the rest room again.

Emma quickly looked away and her face blushed deeply as Trayan smiled to himself, but Trayan did understand Emma's feelings and he placed a hand on her knee and asked her if she would be as good as to get him a cold drink. Emma smiled up at Trayan and thanked him for his understanding however; she was only gone for a few minutes and returned with a cold glass of homemade lemonade that was on sale at the side of the stand.

There she noticed the leader board and she smiled to herself as Daniels name placed in the semi-final slot.

Daniel once again moved to the red tent, once inside he went straight over and had himself a cool glass of lemonade, and then he went and sat on a chair out of the way of the other competitors. After a short while Daniel felt the air inside become stuffy, the heat began to get to him, and so he crawled under the heavy canvass and took in the fresh air outside. Daniel looked around and was relieved to find that he was alone and so he sat on the warm summer grass with his back against a large oak tree and closed his eyes to reminisce on the day's events.

The sun was bright in the sky but there was no time to enjoy it as the noise of the crowd rang out all around, stirring Daniel back into the fight. The young man stood and began to walk around the arena keeping the stand with its cheering masses to the left of him. Daniel soon found a large barrel of water that was being used for the horses on the hot summers day, and he plunged his head straight under and the cool feeling of the refreshing water awoke his senses as it flowed over his hair and down his back. It was just what he needed, he now felt refreshed and ready to face his next opponent, and so he made his way back to the tent, lifted the canvass, and slipped under.

After a short while, Daniel found himself alone in the tent with just one person for company. Daniel looked over at the young man left in the tent with him. He was older than Daniel was, around twenty-four years old, tall but not as big, but his most discerning attribute was his aggressive nature.

The man who was known as Barut walked up and down the tent punching the air as he went, shouting out ,"Yes, Yes," every couple of steps. Barut turned and went over to the refreshment le where he looked around for a cool drink. The day had been very hot and all the drinks were empty, a fact which infuriated Barut and he shouted out at the stewards.

"Where are the drinks, this is not acceptable," and he smashed the empty jugs across the table with his hand. A steward came rushing in to see what all the raucous was, Barut whose face had boiled up red with anger screamed at him. "This is not an amateur competition I should be treated with more respect than this, now go and get me a drink."

The steward bowed politely and held his composure as he turned and left the tent.

Daniel sat at the back of the tent and just watched as the scene unfolded before him and he was not impressed.

A trumpet rang out from outside the tent and soon after the man in the long red gown entered the tent and called out Daniel's name. Daniel walked past Barut and glanced coldly at him as he passed and then exited into the sun.

The crowd settled and the scene was set for the first of the semi-finals. A little breeze had begun to blow and it now stirred the canvass flags used as markers around the perimeter. The cool air was a refreshing treat for the hot and sweaty crowd that had endured the heat throughout the preliminary rounds.

Daniel took up his position on the grass and waited for his opponent from the far end of the arena. There was a loud cheer from the stands as a young man by the name of Bodred moved to his position on the far end of the arena. Bodred was a local man from the nearby town of Tarsdale and it was apparent to Daniel that he was the crowd favourite.
Bodred was a slender young man of about twenty-two years, he had black wavy hair and a tanned complexion and he waved politely to the crowd as he took up his position opposite Daniel. The two escorts left the field and the trumpeters sounded for the start of the match.

Daniel summoned his Braer and waited to see who or what his opponent would be. Bodred summoned his Brannai and under the light of the bright sun, an animal appeared next to him.

Bodred's first Brannai was a Taitu, however it was not as any other one Daniel had encountered before.

Jala, for that was his name, stood some ten feet off the floor. He stood on all fours and had the classic pose of the mountain Gorilla that could be found in the wild parts of the northern lands, but unlike the Gorilla, Jala was covered all over in long wild fur the colour of hay as it is stored in bundles and left on the fields. The Jala's face elongated forward and covered in dark brown tough skin extending down to the jaw. impressively stocked with rows of razor sharp teeth and two downward facing fangs. He also had powerfully built rear legs and long muscled arms.

The Jala looked over at Braer and snorted through his nostrils and then it rolled its upper lip back revealing its white teeth in a threatening gesture. Braer sniffed the air and took in the pungent smell of his rival and then he stood on his rear legs and roared out a warning to the Jala.

The starter entered the arena and took up his customary position opposite the stand and halfway between the two adversaries, then he raised his white canvass flag in the air ready for the start. The gentle breeze blew through the great oak trees, rustling their leaves and the animals looked majestic as their fur shone and bristled in the summer sun. Daniel was aware as to what a Taitu could and could not do and he advised Braer to show caution when the flag finally went down. "Remember my friend, all Taitu have the ability to anticipate the first attack, so do not put all of your strength into the initial blows."

The flag dropped to the floor and the crowd let out a great cheer to mark the start of the bout. Braer took off at a steady pace as Daniel watched on.

As Daniel had anticipated the Taitu remained where he was and waited for the Braer to come on, however when the Braer was within fifteen feet Bodred shouted up at his Jala and the great ape took off at a lightening pace. The hair on its body shook and waved as it set off after Braer, and the speed of the attack took the animal by surprise.

The Jala closed down the distance very quickly and was soon upon the Braer who now met the charge with a charge of his own. Braer had intended to leap forward and catch the Jala between his jaws but the ape had leapt high in the air and as it did, it spun and turned itself skilfully clawing the back of the great beast with its hands, where it now hung on. The Jala was now perched on the back of the Braer and it bit down hard onto the nape of Braer's neck, causing it to let out a loud roar. Braer frantically tried to snap at the beast with his jaws and when that was unsuccessful, he tried clawing at it with his front paws.

Daniel also, stood surprised by the speed of the attack but he was quick to recover his senses and he now concentrated on his friend and in his mind, he called on Braer to roll to the floor. The great beast did so and the Jala jumped free and landed safely on the grass. Blood now streamed down the back of Braer's silvery coat and onto the grass below his feet.

Instantly Braer disappeared and then re-appeared behind Jala and now the great beast swiped out with his deadly claws catching the Jala across the back. The Jala had anticipated the attack just in time and although Braer caught him, the wound was not too deep, as the Jala had leapt to the right.
Daniel urged Braer on; he did not want him to lose his momentum and so the beast shot forward swiping out at the Jala as it jumped and dodged in the air.

The Jala bounded around avoiding the Braer's attacks and it even managed to land several blows to Braer's head in the process, but the Braer was relentless and sooner rather than later, he landed a devastating swipe across the jaw of Jala. The beast knocked back and seemed to stumble under the weight of the blow; Braer seized his chance and pounced on the ape, biting hard down onto the neck of the brave beast.

Jala disappeared in a shower of silver light and Braer stood on its hind legs to roar out the victory.

The crowd had watched the fight intently and during the early stages, they had roared their approval, however at the end they had become quiet as they watched their local hero defeated by the strength and ferocity of the Braer.

It was a strange sight, listening to the arena quieten the way it did. the sun was shining brightly down on the magical scene and yet after the victory roar of Braer, all you could hear was the sound of the leaves as they rustled lightly in the breeze. Daniel called over to his friend and had him follow him to the side of the tent. The five-minute warning sounded and Daniel used the time to inspect the wounds on Braer's back. The cuts were not too deep although they were bleeding badly, Daniel found the barrel of water and with his hands, he scooped some of the liquid up and poured it over the cuts. Just then, Emma appeared at the side of the ropes and looked over at Daniel. The young man spotted her as she threw a small container over to him. Daniel caught it and opened the lid of the tin, inside he found a jelly like substance and as he looked back toward his friend, he saw her making out a sign that he should rub the jelly on the Braer's back. Daniel nodded in appreciation and applied the jelly to the wounds on his Braer. Braer looked to Daniel and said, "Thank you my friend." Daniel looked up and smiled and then he placed his hand on Braer's shoulder, "it is time we were getting back, are you ready to finish the fight?"

Braer's bright blue eyes shone in the summer sun as he stood on his hind legs and looked down at the small figure of Daniel beside him, "this is what I live for."

Daniel simply turned and led the great beast back to the arena.

The judge with the starter flag returned to the centre and raised his flag in preparation for the next round. The crowd appeared over the shock of the loss of the first fight and were now in splendid voice as they tried to rally their hero, and a great roar now went up all through the stands. Bodred responded to the crowd with a newfound optimism and he now stood proudly before them and summoned his next beast.

Daniel looked on intently as a huge Panthrel appeared next to its master. The Panthrel was an enormous beast standing at least eight feet at the shoulder; its body was long, slender and powerful, built for speed. The beast was a sand colour and its fur cut tight to its skin, it also had a long powerful tail embossed with a huge bony club on its end, and at the other end to go with the giant jaws, it possessed to long downward facing fangs.

Daniel had faced a Panthrel before and he had an idea of what to expect as the white canvass flag dropped to the floor

The Panthrel took off at a great pace, its powerful rear legs pushing hard against the grass as it headed toward the tree line. Daniel told Braer to head to the right of the arena so that he could give his friend time to react to the imminent attack. As Daniel had foreseen the Panthrel used its ability to blend into the surroundings and it now changed the colour of its skin to match the trees and the grass that it ran through, and he ran fast trying to circle around to the rear of Braer. Daniel looked for any sign of the great cat but all he could make out were the rustling of leaves and the bending of branches as it ran through the great oaks.

Braer stayed on all fours and sniffed the air with his sensitive nose trying to pick out the scent of his enemy.

Suddenly Daniel spotted movement on the short grass and shouted out a warning to his friend, Braer made ready but could do nothing about the speed of the great cat as it took off and leapt at Braer. The Panthrel intentionally missed with his leap so that as it passed its long slender tail with the large bony end whipped out and caught Braer across the head.

Braer tracked back but before he could regain his senses the Panthrel attacked again, once again leaping into the air and catching Braer on the side of the head. Braer was in a daze and could not use his own ability to disappear and Daniel had to be quick to avoid another clubbing. He shouted out for his friend to stand on his rear legs just in time as the Panthrel leapt once more, but the huge club landed on the Braer's shoulder and he took the blow with ease on the soft tissue of his body.

Both Daniel and Braer searched the area for any sight of the great cat. Daniel could feel Braer's senses returning to him. He called on him to disappear ten paces nearer to the stand, if the cat leapt out now he would surely end up amongst the crowd and it might just give him enough time to work out a counter strategy.

The crowd had roared with approval as the cat had inflicted hit after hit upon Braer and only two people amongst them were not now standing on the feet cheering. Emma feared for Braer for she could not see a way that the great animal could seek out the cat to inflict his own attack and she now had a worried look upon her face.

Daniel spotted a slight movement on the grass to the right side of his Braer and so he called to him in his mind to send out a roar in that direction. It was a gamble that Daniel took but as the waves of sound shot out from Braer's jaws and hit the Panthrel Daniel noticed something he could use.

The camouflage on the cat's skin became distorted and just for an instant as the waves passed over it Daniel could make out the shape of the great cat, a fact he pointed out to his friend. Braer once again disappeared and re-appeared back toward the centre of the arena. The Panthrel turned and now took off, on the attack once more.

Braer tried to focus on movements on the grass, he now used his nose to sniff out the Panthrel's scent, and he roared out in the direction of the movement. The waves of sound passed over the cat as it leapt out at Braer distorting its camouflage. The Braer had triangulated all of its senses and now it had a fix on the great cat and it lashed out with its powerful front claws and caught it across the shoulder, tearing three deep cuts into its flesh.

The cat landed on the grass and blood poured from the wound above its front leg, but most of all it had lost the ability to hide itself and now its sandy body stood out against the background of the arena.

The crowd had up to this point cheered loudly, now instantly fell silent, except for Emma who stood on her own and shouted out encouragement for Braer, a fact which made the whole crowd turn and look at the lone figure as she stood and cheered on her own.

Braer now stalked the cat as it moved around the arena and it growled angrily at it, now that the les had turned.

Braer charged at the beast and the cat was fearless as it too, met the charge with one of his own. However, the injury suffered by the cat had slowed it considerably and the two met together in mid leap. Braer's power and strength now came to the fore and as they clashed, the Panthrel drove back and Braer rolled with it lashing out with his mighty jaws. The Panthrel fought fiercely but Braer held him off with his strong paws until he found an opening and slashed the cat across the head sending it reeling to the floor, were it pounced down and finished it off with a bit to the nape of the neck.

Braer stood on his hind legs and roared out his victory, but there was hardly a cheer from the stands as the crowd witnessed the fall of their hero.

Daniel went over to Braer and patted him hard on the shoulders, before being led to the tent to recoup. On his way in to the tent he met Barut who was on the way out and the ruffian barged into Daniel as the two passed, "watch were you are going, clumsy oaf," said Barut.

Daniel stared hard at the man but did not reply; instead, he composed himself and went into the tent to take some refreshment.
There were loud shouts and roars from the crowd outside as Daniel sat and took some liquid on board, he finished the drink and wiped his mouth with the back of his hand. Just then, the man in the long red gown entered

the tent and told Daniel that there would be a half hour rest before the final bout, Daniel looked over and thanked the man who turned and left.

Daniel took the opportunity to slip under the canvass and once again take in some fresh air. Emma who had a concerned look on her face met him outside and she ran over to him and flung her arms around his shoulders. Daniel grabbed her around the waist and held her at arm's length and then looked own into her eyes, "what's wrong," he said.

Emma looked up as she spoke. "I am worried for your animal; this is too much even for him."

Daniel reassured her saying, "Braer is strong and this completion is what he lives for, anyway we have to remember why we are here, if I do not win this and face Torek then he will regain the upper hand and hunt us down again, and I will not let that happen."

Then iel pulled the girl close to him and gently kissed her on the fore head. The two young people then walked slowly hand in hand through the shade of the great oak trees, until after a short while Daniel turned to Emma and said it was time for her to go so that he could prepare himself for the final. Emma let go of his hand and turned to walk away, then she stopped and looked back to him and called out softly, "The other man that you face in the final, he has a Braer and it has a terrible temper, warn your friend."

"Leave him to me, Braer can look after himself." said Daniel and he gave her a reassuring smile.

Once Daniel was back inside the cover of the canvass tent he went and sat down on the lone chair that was left by the Marshall's, there he closed his eyes and reminisced over all that had happened to him and Braer over the past months. The attacks, his time alone in the wild and his rescue of Emma all steeled him ready for the final bout against a bully and a ruffian and he was in no mood to give way. Daniel now stood and there was a stern conviction on his face as the marshal in the long red gown now entered the tent. Daniel looked over at the man and nodded, he was ready.

The marshal led Daniel to the arena and as he entered he was surprised to hear the crowd cheer and clap for him, in fact they had all stood in admiration for the young man and Daniel felt a sense of pride as he stepped up to his mark on the grass.

The marshal in the blue gown now led out Barut and there was a noticeable drop in the level of support for him, a fact that did not interest him in the slightest.

Before the contest could begin, there was a ceremony to perform and the trumpeters now entered the arena and blew out a loud ceremonial fanfare before they left replaced by the chief judge of the tournament.

Bartholomew stood in front of the stand and in a deep and powerful voice; he called out to the multitude. "Ladies, Gentleman, and all the children of our audience, welcome to the final bout of the day. I must say we have been entertained by some of the finest competition witnessed here at the arena in Little Dale and today we will find out who the champion of all Arnorst will be."

The crowd cheered loudly and settled down by Bartholomew who lifted his hands to wave the crowd to silence. "My friends I will not keep you from the entertainment suffice as to say, enjoy."

The old judge then turned and walked to side of the stand and great cheering rang out as the starter with his white canvass flag made his way to the centre of the arena. Daniel summoned Braer who now appeared next to him. Daniel turned to face his friend and Braer looked down at him with his bright blue eyes. Daniel looked straight into the heart of his mighty friend and spoke to him. "You have been cut and bitten, you have been attacked by all forms of enemy and yet you are still here, that is because you are the lord of all Brannai and nothing he can do can hurt you. Today is our day, our victory and we will do it together."

Braer filled with a pride that lifted his soul and he stood on his hind legs and roared out to the heavens.

Emma and Trayan sat down in their seats and Emma placed her hands nervously on her lap, Trayan looked over at her and placed an arm around her shoulder to comfort her.

Barut now summoned his beast and it appeared next to him. The animal was a Braer as Emma had pointed out, however he did not look like Daniels Braer. Barut called him simply, beast for that was what he was.

Beast stood twelve feet on his hind legs; covered in dark thick brown fur all over his body except for his face, and his body was round and very powerful. He possessed sharp claws on his feet and paws, and sharp teeth inside the jaws of a large rounded head.

Barut egged his beast on and appeared to try to rile the animal up by screaming at him in a wild frenzy.

The starter raised his flag and the two animals made ready, however the flag was only half way down when Beast took off, churning up the grass and sending sods high in the air. The two met in the centre of the arena right in front of the stand and the noise of the collision was thunderous as their bodies clashed together.

Beast lashed out wildly with his paws, right ,left ,right and then left again all the time trying to get close enough to bring his jaws into play. The attack was savage and Braer fell back under the barrage. Then Braer roared right into the face of the Beast and dug his rear feet into the soft ground, halting the animals advance. Braer pushed off with his rear legs and at the same time swiped out with his front claws catching Beast across the head. They were devastating blows but the Beast was in such a fury that it did not appear to feel them. Blood poured from the wounds on its face the wild animal came on slashing Braer across the arms. Daniel understood what was happening and he called out to his friend who now disengaged by disappearing back ten paces.

Daniel spoke to his friend through his thoughts, "this animal will not stop until he is dead do you understand?"

Braer did understand and he looked at the Beast as it now charged at him again. Braer's face changed and a rage built up inside him as he charged at the oncoming animal.

The two clashed once again and none gave any quarter to the other, they simply fought like wild animals in the centre of the arena, until Braer's superior strength told and he finally caught Beast with a ferocious swipe across the jaws killing it instantly.

The crowd did not know whether to applaud or not, overwhelmed by the shear ferocity of the bout and now all that left was Braer who stood bloodied on the grass, breathing heavily from the fight.

Daniel summoned his friend back to him and looked worryingly at the cuts to his arms and chest, and now went over and hugged him around the waist as it stood on its hind legs panting hard.

The marshal had entered the arena and now signalled the five-minute warning by waving the flag over his head. Daniel just waited, giving his friend time to catch his breath and as he looked over at Barut, he could see the man raging with temper and he wondered what was in store for him and his Braer. He did not have long to wait because Barut now summoned his final Brannai.

Appearing at the side of Barut was a huge bull like creature; standing at least ten feet at the shoulders the animal covered in fine black close cut fur with two huge forward facing horns on the top of its huge head. However, what was unusual about him was the fact that it stood upright on two powerful hind legs with hooves and the front legs where more like powerful arms as they hung at its side with grotesque hands on the ends.

Daniel recognised the beast as the one that Braer had fought just before he had evolved, although this beast was not as big and did not possess a club.

Daniel looked up to his friend and simply smiled at him and Braer could sense a confidence run through him. The marshal now raised his flag and the crowd settled down to the final fight of the day.

The flag dropped to the floor and the Bull set off after Braer.

For such a cumbersome beast, the Bull ran at a good pace trying to get up a head of steam for a charge. Braer too set off but did not reach his full potential before disappearing and re-appearing on the right of the arena causing the Bull to change his point of attack. As soon as the bull turned, Braer disappeared again, causing the animal to change his attack. Each time the Bull lost momentum until finally they were only a few feet apart and now Braer rushed in, clamped the bull's horns with his claws, and pushed it back. Braer took two blows to the midriff by the arms of the Bull but he shook them off with distain and twisted the horns throwing the beast to the floor. Once down, Braer pounced on top of the beast and bit down hard onto the back of the neck crushing through skin and bone. The Bull let out a gruesome deep howl and its eyes rolled back in their sockets as it disappeared in a shower of silver.

Braer stood and roared out a victory and Daniel ran over to him with joy on his proud face. The crowd all stood and cheered wildly and Emma left her seat and ran down the steps and onto the grass of the arena itself, running over to Daniel and embracing him around the shoulders, ecstatic with happiness. Daniel could not believe it, he was champion of all Arnorst and he hugged the young girl with all his might. As Daniel twirled Emma around in the air, he saw Braer standing over the spot where he had defeated the Bull and Daniel now put Emma onto the floor, smiled at her and then walked over to his friend.

"Thank you my friend for the finest moment of my life. To watch you victorious in the centre of the arena, you truly are the lord of all Brannai." Daniel then bowed low in front of the huge beast. Braer said nothing, he just returned the bow but inside he had a deep respect and love for the young man standing in front of him.

Trayan too had made his way down onto the grass of the arena, once Daniel had spotted him the two embraced, and the old man patted him firmly on the back.

"Well done, you and your animal fought well, I am proud of the both of you."

As the celebrations went on, the podium returned to the grass, and assembled in front of the stone stand. The wooden framework draped with colourful canvass banners and poles erected and placed at each of the corners with white red and blue flags now flying from their tops.

Bartholomew had donned a long ceremonial gown of gold and yellow and was wearing a long gold chain around his neck, the symbol of his status as mayor of the township. Trumpeters had placed themselves either side of the podium, three on one side and three on the other, and when they held their instruments up long gold flags hung down on gold tassels from the bright brass tubes. The musicians then blasted out a sound that brought everyone to order ready for Bartholomew to take the stage.

"Ladies and gentleman," he cried out, "If I could have your attention for one last time. Thank you for your support it would seem that the tournament was once again a huge success, and we are blessed by the beautiful weather. Firstly I must congratulate all of this year's entrants, the level of competition has been breathtaking as well as the level of sportsmanship."

The crowd stood and applauded the last words with gusto. "It leaves me with nothing other than to crown our champion."

The old judge then turned and beckoned Daniel onto the stage. Daniel was standing with Trayan and Emma and now he let go of the young girls hand and walked over to the podium. The cheering and clapping began as he started to walk up the steps and once at the top he politely waved to the crowds of people.

Bartholomew shook Daniel's hand, presented him with a bag of silver, and placed a Reith of flowers around his neck, before handing him the tournament cup.

The cup was not a cup as such, but a magnificently carved, silver eagle with two bright blue gems for the eyes that sparkled brightly in the summer sun, and its wings folded gently around a person as if to protect it.

Daniel looked around and now beckoned his Braer to come and stand before him on the grass in front of the wooden podium. The beast walked slowly and majestically forward and then, when he was right in front of the podium he stood on his hind legs and Daniel lifted the trophy into the air.

The crowd clapped wildly and everyone, including Bartholomew and the trumpeters joined in, in the adulation of the champion.

The celebrations went on when the trio where back at the inn and a party was laid on by the innkeeper that lasted the whole evening. The silver eagle placed at the centre of the table, which was laden with a feast fit for a king. It seemed that the whole town were invited and such was the crowd that the innkeeper extended the feast to his extensive rear gardens. He did not mind for his inn was now the centre of the town and he envisaged reaping a fortune from the popularity that Daniel had brought to his humble abode. All the town's dignitaries were there and the vaults of the Kepegest were drunk dry by the end of the night.

The following morning Daniel and the rest of the guests awoke to the clatter of glass and debris. Jeremiah began the cleanup operation in the gardens to the rear of the inn, but to their surprise when they arrived downstairs they found that the inside of the inn was spotless and a breakfast had been laid out on the le with the silver eagle as its centre piece. Jeremiah rushed in to meet Trayan and Daniel as they entered the breakfast room and fussed over them, thanking them for the prosperity that they had brought to his door. Emma joined the le just a little after her bedroom overlooked the front of the inn and the noise had not been so noticeable, Emma would have slept through the noise even if she had been in a back room, a fact Trayan and Daniel knew well.

At the le the plans were made for the next stage of the plan to defeat Torek. Trayan spoke up, "The final tournament will take place in Kingdale in three weeks time and I think we should make our plans to head in that direction by the morning."

Daniel looked over at his friend and with quietness in his voice he said, "This could be the last fight that I and Braer have and I would like to visit my mother before I try. If it is alright with you I would like to hire myself a horse and travel down alone and I can then meet with you in Kingdale in, say two weeks."

Trayan did not seem to put out by the request and thought in his mind that it would actually be safer for the young man to be far from the town of Kingdale just before the tournament was being prepared, and so he agreed.

The following morning Daniel, Trayan and Emma met outside the inn and said their farewells to Jeremiah who insisted that they return once Daniel, crowned champion at the tournament in Kingdale, a fact that he was sure would happen. The trio then set off for the outskirts of the town and at the top of a hill overlooking the town below, on a dry dusty path, Daniel stopped and looked back at the scene below him. Trayan went over and took a hold of the reins of the horse that Daniel had purchased and he now walked the tall black elegant beast away without a word, leaving Daniel and Emma alone.

"You know what I have to do," said Daniel and Emma pulled herself close to him and with tears in her eyes, she kissed him and then flung her arms around the shoulders of the young man and the two embraced for what seemed an eternity.

Brannai

The sun was high in the sky and it brought the promise of a fine day as Daniel sat proud on top of his mount. He turned his head back to Trayan and Emma as they stood overlooking the town of little dale and he waved them goodbye, and then he turned his horse and sped off, south to his home.

BEFORE THE STORM

For the first couple of days Emma was sullen and not the best of company and so Trayan decided that the best thing to do was to take her mind off Daniel. He and Emma made camp at the side of a picturesque part of the land called the Meadow; this was a part of the land just north of Little Dale near to the coast. The river Asner began its long journey here before it would eventually turn south and join forces with the mighty river Godwen turning that into the main waterway of Arnorst. The land covered in large oak and fir trees and the grass was green and fertile and populated with all manner of wild flower that at this time of season were in full bloom.

The river looked inviting under the heat and gaze of the summer sun, birds, fowl and insect worked busily gathering up food and enjoying courtship on the tranquil waters. Trayan decided the ideal time for some fishing arrived, a past time that he was partial to and one that he knew Emma was particularly good at and so he fashioned two rods from branches of nearby trees and attached the line that he always carried in his backpack. To the line, he fixed flies of his own design and with Emma; he went and stood on an outcrop close to the water's edge. He weighted the line and taught the young girl how to cast off and drop the fly into a shaded part of the river were bushes on the side protruded out, casting a shadow over the glistening water. It took several attempts however, Emma was a willing learner and revelled under the tuition of the old man, until eventually Trayan decided that she had become proficient enough to leave alone.

The weather was warm and lazy and the two friends fished happily for hours, casting and re-casting into the slow running waters of the river Asner. By late afternoon both Trayan and Emma had caught enough fish to enjoy a healthy meal of fish roasted on long skewers over an open fire. "It is time that we continued with your training as a trainer of Brannai and not just fish." Said Trayan, as he and the young girl sat and finished off their meal on rocks around the open flames. Emma looked up and smiled at Trayan for she understood what it was that he was doing for her, however secretly under her smile she only had thoughts for Daniel and where he was and what he was doing right now.

One important thing about the Meadow was that it was also the site of an arena, and now Trayan took Emma off into the trees to continue with her training of Brannai.

Trayan took up a position about fifty paces away from where he had asked Emma to stand and now he looked over to the young girl and spoke softly to her. "I will summon a beast; you are to defend yourself with whatever animal you deem has the best chance for a victory."

Emma nodded in receipt of the order and readied herself. Trayan clapped his hands above his head and summoned a small bat like creature that flew slowly around the area around him until it stopped and perched itself on a nearby branch. Emma looked long and hard at the animal that Trayan had summoned and her mind raced with pictures of different Brannai, until she settled on one. She concentrated as taught and then with a small flash a bird appeared next to her.

The bird had a striking orange colour on its back and beige with black spots all down its front and long curved talons on its yellow feet. Emma bowed her head to the bird and the bird bowed its head back in return.

Trayan looked over to Emma and gently nodded his head in acknowledgement of her choice of foe and then he turned his attention to his own beast and waved the small bat like creature into flight.

Emma too waved her bird off and the young falcon now took to the sky. The falcon flew straight and true but did it with an unbelievable speed, it shot through the trees and branches at a blur and was so fast it was hard to keep up with the naked eye. The bat on the other hand flew in short jerky movements and emitted loud clicking sounds as it darted in the air above Trayan's head.

The bird attacked the bat with its sharp talons held out and as it neared, it turned itself onto its side. The speed was phenomenal and just as it was about to strike the bat managed to dart out of the way. The falcon turned in the sky and readied itself for another pass, and at the same time, Trayan called to the bat.

The falcon raced in for another attack sweeping past leaves and branched as it went and as it neared the bat, something happened. The falcon appeared to waver in the air and it became disorientated, so much so that it could direct itself properly, until with a loud thud it crashed head first into the trunk of a large oak tree. The bird flopped in the air and then disappeared into a shower of silver light. Trayan bowed his head just a little to his bat, which bowed back and then disappeared.

Emma looked a little dismayed as she walked toward Trayan, they met in the centre of the clearing and the old man put an arm around her shoulder and asked her to walk with him.

"The bird you chose was an excellent advisory; however you need to be able to recognise the strengths and weaknesses of your animal and the one you face." Emma looked down to the floor; Trayan then stopped her, placed his two arms around her, and looked her in the eyes. "You have done very well, your choice was excellent, it is just your execution that requires a little help."

Emma smiled, but then asked him a question. "How did my falcon just crash into the tree, it is a better master of flight than the bat."

Trayan did not answer at first; he just walked her back to the camp where they sat down next to the bank of the river. Trayan sat on the dry warm grass and pulled out an old pipe, "tell me, what you know of the bat."

"Emma sat down and then answered the old sage. " The bat cannot see, it uses a series of clicks to find its way, oh! And it has small razor sharp teeth in its mouth and claws on the end of its wings."

Trayan thought for a while and then spoke. "The clicks and sounds that you hear the bat making can also be used as a form of attack, if directed properly they can cause disorientation in a foe. The problem you face is having the ability to understand the strengths and weaknesses of various Brannai; this is something you must study."

Emma acknowledged the fact with a nod of her head, she simply did not know enough, but that fact would change for she was determined to make a go of it.

Her thoughts then slipped to Daniel and a worried look came on her face, she looked over to Trayan as he was smoking his pipe and asked, "Do you think Daniel has a chance of defeating Torek."

The old man blew a ring of smoke into the evening air and then he smiled at the girl as he answered. "Daniel has a fine animal and a strong character, he certainly stands a chance of winning the tournament, and he has the uncanny ability to find an opponent's weakness that is for sure. Can he beat Torek after battling through the heats, with just Braer, I am not sure if anyone could do that." Then the two turned their heads and looked out over the river, and their heads filled with thoughts of trepidation of what is to come.

SKORDIK INGERSEN

Skordik Ingerson arrived at the town of Tarveld, the weather was cold and the snow had been falling for the past four days and lay heavy on the floor. The wooden roofs of the houses sat; covered in a thick layer of snow giving the old town a Christmassy look; even the run down fences and barns had a tranquil feeling about them. Skordik, however was not here to look at the scenery, he was a mighty warrior in search of an advisory who could finally match up to his beast and his travels had finally led him to the town of Tarveld, home of Nilmar Bergesson the Brannai champion of the frozen lands of the north.

The tournaments were all over and the land had settled down to endure the cold winter that lay ahead, Skordik stood in the centre of the town with the snow blowing heavily into his bearded face and the coat of animal skins on his body blew in the wind.

"Nilmar, Nilmar Bergesson, I am Skordik of Barveld and I have travelled these lands for the past five seasons, searching for warriors like myself. I have battled and defeated many advisories and yet none has lived up to the power of my beast. I call on you to stop cowering in your hut and face me, here and now on the field of Battle."

There was silence for some time and all that could be heard was the barking of the dogs and the noise of the cold wind as it blew through the surrounding trees and out houses. Just then came the creaking of wood as a door was jarred open to the right of were Skordik stood and there on the snow-covered porch stood Nilmar.

Nilmar was a tall man, clean-shaven with thick blond hair and a rugged face that scarred by the cold north wind that was common in this land. He looked over at the large figure of Skordik standing in the snow and he called over to him.

"I know of the great Skordik, but where was he when the tournaments were being held, hiding in the mountains and the fjords, afraid to face me."

Skordik felt the blood boil in his body and with his temper rising inside of him he shouted back his reply. "I am Skordik of the north, the true champion of these lands, tournaments are for those who seek fame and money, and I battle for victory."

With that, Skordik raised his hands to the white sky and roared out such a noise that it echoed around the small town sending loose snow sliding down off some of the roofs and onto the floor below. At the same time, a huge beast appeared and stood next to him.

The animal was like a huge ape; it stood twelve feet off the floor covered in thick white fur. It arched its back in a classic pose and looked over with his bright blue eyes as Nilmar stood in the doorway.

The beast was an impressive sight with its powerful arms and legs and the snow now started to stick to the grey leathery skin of its face as it snorted out hot air through the holes in his nostrils.

Nilmar took the few steps down to the battlefield and then he knelt down on one knee and looked the heavens with his head. He then closed his eyes and summoned his beast. As the storm blew, a great beast appeared next to him, Bergrid the champion of the north. Bergrid was a pure white Braer, fifteen feet tall with huge claws on the end of his feet and hands. His face was long and the skin hard and his mouth lined with an impressive set of pure white razor sharp teeth.

Skordik was carrying a large pack and he now through it to the floor and readied himself for battle.

Around the small town, heads had appeared at windows as people now gathered to watch the spectacle.

"BERGRID," shouted Nilmar, and the beast took off churning up the snow as it charged at his foe.

Skordik remained calm as the great white Braer raced through the snow towards him, "Indrik, feel its power and be ready." The great ape looked down at Skordik, blinked calmly with his bright blue eyes, and then returned his gaze to the oncoming Braer.

When Bergrid was ten paces away from Indrik, he vanished and re-appeared behind him and now he lashed out with a swipe from his powerful front claws. Indrik however had anticipated not only the disappearance but also were he would re-appear and was now already in the air, spinning and bringing his mighty hand down onto the unguarded head of the Braer. The hand connected with a loud thud and the force was such that it disorientated Bergrid. For a second the Braer had no sense of direction and it swayed around in the snow, but the force of the blow had awoken anger inside of him and he lashed wildly with his claws in all directions. The sudden lapse was just the opening that Indrik needed and now he skilfully manoeuvred himself to the rear of his opponent from where he now launched his own attack.

Indrik did not make a sound as he leapt into the air and landed on the back of Bergrid. The white Braer reared up and roared with a fury but the ape had a good hold around the Braer's neck and he wrestled him to the floor punching all the time with one free hand. Bergrid snarled and bit wildly with his jaws but could not manage to find the target, suddenly Indrik managed to grab hold of Bergrid's jaws and now he tried to pull them apart with his powerful arms. The Braer struggled and fought with all his might but he could not shake off the beast, and then with one final mighty heave from the ape his jaws gave way. There was a loud crack as the jaws snapped and the Braer's body went limp and lifeless until it eventually vanished in a shower of silver light.

Indrik did not make a sound, he simply strode over to where Skordik was standing and then he bent down and picked up the man's' backpack and handed it to him and then the pair turned and walked slowly out of the town leaving Nilmar distraught on the snow covered floor.

Indrik looked up at his beast and spoke to him. "There is nothing left for us in this land, there is nothing left to conquer. It is time we found new enemies, we will head south my friend to the land of Arnorst, there is someone there who calls himself the lord of Brannai, and we shall see if it is a just boast."

With that, the great white ape disappeared and Skordik began the long journey south to the land of Arnorst.

It took Skordik several weeks to travel down to the southern lands, the further south he went the warmer the weather became. The heavy trappings of furs discarded and tied to his pack, leaving the man with long trousers and a thin shirt made of fine wool. Along the way, he would ask for directions to the land of Arnorst at towns and villages he encountered, seeking any information, he could gather on the lord of all Brannai. Skordik learnt of the name Torek and of a castle called Ballen, and now late into the summer season he headed south.

Torek stood contemplating the change of events that had happened to him over the past week, the boy had been in his grasp until the fates had intervened and now his advisory had grown. He stood looking out over the land to the north from a window in the high tower of his home and thoughts raced through his mind, he was angry with himself, he should of finished the boy off, however when they meet again the lad will not be so lucky, His Braer will be no match for both of his own beasts.

As he conversed with himself over the fate of Daniel, he spotted a lone figure walking over the hills, heading straight for his castle. The thought of such a sight normally did not even warrant an interest, except that there was something different about this man as he came closer and therefore more visible. This stranger was clearly not from these lands and there was something else about him that Torek could not put his finger on and yet found intriguing.

Skordik ventured near to the northern edge of the castle walls and as he did so he sensed that, he was being watched and he smiled to himself. He knew that the entrance to the castle was on the far side, he could tell by the lay of the land and by the moat that ran around the shear sides of the northern face of the stone tower, besides entrances were not for him, he could say what he had to from where he already was.

Skordik stopped on the banks of the moat and shouted out to the top of the tall tower. "I am Skordik, conqueror of the frozen lands of the north and I have come to do battle with Torek, who calls himself lord of the Brannai. I know you have watched my approach and I now call on you to stop cowering behind your stone walls and face me."

Torek was not affected by Skordik in fact he found him intriguing and interesting, and with no emotion on his face he turned and walked slowly down the narrow stone steps of the tower and out into the courtyard. There he had his servant prepare his horse and then he mounted it and calmly strode out of the gates.

Torek found Skordik sitting on a small mound to the rear of the castle and the man did not rise when he approached. Torek stopped a few paces away and looked down onto the face of this outlander. With no tone in his voice and no emotion on his face, he spoke from the saddle of his finest black stallion.

"There is an arena just a short ride, you may walk behind." With that, he turned his horse and walked slowly to the east.

Skordik's face was stern as he now stood and walked after Torek, maybe here there is someone who can stand up to the power of his beast, someone like him.

The arena was a very drab area of parched grassland, dotted with the occasional tree and shrub and was in sharp contrast to the very beautiful land that surrounded Ballen Castle. Torek dismounted and then tied the reins of his beast to one of the isolated shrubs, and then he calmly walked over to the centre of the dry grassy land where he turned and waited for Skordik.

Skordik took up a position opposite, removed his backpack, and threw it to the floor. He then looked over at Torek and then raised his eyes to the heavens and roared out loudly, scaring some nearby crows that were resting in the top branches of a nearby oak tree. His beast, the mighty

Indrik then appeared at his side and stood in the classic arched pose of the wild mountain gorilla, which it imitated in shape.

Torek's face was unmoved as he looked over at Skordik and his Taitu and now he decided to summon his own. He raised his hands above his head, suddenly dark clouds began to form directly over him, and then there was a bright flash of lightening that struck the ground next to where he stood. When the flash and the dust began to settle, there next to him stood the tall and powerful figure of his bull.

Torek did not take his eyes off Skordik as he spoke softly to his beast. "This is no tournament, I want this over swiftly. You can use all the power you wish, but remember we are dealing with a Taitu." The bull snorted through its nostrils and then advanced slowly toward the ape.

Skordik had Indrik wait, watching all the time as the bull walked toward him. When the bull was about twenty feet from Indrik it stopped and then raised its head to the sky and bellowed loudly. The bull then hammered his club into the floor and shockwaves ran through the ground to where Skordik and Indrik were standing. The force of the waves threw Skordik to the floor and even caused Indrik to lose his balance.

Repeatedly the bull hammered his club into the floor until Indrik realised that his master was being thrown around with such force that he was liable to injure himself and so with a fury that had built up inside him he now launched himself at the bull. Indrik leapt into the air, a mistake he would only make once, for the bull was ready and had already prepared for the attack, and he stood with one mighty hoof in front of the other and brought his powerful horns to bear. The Taitu could only manage to twist slowly in the air as it realised its mistake and one of the horns raked down the left side of his body. Indrik landed awkwardly under the blow but did not have time to recover as the great bull closed in on him and started to rain down blow after blow onto the unprotected back of giant white ape. Indrik somehow managed to twist his way onto his feet and he now staggered a few paces away from the hammer blows that had rained down on him. The bull on the other hand had let the animal get to its feet for he now had a few yards of space between him and the Taitu and now he charged with all his might and rage. Indrik could not anticipate the oncoming rush, too disorientated and now he took the full force of the beast in his chest. Indrik flew through the air until it disappeared in a shower of silver light before he even hit the floor.

Skordik sat with disbelief on his face as he now watched Torek striding toward him. Torek paced slowly and purposefully toward him and as he did, he slowly drew his long silver sword from its scabbard and pointed it at the man on the floor. Torek stopped a step away and held the tip of the sword to Skordik's throat.

 "This time I will leave you with your life; there had better not be a next time." With that, he turned and walked over to his horse were he undid the reins and mounted it. Torek did not turn back as he headed back to his castle, satisfied with his work, for whatever tension had been built up inside of him had now been released.

KINGDALE

It had been two weeks since Daniel had left Trayan and Emma on the hilltop above Little dale but to Emma it seemed a lifetime and now as she and Trayan approached the town of Kingdale she became nervous and frightened. This was to be the final scene, the ultimate fight to the death and she was scared. She stood on a hilltop next to Trayan and looked down on the bustling town, and she grabbed Trayan around the waist and pulled him close to her. Trayan took in a long and deep breath as he looked at the ominous castle that stood on a lonely hill overlooking the town and his thoughts drifted to that night when Philip faced Torek alone and brave on a deserted field not far from where they now stood.

"Come, let us go and make preparations." He said, and he led Emma along the green hills to a dry path that led to the outskirts of their fate.

The town of Kingdale was a huge conglomeration of stone houses built in an outward spiral away from the centrepiece, the arena. The houses were a mixture of design and coloured stone, some had thatched and others hard roofs, others were constructed entirely of wood with dark wooden beams, all in all it was a town that had been added to and added to over the years as its popularity had grown. Overlooking the whole spectacle was the impressive and ominous Ballen castle with its high walls and ramparts and the high tower that reached up to the sky, dotted with narrow windows. The whole scene of town and castle where placed on the coast adjacent to the great sea and there were all manner of sea birds flying and squawking over the rooftops and some had even made their nests on the thatch of some of the houses. Trayan took Emma to the " Beleaguered traveller;" it was an inn that he had used many times during his travels with Philip and as soon as he was inside the old innkeeper recognised him and ran over to welcome him with open arms. Mathias was a small man, and held a good physique for someone of his advancing years. He still had all his own teeth and a good crop of brown hair. "On all that is holy, my dear friend Trayan, how are you." Mathias was indeed glad to see Trayan after all it had been many years since the old man had dared to venture to this part of the land, not since the days of Philip had he stayed in the town of Kingdale and the welcome he received was overdue.

"Before I ask you of your business on this fine day, let me set out a table for you and your companion." Mathias then looked over toward Emma encouraging an introduction. Trayan noticed the pause and the manners shown by Mathias and so he introduced Emma to him. "This is my good friend and travelling companion Emma Shelton." Emma thought it strange, Trayan had never used her second name before when introducing her to someone new, but for now, she overlooked the comment and offered her hand to Mathias. The old innkeeper seemed to revel in the pleasantries and he now took her hand and kissed it gently on the soft skin. Then they were led through the inn to the back rooms were Mathias had several wooden les laid out with le cloths and flowers ready for evening dinner. There he asked Trayan and Emma to make their selves comfortable whilst he lit a small fire in the room and then went to prepare some food.

After some minutes, Mathias returned with some fresh loaves and a selection of cold meats and cheese and then he sat with them eager for the news as to why Trayan had returned to the town of Kingdale.

"We are here for the tournament." Said Trayan, and the innkeeper looked quizzically over at Emma. "You misunderstand my friend; Emma is my apprentice, she is on the road to becoming a fine trainer." This comment brought colour to the young girl's cheeks and Mathias nodded over to her in appreciation.

Trayan continued, "We are here to make preparations for a friend of ours, someone I am sure you will be glad to meet when he arrives, his name is Daniel and he is Philips son."

The news brought a shocked look onto the face of Mathias for he did not know that his friend had a son.

"If there is anything I can do to make your stay more comfortable, you only have to ask." With that he stood and begged his leave for he had to make preparations for the evening meal. Trayan and Emma were both given separate rooms, the finest in the inn with a large comfortable bed and a le decorated with an evening candle of scented wax.

It was late in the afternoon when Trayan and Emma were ready to travel down to the arena to sign Daniel in as the champion of Arnorst.

The arena was an area of flat open grassland about two hundred paces long and one hundred paces wide, but the most striking landmark was the hand built wooden stadium that surrounded it. It rose high into the air and encircled the arena in an oval, the pinnacles of each section of the building were topped with coloured canvass flags and it dominated the town, becoming the centrepiece when viewed from the castle or the surrounding hills. Inside there was seating for fifteen thousand people, and when the stadium was full the noise from the excited crowd would fill the whole of Kingdale and even travel up to the castle on the top of the hill.

Trayan and Emma arrived at the arena and were directed to a section that was being used by the officials. There was an old man with bright silver shoulder length hair who was dressed in a long green and silver gown and he immediately recognised Trayan as he approached the long oak le where the judges sat.

The old judge looked up at Trayan and then he turned his gaze to Emma. "Here for the tournament my friend, it has been a long time since you have graced this town, if I could have the young girls name."

Trayan, once again had to explain that it was not Emma for whom he represented, but another who had yet to arrive, however Trayan did not mention to the old judge that Daniel was the son of Philip.

The judge explained that the tournament of champions was to commence in four days time and wished Trayan luck.

"Well, that was uneventful," said Emma, "I hope Daniel arrives soon so that we can prepare." Trayan too hoped the young man would arrive in order for him to give the lad some valuable tuition, but Daniel was overdue and the old man was slightly worried.

News of all the contestants soon reached Torek, and he mused over the names as he looked down the list that had been sent to him on a piece of official parchment . Just four names this year, people were becoming frightened he thought, that is good. Torek read out the names in his mind, Nilmar of the frozen lands of the north, Beruzen of the Great Plains, and Tien of the lands from the Far East, but when he came to the last name, he pushed back the wooden hand crafted chair on which he sat and stood. The boy has become his father, just as brash and disrespectful, he has come as the champion of these lands hoping to challenge me in front of my people, we shall see if he can live up to that reputation. Torek then called his servant Sebastian and ordered a quill and some parchment; it was time for an official reply.

Trayan and Emma were sitting at a le in the inn enjoying breakfast the following day when Mathias came in holding a wooden tray full of fresh bread rolls and two plates of eggs, bacon and cold meats. The innkeeper placed the tray on the le and then he took a piece of paper from a pocket in his coat and placed it on the le in front of Trayan. "I thought you should look at this, it is from the castle."

Trayan ignored the food and opened the paper and the colour in his face drained away leaving him as white as a ghost. Emma had begun to tuck into the plate of food, when she saw the change come over her friend. "What is it?"

Trayan simply passed the paper over for her to read herself and Emma held her hand to her mouth, as she understood the words.

By command of his most high lord Torek, he regrets to inform the council that due to his very busy schedule he has issued this proclamation.

The battle, and the right to be called Lord of the Brannai, shall take place no longer than one hour after the final of the champion of champions.

He regrets any inconvenienced this may cause.

Signed, J P Thoroughgood.
Chancellor of the board

Emma could not hide the shock on her face. "He cannot do this, can he?" Trayan looked over at the young girl but could offer no comfort to her. "I am afraid he can do anything he wishes, as Lord of Brannai he controls the bouts. I am afraid that even if Daniel manages to reach the final, his beast will be in no fit state to fight off two of Torek's animals.

Trayan looked dismayed and he pushed the plate of food to one side, suddenly he was not hungry. Emma too struggled with the plate of food, where was her friend? Three days left and still he had not shown up.

Two more days passed and the town became filled to the very brim, people travelled from outlying districts and lands to be there. All the inns were full to the limit and there appeared an excitement in the air as everyone gathered to witness the champions of other lands do battle with the champion of Arnorst and eventually Lord Torek himself. Trade was booming as shopkeepers stayed open from the break of dawn until dusk, selling all manner of foodstuffs and drink to the bustling crowds. Taverns were open from the time the sun was high in the sky until it set late at night and there was a party atmosphere all over the town.

At the "Beleaguered Traveller", a party atmosphere was the farthest thing from the minds of Trayan, Emma, Daniel still had not shown, and now there was genuine concern for his safety. "I do not know what to make of it, the boy knows the dates and the venue for the tournament, I only hope that nothing has befallen him and that when he does arrive he has a good excuse." Trayan was speaking to Emma as they walked through the streets that wound their way to the stadium. Emma was more than worried, she feared that one of lord Torek's henchmen had caught up with Daniel and now he was lying at the side of some dry path with an arrow in his back, and that very thought suddenly brought a tear to her eyes.

Trayan took Emma to the stadium, for as was tradition on the eve of the biggest tournament in the kingdom, another tournament held; open to beginners and Trayan thought that it would be an ideal opportunity for Emma to witness more variety of Brannai in her effort to become a trainer.

Trayan had felt the pain and saw the tears that the young girl had cried and as they walked through the bustling streets of Kingdale he put an arm around her and comforted her on the approach to the stadium.

Once inside, the tension faded just a little as Trayan and Emma became caught up in the atmosphere. The sun was shining brightly, casting a shadow over one corner of the arena that would move around as the day progressed. The crowd were in good voice and they cheered as different animals fought against each other and as Emma watched, her mind drifted to Daniel.

The contestants were similar in age to him, some were obviously younger and it made Emma realise that Daniel should be here, with these trainers, not fighting for his life against veterans and Lords, and she feared for him. The day passed off quietly for Emma, although the entertainment was of an excellent quality and the variety of Brannai on show was superb, her mind always turned back to Daniel. Why was he not here? It was too much to bear, and in the midst of the shouting and excitement, Emma stood and with a panic on her face, she turned and pushed through the crowd. The dread and the doubt had been building up inside and now in the midst of the battles in the stadium it had burst out of her, taking a hold of every nerve in her small body. She ran, down the wooden steps to the exit pushing past stragglers on the stairway as she went, there she faltered and looked nervously in both directions, before taking off west, down the winding streets to the edge of the town. Emma was in such a panic she did not hear the voice of Trayan as he called hopelessly after her. She ran as fast as her legs would carry her, and all that she could see was a picture of Daniel lying alone on the floor with an arrow sticking out of his back and the blood oozing from the wound and flowing onto the dry, bare path beside him. Sweat poured from her body as she ran and the tears that she cried blurred her vision, then suddenly she felt a hand on her shoulder and she fell to the ground as the hand pulled her sharply back. The young girl tried to get back up and she stumbled and tripped in her panic to continue. Trayan managed to grab a hold of her shoulders and now he held her down on the floor. "Emma, EMMA!." He had to shout to make himself heard and now he pressed down firmly with his strong arms and pinned her to the floor. Emma was shaking all over, she realised she could not move and slowly her eyes began to focus. She looked up and the blurred image of the man before her slowly came into focus, until at last she saw Trayan before her.

"Daniel!" Her voice was weak and pathetic, but Trayan eased her. He released the hold that he had on her and then spoke in a soft and comforting voice.

"My dear girl, you should not worry, Daniel is fine, I can feel it, here inside." In addition, he held his hand to a place on his chest over his heart. Emma looked up at the old man and then she reached out with her hand and placed it over his, and then she reached up with both her arms, pulled herself toward the old man, and wept hopelessly on his shoulders.

Trayan walked Emma back to the inn on the edge of town and called for Mathias to brew up some hot sweet tea. As the young girl cupped the tea in her hands, she felt the warmth of the brew flow through her body and when she took a drink the hot liquid seemed to flow to every extremity of her being.

"I have been such a fool, you must think I am blithering mess, just the sort of hopeless girl you thought I always was."

"You are nothing of the sort; you simply have a courageous heart." Trayan placed one hand on her shoulder as he spoke to her and the look on his face was comforting and reassuring to her. He had not realised until this very moment just how much she loved Daniel and he felt deeply for her.

After about an hour, the tension in the inn lifted and Trayan thought that now was a good time to speak and so he turned and faced Emma at the le. "The tournament is tomorrow; we will make preparations as normal and hope that Daniel has not left it too late. If he does not show by the time the first bout takes place we will leave and begin a search of the land."

He spoke calmly and with such an utter determination in his voice, that Emma simply nodded in response. He then added, "Tonight we shall have our supper and retire early and we shall see what tomorrow will bring."

Mathias who until now had watched from the distance of the stone fireplace, made for the kitchen and began working on a hot filling meal, something he had a particular talent for.

The meal went off in a qiuet and sombre mood with not much being said between Trayan and Emma and as previously agreed they retired early for bed.

Emma's sleep interrupted with dreams of Brannai and battles and with scenes of fighting, always involving Daniel. Sometimes he would fight off several foes with his sword and at others, he would be struck down with an arrow from a hidden advisory, hiding in some bush or from behind the branches of some tree. She tossed and turned all night long until the warm rays of the sun danced on her face as it forced its way through the gaps in the flowered curtains that hung over the wooden window frames in her room, the morning of the tournament had arrived.

BATTLE

Trayan was sitting at the breakfast le talking to Mathias when Emma came slowly down the stairs; she looked over at the two men and gave them a small and nervous looking smile. Mathias acknowledged the young girl and he stood and pushed back his chair and offered it to Emma in a very courteous way. Emma thanked the kind innkeeper and took her place at the le opposite Trayan. Trayan then moved as if to speak to Emma but she held out her hand and took hold of his fingers with the lightest of grips, "thank you for what you did for me yesterday, you are a kind man."

Trayan squeezed her hand gently in acknowledgement and then ushered the girl to eat.

Mathias had made some fine scrambled eggs and had served them in a fine wooden bowl that sat in the centre of the le next to a wooden plate of a selection of sliced cheese and small freshly baked loaves. Emma and Trayan ate their fill as if it was the last meal that they would ever have together. After eating she looked over the le at Trayan and was about to speak but Trayan appeared to know what she was about to say and he looked grim as he shook his head, "I am sorry but there has been no word nor sign of him, Mathias has sent servants out into the land just to the south to watch out for him, they have returned with no sightings."

Trayan could see the worry on the girls face and he shared her concerns over Daniel's safety, but for now, he could not show her, he had to be strong and so he told Emma to get herself ready, they were going to the stadium.

Mathias packed them a light lunch and wished them well before they set off through the narrow streets following the bustling crowds as they made their way to the stadium.

The crowds of people were making their way through the wooden gateways that led to the inner stands, but Trayan and Emma stood alone outside and waited.

After some time the paths that led to the stadium became empty of people and the noise from inside began to grow as the expectation of the day's events reached a high buzz. Suddenly Emma turned her head; she could just make out the noise of hooves on the dry ground and now Trayan too could hear them and they both held their gaze to the end of a long dry path ahead of them.

From the far end a horse and his rider came galloping down, the horse was covered from the neck to the shoulder in teams of moist white sweat and on its back rode Daniel, dressed in black breeches and a white cotton shirt covered in mud.

He raced to where Trayan and Emma stood and then as calm as you like he dismounted and said, "Not to late am I."

Emma ran over, flung her arms around his shoulders, and laughed loudly. Trayan went over and clasped the young man on the shoulder, "You can tell me what happened later, for now you have a tournament to win." The three companions then turned and went into the stadium. Trayan led Daniel along a path and into the bright sunshine, once inside he pointed to an area at the far end of the arena where the other competitors had gathered. Trayan then stopped and took hold of Daniel's shoulders, "whatever has happened to you over the last weeks is behind you, now you and your beast face the greatest of tests. Torek has insisted that the champion of the day's event will face him no more than one hour after the final battle, be sure and be swift, try to conserve what energy you can." Daniel nodded to him and then he turned his attention to Emma who was standing with a worried look on her face.

"I will win this, and I will bring Torek down in front of these good people." The sweat had built up on his forehead and his chest was heaving from the rush, he looked Emma in the eyes and then turned and walked quickly over to the waiting area.

A great podium stood in the centre of the arena, decorated with canvass flags and there was a coat of arms hand painted on the front, a silver eagle crossed with two black daggers. The canvass flags that hung from the corners were coloured silver and black; all were in the colours of Torek.

A great cheer went up from the crowd as an old man dressed in a long green gown emerged from the edge of the stadium and walked to the podium accompanied by six trumpeters, three either side dressed in short red jackets and black leggings. The man was rather short and balding on top, but he held himself with a grace that showed his high standing. Slowly he walked up the few wooden steps that led to the platform of the podium and then once there he smiled and raised his hands to the sides. The crowd settled down and waited as the trumpeters raised their instruments to their lips and blew out a fanfare.

The old man in the green gown known as Gregory, and after the trumpeters had finished he took in a deep breath ready for the opening speech.

"Ladies and gentleman, welcome to the final of the champion of champions."

A great cheer went up from the crowd and they all stood in unison, clapping and throwing hats and kerchiefs high in the air, until Gregory had to raise his hands in the air to quieten them.

"This year we have four champions who will battle for the right to challenge Torek as lord of the Brannai. I shall now read out the names of those champions." Gregory took out a piece of parchment from a pocket in his gown, it was rolled and tied with a blue ribbon and was sealed with the stamp of his office in red wax. The crowd settled down and listened as Gregory removed the ribbon and broke the seal.

"From the frozen lands of the north I present Nilmar." The audience clapped profusely as Nilmar walked from his position at the corner of the stadium and stepped into the bright sunlight, taking up a stance in front of the podium.

"Next from the great plains of the northern lands I give you Beruzen." Beruzen was a huge man who stood almost seven feet tall, he was completely bald but possessed a massive frame and he was clad in the wild furs that were native to his homeland. The man stepped into the sun and began his walk to the podium. The crowd clapped the man as he took up his position next to Nilmar and then they settled down ready for the next competitor.

"Third on the list of illustrious champions is Tien from the lands to the east."

Tien was a small man of about twenty-five years and was dressed in a fine black silk shirt and loose trousers. The man stepped into the arena and walked just a few paces before he stopped and bowed to each corner of the stadium and then finally to Gregory on the podium, then he continued his walk and took his place alongside Nilmar and Beruzen. The crowd appreciated the man from the east and they all clapped loudly for him.

"Finally, the last of the competitors, from the small town of Dantaal I present the champion of Arnorst, Daniel!

The crowd all stood and roared as one as Daniel began his approach to the podium, and he smiled and waved as he walked across the dry grass. The cheering took some time to die down and Gregory, purposely allowed it to pass until simultaneously the crowd settled back into their seats. The four champions stood in front of the podium and waved to the four corners of the stadium as the trumpeters blew a fanfare. Gregory then explained that the four names were to be wrote down on pieces of parchment and placed in a bag; there then drawn by him to match them into bouts.

Another man who now entered the field also dressed in a long gown assisted Gregory but this one was blue, the colour of the Brannai. The assistant had brought out a quill, some parchment, and a small blue velvet bag, which he now offered to Gregory. The old man placed the parchment on a wooden Pugh in front of him and then proceeded to write down the names and place them in the velvet bag. The four champions turned to face the podium and waited in anticipation along with the crowd as the names were drawn.

Gregory put his hand into the bag and pulled out the first name. Then he called out, "Beruzen." The crowd applauded mildly and then waited for the second name. Gregory dug deep into the bag and then he called out, "Daniel." The crowd once again stood and cheered and Daniel then turned to Beruzen and shook the big man's hand in friendship. That meant that Tien would fight Nilmar however, Gregory still put his hand into the bag and drew out the two remaining names to show that it had been an honest draw.

The four champions where then shown to opposite ends of the arena, Beruzen and Daniel went to the north end leaving Tien and Nilmar to the south. There was then a great flurry of people as men rushed onto the field to dismantle the wooden podium whilst others including children ran out with flags of blue and white canvass and placed them all around the perimeter of the arena. Trayan and Emma had taken their seats close to the field and near the centre line of the arena and now, they settled down for the start.

As Daniel and Beruzen were the first names drawn out, they would be the opening bout of this year's tournament, and so with the arena cleared the trumpeters entered the stage and blew out a fanfare. Daniel was led out to a position at the north end of the stadium, whilst simultaneously Beruzen led to the south. The trumpeters left and Gregory entered and took up a position in the centre of the arena but adjacent to the edge. "Gentleman, summon your Brannai." He shouted out the words and a great roar went up as the two animals appeared next to their trainers.

Braer was magnificent, and as he stood on his hind legs, his silvery fur shone in the sunlight and every muscle in his body looked toned and ready, and he looked down at Daniel with his bright blue eyes and then in the softest of tones he said, "Together."

Brannai

At the far end of the arena Beruzen was joined by his animal, a large brut of a beast. A wolf, but no ordinary one as Daniel was to find out, this animal stood eight feet at the shoulders, and it had dark brown fur and huge claws on the end of its feet. The beast had the bright blue eyes of the Brannai but its facial skin scarred with old cuts from previous battles that cut across its eyes and mouth. The teeth were sharp and yellow and saliva drooled from its mouth onto the grass below.

Daniel already knew what to expect from his advisory and he readied himself as the white canvass flag raised ready for the start.

The flag dropped sharply to the floor and Braer took off in a charge at his foe. However, Daniel noticed that the wolf had not charged and he called Braer to a stop. The large wolf stalked just in front of Beruzen, snarling and growling in the direction of Braer and even on this hot summer's day, steam poured from the openings in his nostrils. Daniel watched intently, these were not the tactics of the wolves he knew and now the two animals closed in on each other, and began to circle around looking each other up and down.

The wolf suddenly charged at Braer and leapt up at him, Braer caught the beast between his large front paws and the two animals heaved against one another pushing in a trial of strength, their faces were only inches apart as their jaws snapped and bit. Finally, Braer pushed off with his powerful back legs and threw the wolf to the floor. The animal rolled as it landed and when it stood back up it growled fiercely back at Braer. Beruzen then called to his beast and the wolf turned around and ran back to where he was standing and then it turned back to face Braer once again.

Something strange happened next, the air around the wolf grew cold and a mist began to form hiding its form in a haze and then from out of this haze there came a flash of bright light and the wolf, suddenly became two. Daniel smiled and he shouted over to Braer to prepare.
However the mist did not disappear and now there was another flash of light and each of the two wolves split again until there was four of them and then once more until finally the mist evaporated away leaving eight

wolves facing Daniel and his Braer. Each wolf was a replica of the first, each stood eight feet at the shoulders and each one now growled and snarled and belted hot steam from its nostrils.

The look on Daniels face had changed and now one of genuine fear replaced it.

The wolves walked forward in unison until when they were on top of Braer they split up, encircling him, four were in front and the others split evenly behind him. Braer was on all fours and did not know where to face and now he roared out in defiance. For the first time Daniel was unsure, there has to be a weakness he thought, but as he dallied, the wolves attacked. The four at the front growled, barked, and came forward as one. Braer met them with growls and swipes from his front paws and as he did so, the wolves at the back quickly snapped in. One wolf managed to grab hold of Braer's right leg with its powerful jaws and instantly Daniel called for his friend to disappear to give him time to think. However, Braer found that he could not disappear and he struggled against the wolf on his leg. Another wolf at the rear now managed to take hold of Braer's other leg and the great Braer began to lose his balance. Daniel screamed out to his friend in a loud roar and Braer responded.

Braer suddenly ignored the four in front and turned his body backward, were he swiped out with his mighty claw catching one of the holding wolves across the shoulder, and then he kicked out with his other leg freeing it momentarily.

As soon as both legs were free, he found that he could disappear and so he did, just as the others closed in. Braer re-appeared ten feet away just as another wolf had leapt into the air ready for an attack on the back of his neck, but somehow he managed to turn just in time and with the back of his paw, he deflected the beast onto the floor.

As Braer knocked the wolf to the floor, he felt something strange, although the wolf was strong there was something different about the way in which it fell and thoughts raced from Braer to Daniel. Daniel watched as the animal fell and realised that for such a big animal it had been knocked over quite easily and he thought to himself.

Daniel had to be quick because the wolves were gathering for another attack, and his mind raced with ideas and possibilities, when the wolves attacked they were strong and powerful and yet when Braer attacked them he appeared to knock them away with ease, that's it!

Daniel called out to his friend through the thoughts in his head. "There are eight of the beasts but if you attack them, individually they only have an eighth of the originals strength, you must strike out, and run and move, take them out one at a time.

Braer roared out and now he took off throwing dry sods of grass high into the air as he charged forward. The wolves tried to close the great Braer down by cutting him off in small packs, but by a blend of disappearing and speed Braer slowly managed to single out individual wolves and when he did he ripped them apart with his mighty front claws. Every now and then, a lone wolf would catch Braer side on and then it would jump at him burying its teeth into his flesh. The remaining wolves tried to stay in small groups for protection and when they attacked they managed to inflict some damage; however when Braer attacked them even in groups, such was his power that they were killed almost instantly. After several minutes there was only one of the wolves left but Braer was breathing heavily from the exertion, and was bleeding from several cuts on his arms and sides. Daniel had to think of a way of preserving his strength, he needed this fight to be over quickly and so he called Braer over to him. "The one animal that is left I believe is the original, however his strength is greatly depleted, conserve your energy and let him come to you." Daniel spoke to Braer but never took his eyes off the wolf at the far end of the arena.

Beruzen was furious with his pack and now with only one left, he bellowed out in a deep and powerful voice, "KEDRA!"
The wolf was unafraid and now it turned its head to the sky and howled, then with a growl and a deep snort of hot steam from his nostrils it ran at Braer.

Braer did not meet the charge with his own; instead, he waited on all fours and let the animal charge at him from the full distance of the other end of the arena. As the wolf closed in and readied itself for the final leap Braer took off and together they met in a clash of bodies and teeth and claws. The Braer's greater power told and he forced the wolf back, throwing it to the floor and as it landed, the Braer bellowed out a mighty roar that sent the fur on the wolf down as if caught in a strong wind. The wolf cowered but then regained its composure and half-heartedly jumped at Braer.

Braer caught the wolf around the throat with his jaws, killing it.

The crowd went wild with emotion, they had never seen the like before and they now stood and cheered. Emma was caught up in the mayhem and she to stood and shouted, Trayan on the other hand was worried, it was only the first fight and although Daniel was victorious his animal was breathing heavily and also bled from several cuts. Just then, the roars of the crowd turned to murmurings as an entourage of people entered the arena at the south end and took up the seats that had been reserved for them; Torek sat down with a smirk on his face.

A lone judge now appeared in the centre of the Arena and called out a five minute warning to the two trainers.

Daniel had noticed Torek's arrival, however he did not show it, instead he turned his attention to his friend Braer. "How are you feeling my friend?"

Braer answered him with a strong voice, "I am fine we always knew this was not going to be easy."

Daniel smiled up at Braer and applied some of the ointment that Trayan had given him to the cuts on the great beast's body.
Then the lone judge returned to the stadium with a white canvass flag in his hand, and the expectation in the crowd grew.

From the south end of the stadium, Beruzen summoned his final beast, an enormous brown Braer. The beast was as big as Daniels Braer but bit looked much thicker set covered in long heavy fur, it was also more rounded than Daniels and had a fuller face, Beruzen called him Ruben after his own father.

The crowd waited in anticipation to see what Daniels other Brannai would be, but they soon murmured and whispered amongst themselves when they realised that Daniel only had the one.

The judge raised the flag and the two contestants readied themselves. Daniel spoke to Braer without looking up at him, "let the animal come on to you, I would like to see how it moves."

The judge then lowered the flag to the floor and Beruzen ordered his beast to attack. Ruben was surprisingly quick for such a large animal but he was no match for Braer and now Daniel urged him into action. Daniels tactics were to get in and out quickly using Braer's superior agility and so as the two animals closed in on each other Braer disappeared and then re-appeared next to Ruben were it struck out with its front paw catching the animal on the side of the head and then Braer retreated out of harm's way before Ruben had time to react.

The tactic appeared to be a sound one, for Ruben to, could disappear, however Braer could react much quicker than his thicker set foe, and so Braer remained untouched whilst Ruben was being struck repeatedly. Unfortunately, there was a floor in the plan, as Daniel watched he soon realised that Braer was doing a lot of running around and although he was striking the other animal it did not appear to be affecting it and he wondered why.

Then it dawned on him, it was precisely the fact that the other animal was thicker set that was saving him from being hurt. "He's fat," but the words he was thinking slipped out embarrassingly from his lips.
If Daniel allowed these tactics to continue there could be only one outcome and he was not going to let it happen, he had to come up with something different and quickly, sooner rather than later Braer would tire

and Ruben would begin to catch him. Rubin did catch Braer, the two animals disappeared and re-appeared on the same spot, immediately Ruben grabbed Braer around the middle and the two were caught in a massive hug. The two animals snapped at each other with their jaws, but it was Ruben who had the better grip and now he squeezed Braer, the colour began to drain from Braer's face and he felt as though his ribs were about to break.

He may have been slower and thicker set but Ruben was a powerful beast and Daniel could see his Braer struggling for breath, he had to act now. "Braer, use your feet, push off from the floor."It was a chance but Daniel could think of nothing else and so Braer, hearing the words of his friend dug his feet into the ground and pushed backwards. Ruben was squeezing and trying to force Braer back when Braer pushed off from the floor and the two of them went crashing to the ground. The jolt managed to loosen Rubens grip and Braer rolled free.

Daniel spoke to his friend through his thoughts, "go only for the head." It was the only part on Rubens body that did not appear to be covered in heavy layers of fat and so Braer started a new attack.

Braer recovered his breath quickly and then he ran at Ruben, when he was close enough he lashed out with his front claws catching him across the head. Ruben countered but Braer was too quick, pulled back out of the way, then moved back in, and lashed out again hitting the same spot as before. Ruben became furious and struck out wildly at Braer; the two animals stood toe to toe hacking and swiping with their great claws. It was a terrifying sight but Rubens strikes were random whilst Braer concentrated on only the head, a tactic that soon paid dividends as Ruben became disorientated and his swipes began to miss altogether. Braer seized his chance and went for the throat of the great beast; he dug teeth deep into the jugular and ripped out the source of his life. Ruben dropped to the floor and then disappeared in a shower of silver light.

The crowd stood, they cheered and clapped and threw whatever they were holding high into the air, their champion was through to the final and with only one animal. "A miracle that's what it is, pure genius, would you believe it." The accolades shouted across the stadium as the people began to believe that their champion could go all the way.

All except Torek who sat still and calm in his seat, he had a slight smirk on his face because as he looked on at Daniel and his beast he knew how weak the Braer was becoming and that this fickle crowd would soon be dancing to his tune.

Trayan and Emma both left their seats and raced down to meet Daniel, it would be at least a half hour before he would be called to fight again and they had not had much time together since his last minute arrival.

Daniel was ushered to an area at the corner of the north stands and it was here that he found Trayan and Emma waiting for him. Emma immediately broke through the roped area that separated Daniel from the baying crowd, rushed up to him, and flung her arms around his shoulders. Daniel lifted her off her feet and swung her round before looking into her eyes and smiling, and then he looked over at Trayan who was standing on the other side of the rope and he put Emma down and went over to him.

"My boy, that was a fine fight, you have done very well, but your beast," at that point he paused and with a worried look on his face, he continued. "Well, does he have the strength to see this through to the end?"

Daniel simply clapped the old man around the shoulder and with a smile as big as you like he said, "I told you before Braer is the finest Brannai in all the land, there is nothing that can beat him, oh and don't worry about Torek I have plans for him."

There was loud cheering and clapping as the other finalists appeared on the grass, ready for the other of the two bouts and Trayan urged Daniel to come and sit with him and Emma, unfortunately the rules of the tournament stated that the winner of each bout could not gain an unfair advantage and so he was restricted to the roped off area at the back of the north stand.

Every effort had been made to provide enough comfort for Daniel, there was a refreshment area and a comfortable bench. Daniel had a word with one of the stewards and Emma was allowed to sit in with him, Trayan politely refused, using the excuse that he wanted to see the other match. Trayan still wondered what had happened to the boy over the last weeks and why he was so late, but he felt it more important that Daniel and Emma had some time together, and so he left them and retired to watch the other match.

Daniel needed a drink after the long journey he had undertaken and as well as the tough fight, he had just been involved in, and so he took a tall goblet of cold lemonade and finished it off in one. He then began to inspect the array of sandwiches that were on display when Emma came over to him. "So, are you going to tell me what happened, we have both been very worried, we, well I, thought that one of Torek's henchmen had caught up with you and all I could see was you laying in a pool of blood with an arrow sticking out of your back."

Emma was about to continue when Daniel turned to face her, he saw the look on her face and so he grabbed her gently on the shoulders and as he looked deep into her eyes he spoke softly to her. "I am fine, as you can see. I had some business to conclude, it took longer than I expected but in the end, well you shall see later."Then he just leant down, pulled her to him and kissed her softly on the lips, and her heart melted.

They embraced for a short while until a feeling came over the young man not of passion but one of isolation, gentle he pushed Emma away and she was about to ask why, when she too noticed that they were all alone in the area. Daniel turned around, but too late, a blow from a wooden club took him across the base of his neck and he fell to the floor. Emma screamed aloud but was soon held in a strong grip and a hand was roughly pressed around her mouth.

Daniel moved about the floor, his head groggy from the blow and as he looked up, he saw Emma being held by a scruffily dressed man with a dark unkempt beard. He tried to get to his feet but he was knocked back down to the floor, as he looked up there were three men standing before him and now they started to beat him. "Remember only were it does not show." One of the men spoke as the other two hacked at Daniel's arms and legs. Emma struggled, but try as hard as she might she could not break free, she could only stand and watch.

The men finished what they had to do quickly and then released Emma and hurried out of the area, Emma ran over and screamed out for help and she bent down to try and help Daniel to his feet. Daniel winced at every touch of Emma's hands, they had done their evil work well, because there was not a mark on Daniel's skin, but his joints were battered and bruised. Emma cried as she called out for help and with tears in her eyes she said, "You have to call this off, you cannot continue."

Daniel still tried to smile to her as he replied, "My animal has gone through far worse than I, now I owe it to him to continue." And with that, stewards arrived and fussed over what had happened, and helped him on his feet.

Shortly after Trayan arrived with Gregory and they were both told the news of what had happened. "This is the work of that evil bastard Torek." Said Trayan, but Gregory calmed the old man down and then stated that Torek had never left his seat, "the whole crowd were witness to that fact."

Gregory looked over at Daniel and could see the pain that he was in. "Do you wish to abandon your quest, my friend."

Daniel looked up and there was a fury on his face as he spoke. "I am going to win this tournament and then I am going to fight and beat that murderer."

The other match had been a close affair, however it had been Tien who had pulled through and it was he who would meet Daniel in the final. It had been another half hour but Daniel was still moving uneasily as the steward came to accompany him onto the arena, his arms and legs felt heavy, however as he entered the stadium and stepped into the sun he straightened himself up and tried to walk as normally as he could. Trayan had taken his seat with Emma sitting beside him and as he sat down he glanced over at Torek. The man was expressionless and did not return the look, but Trayan knew it was he who was responsible for the cowardly attack on Daniel and the blood inside his body boiled with anger and revenge.

Daniel was led to his spot on the grass at the north end whilst Tien was led to the south. The master of ceremonies, Gregory, now appeared and walked to the centre of the stadium to introduce the two contestants. Ladies and gentlemen we have been fed a feast of the finest fighting yet seen on this soil and only leaves me now with the simple task of introducing the two winners. "From the east, a master in his own land I give you TIEN." There was loud applause and clapping for the young man and he responded as usual by bowing to each corner of the stadium. "Finally from your home land of Arnorst I present Daniel." The crowd were off their seats shouting his name repeatedly, Daniel, Daniel, Daniel.

The young man tried to wave to them but as he lifted his arm a pain shot through it and into his body. Daniel managed a smile and tried to appear as though nothing was untoward but inside he was aching all over.

Gregory dismissed himself as the cheering of the crowd continued and he was replaced by the starter with the white canvass flag.

Daniel summoned his Braer but when he appeared it was obvious that something was wrong. Braer looked down at Daniel with sadness in his bright blue eyes and he spoke to him and his voice was unsteady and fearful. "Daniel, what is this, my arms and my legs they feel as though they have been." And then it dawned on the mighty beast and the look on his face changed from fear to anger and rage. His voice became loud and he stood on his hind legs, "What have they done to you, I will rip them apart," and he roared out loud with temper.
Daniel looked up at his friend and placed a hand on his thigh, and then with a calm look in his eyes he spoke softly to him. "My friend what they have done is only on the outside, they can never take what is on the inside, and that is the love I have for you."

Braer came back down onto all fours and stared into the heart of the young man. "I am yours and you are mine, together we shall overcome all that is put before us." Braer used the very words that he said to Daniel on their first meeting long ago in the wood by Dantaal, and then the beast turned and looked over at Torek who sat unmoving and coldly in his seat at the far end of the arena.

Tien now summoned his beast to the arena and he did so by closing his eyes and joining his hands in front of him as though in prayer. Beside the young man a great white animal appeared. The beast looked like a tiger from the hot land to the north east but they were striped and their fur was close cut to their bodies, this animal had long fur that was pure white and it stood nearly ten feet off the floor at the shoulders. It had enormous paws each equipped with a set of razor sharp claws and he possessed a set of impressively large sharp teeth, with his bright blue eyes he was a truly majestic creature.

The starter now raised the flag above his head and the two advisories made ready. The flag dropped to the floor and the battle began.

Daniel urged caution to begin with until he could gain a measure of this new Brannai and so Braer stalked slowly away from him. The white tiger on the other hand moved off and Daniel was impressed with the grace and speed of the animal as it moved across the grass toward him. Braer laboured as he walked but he kept his eyes on the great cat all the time, which was an easy thing to do since it was pure white. Tien made the first move, he ordered his cat to attack and now it made straight for Braer. The movement of the big cat was sublime and under its thick fur you could sense the muscle tone and the power and now as it neared Braer it readied itself for a leap. Daniel though was not ready for what happened next.

Braer faced the cat and bared his teeth ready for the attack, but when the cat leapt into the air it did it with such speed that it had leapt, struck out and landed without Braer even making a move and Braer was left with three deep cuts across his face where the claws of the big cat had gouged over him.

The cat had landed and had moved out of range in a graceful run. Braer rubbed his paw over the wound on his head but his arms and legs ached with each movement and now the cat was moving in for another strike. Daniel called to his friend to move, but Braer was labouring and the cat-sensed victory, so it moved quickly into position and once again leapt at his foe. The speed appeared even quicker than before, whether that was because of the cat or whether it was down to Braer did not matter, for the cat raked across Braer once again cutting more gouges into his already bloody face.

Daniel could not believe it, his animal was on the brink of defeat and it was his entire fault, he had been caught unawares and now his wounds were killing his friend.

His mind drifted back to when he was a boy and he had first met Trayan, and now the words of the old man filled his head, "what the Trainer is the Brannai will become." The words seemed to run through his head repeatedly, until Daniel realised what they meant and now through his mind he called to his friend. "I need you here by me now, as quickly as you can." Braer disappeared twice until he stood next to Daniel and the young man now spoke to him. "The wounds I have are mine, they are in me, you do not have any, it is my pain that you feel. If you break the link between us you will regain your strength."

Braer looked into Daniels eyes and new he spoke the truth and so Braer closed his eyes and concentrated.

Suddenly Daniel felt all alone, Braer was standing there before him but he could not feel him and he felt emptiness inside and a tear welled up in the corner of his eye.
Braer lifted his head and looked at Daniel standing there before him and then he turned and ran with power and with lightening fast speed. Daniel shouted to him as he left. "Remember you are on your own."

The tiger had already begun another attack but now he faced a Braer that was angry and the new speed took the cat by surprise, he had only just began his leap when Braer vanished and re-appeared and now he swiped out with his own mighty claw and caught the cat across the head. The cat reeled from the blow and Tien tried to compose his animal but Braer was already on top of him and now he struck out, hitting him time after time across the head and shoulders, causing fatal wounds that bled profusely. Tien called out in a panic-stricken voice, "SHANTU." However, it was already over and the great white cat disappeared in a shower of silver light.

The noise in the stadium erupted as everyone realised that Daniel had won and they all cheered for their champion, and the songs rang out Daniel!, Daniel!, Daniel!

The starter walked onto the grass and signalled the five-minute warning and it gave Daniel some respite. Amid the cheering of the crowd it was hard for Daniel to make himself heard, "You were magnificent," he said as Braer came and stood beside him, and Daniel reached up to his friend to touch the bleeding scars that were on his face. His arms were still in great pain and so Braer lowered his head and allowed Daniel to rub ointment on him. Daniel looked at his friend, Braer was bleeding from cuts to his hind legs, there were grazes and gouges on his sides and face, and suddenly as Daniel looked at him he was overcome with sadness at what he had done to him.

Braer did not need to be joined with Daniel to see the hurt and pity on the young man's face and as he looked at him he spoke, and his voice was fierce and steady, "This is what I fight for, wounds can be healed but pride cannot and I feel a pride when I fight for you, together we will defeat whatever comes at us and then we will take on and defeat the so called lord of the Brannai." Braer then turned around and lay next to Daniel on the dry grass, and the warmth of the sun felt good on his soft silvery fur.
The starter then re-appeared and took up his position on the grass and once again raised the white canvass flag in the air above his head.

Braer got up off the floor and stood ready, next to Daniel, ready for whatever would come at them.

Tien joined his hands together one more time and as he closed his eyes, his final Beast appeared next to him. Tien had summoned a snake, the creature had curled itself up and so its full length was hard to tell, however it was as thick as Daniels body around the waist and its head was huge. The snake had the bright blue eyes of the Brannai and it now reared itself up showing off its beautiful markings of red and yellow, and it flicked out its long tongue, trying to gain a taste of its opponent.

Daniel tried to look the beast over but he could not see any sort of rattle on the end of its tail and he wondered what surprises would be in store.

The starter dropped the flag to the floor and the final battle was under way.

The snake unwound itself and slithered eloquently across the grass revealing its full length, it was at least thirty feet long and it moved at a great speed. Braer had fought a snake before and was wary, and so he did not run straight at it, instead he stalked waiting for the snake to make the first move.

The snake did make the first move however, it was an unusual one, as it slithered across the grass it suddenly reared up and then drove straight into the earth, were it buried itself and disappeared from sight. Braer walked slowly around sniffing and listening but he could not make out where the beast was.

Suddenly the snake shot out of the ground right behind Braer and as Braer turned to face it, the snake struck out. The huge beast reared itself up and struck with two long pointed fangs that hung from its upper jaw and it buried them deep into Braer's leg.
Braer pulled back in pain and the snake once again drove itself down into the ground and disappeared.

Braer let out a roar for the pain in his leg was excruciating and in a panic, he searched around for the snake. Braer began to run but his back leg felt as though it was becoming numb and he began to limp. Braer stamped around trying to bring the snake up so that he could fight it one to one, but that was not Tien's strategy and now the great snake shot out of the ground once more. This time it appeared at the side of Braer, Braer struck out with his front paw to try, claw at its body, but the snake was immensely swift and agile, and it dodged the swipe and struck out once more with its fangs catching Braer on the front leg. Once again, Braer howled in pain, it wasn't so much the bite as the searing heat he felt as the venom worked its way slowly through his limb.

Daniel could do nothing, he was not joined to his friend and so he shouted out in anger, "BRAER!"

Braer limped around and it was that particular movement that Daniel then noticed something, as Braer limped all his weight fell onto his good arm and leg and as it did the ground around shook.

Could that be it, he thought hard but it seemed the only solution as to how the snake knew where to emerge from under the ground.

Daniel shouted over to his friend but his voice was hard to hear above the din of the crowd as they screamed and awed at the spectacle, luckily for Daniel, Braer managed to make out his friends voice and he turned and looked over at him. Daniel waved for Braer to come to him and the animal slowly made its way over. Daniel shouted up at Braer, "it can feel your footsteps on the grass, tread lightly and use." He was about to say use your disappearance, but it dawned on him that they were now separated and that was impossible.

"We must join once more; I can only help you if we are joined."

Braer closed his eyes and concentrated and Daniel felt the power of his friend flow through him once again. "Now go," said Daniel, and Braer limped away. The feelings of Daniels beating returned to Braer's limbs and coupled with the venom in his body he looked a forlorn sight as he moved slowly across the grass.

Daniel searched the arena for signs of the snake and then he saw it, there to the right of where Braer was standing, about thirty paces away, it was just noticeable. The grass was moving, swaying rhythmically in a line and Daniel could see that the snake was searching for Braer. Daniel called to his friend through his mind, stamp down hard on the floor and as he did Daniel saw the wave of movement alter and turn toward his friend.

Daniel talked to Braer, "get ready my friend we may only get one shot at this." Then Daniel concentrated on the land around Braer.

Braer was facing the other way, Daniel saw the earth bulge up behind him, and he shouted out at Braer, "NOW."

Braer disappeared just as the snake burst from the ground below, and he re-appeared behind it. Braer was immobile but he had timed it to perfection and he struck out with his jaws and clamped them around the neck of the snake. Braer bit down hard and snapped the neck of the great beast in two.

The snake disappeared in a shower of silver light and the stadium; including, Gregory, Trayan and Emma erupted into a cacophony of noise. Daniel fell to the floor in triumph; he placed his hands over his eyes, he had done it.

Only Torek and his entourage did not stand and cheer at Daniels remarkable achievement, they simply stood and walked to the exit, however you could detect a satisfied look on his face, he felt as though everything was going to plan.

Daniel was led to an area at the side of the arena whilst preparations were made for the victory ceremony and it was here that Emma and Trayan met Daniel. As soon as the young girl saw Daniel she ran over and flung herself around his shoulders, he winced from the pain but did not show it, he was happy and wanted to enjoy the moment. Trayan stood before him and his pride for the young man was evident, he stood proud and tall and now he walked over to him and as Emma stepped back, Trayan clasped the man around the shoulders and hugged him like a son.

Daniel was surrounded by well-wishers, the area was not cordoned off and many members of the vast crowd had gathered there to try and get a look at the new champion, the man who would take on Torek. Stewards were ushered in to separate the crowd from Daniel and his friends, they opened up a path that led to the outside, it was time for the ceremony to begin.

The podium had been erected once more and flags had been placed all around it, there was also wooden posts laid on the grass joined by heavy rope in a route from the holding area at the side of the arena right up to the podium itself. Trumpeters now lined the route and as Daniel emerged from the side, they all blasted out a fanfare in his honour. Trayan and Emma watched as Daniel took the path on his own, his steps were slow and deliberate, he wanted to show as little pain as possible to Torek, he need never have bothered for Torek had left the arena, and so Daniel walked out into the bright sunshine.

The crowd cheered and clapped loudly, Daniel was a popular winner, he was one of their own, a commoner just like them who had risen to the dizzy heights of champion of Arnorst.

Daniel walked up the few steps that led to the platform at the top of the podium and there to greet him was Gregory, dressed in his long gown and decorated around his neck with the gold chain of office.

Gregory shook Daniel's hand before turning to face the front of the podium, there he cleared his throat and addressed the multitude.

He waved his hands to calm the crowd and then he spoke to them, "Never before in the history of this tournament have we witnessed such bravery and such commitment in the face of such adversity. To come through such conflict with just one Brannai was truly an amazing feat and I hope you will al join me in congratulating our champion, from the small town of Dantaal, May I with great pleasure present, Daniel."

The crowd all stood and along with Gregory, they put their hands together and clapped him. Daniel bowed to Gregory and then turned and bowed to the whole stadium. When the clapping began to die, Gregory turned to Daniel and presented him with the winner's trophy, a golden statue nine inches tall depicting an eagle with blue eyes with its wings folded around the body of a man. Daniel took the statue and raised it into the air with two hands and the crowd cheered, roared, and threw ticker tape down onto the grass.

Daniel then waved the crowd to silence as he took up a position at the front of the podium. "There are so many people I would like to thank, for winning this has not been all of my own doing, none of this would have been possible without two of the greatest friends anyone could wish for," and now he waved to Trayan and Emma who stood in the shadows at the side of the arena to come forward. The two people stepped out into the bright sunlight amid cheering and clapping as it rang out around the stadium.

When the clapping had died down, Daniel spoke out aloud once more. "This trophy depicts and eagle with his wings folded around a man, shielding and protecting, I would like to present to you my shield and my protector and most of all, my friend." Daniel then closed his eyes and there in front of the podium appeared Braer, his leg and front paw were hurting from the venom and his body was ravaged with cuts but he now, somehow managed to stand on his hind legs and proudly lift himself up to his full height as the people in the crowd roared out in celebration.

The celebrations went on for some time even after Daniel was led away to the private area at the north end of the stadium where he had been beaten earlier. The crowd dispersed for refreshments, the entertainment was not quite over, for there was the small matter of the battle to determine the lord of all Brannai.

Gregory had posted stewards at the entrance to the area he did not want the same thing to happen twice and so Daniel, Emma and Trayan stood alone to wait.

Trayan looked over to Daniel and all manner of happiness had left him for now was the serious business of the final fight, he sat at a long wooden table that had been filled with sandwiches and drinks and spoke to the young man as he paced across the floor, "You cannot go ahead with the duel, your animal is too badly wounded, and as for you, well you can hardly walk."

Daniel fought back but there was no real conviction in his voice, inside he knew that Trayan spoke the truth. "I will not give in after achieving so much." He looked to Emma for support but there was none in her eyes as she looked back at him. Daniel turned to face back to Trayan but as he did pains shot down through his legs and he stumbled. Trayan moved to help the lad but Daniel held out his hand to stop him. Trayan spoke, almost pleading with Daniel, "If there was even a small ray of hope, I would say yes, but just look at you, as with the trainer so the Brannai will become."

Daniel's head dropped at with it all hope faded and the area was filled with an empty silence.

Just then a person appeared and stood at the rope of the entrance to the waiting area. The man simply stood and waited until Trayan noticed him there and looked over at him. Daniel turned and called out, "Tien, what are you doing here?"

The small man bowed politely to Daniel and then to Trayan and Emma in turn, "May I impose on your humble gathering."

Trayan went over and invited the young man in and then he stood next to Daniel and Emma and the three of them looked quizzically at Tien.

"I must apologise for this intrusion, however things have been made aware to me that I did not know, and I for my own part feel that I must act upon them." Daniel looked at Emma who shrugged her shoulders; Trayan went and sat back at the le.

Tien continued, "I will speak plainly, I have learned of the cowardly attack that took place before my encounter with you, and now I would like to offer my services to you." Daniel still did not know what Tien was on about and he answered back to him, "services."

Tien took a small bag off his shoulders that he had been carrying and now he reached inside and took out a small vial. "This is an antidote to the venom of Tangra, my Phythian; it will heal your animal. I offer it to him as a mark of respect."

Daniel did not know what to say and so Tien went over and placed the small glass bottle on the table in front of Trayan.

Tien had not finished, "There is something else, I would not have fought you had I known what you have been through, and so I would like to alleviate you of your pains." Daniel was left speechless; he did not know what Tien meant.

Tien once again reached into his bag and took out a small jar that contained an opaque looking jelly and then he walked toward Daniel and asked him to remove his shirt and his trousers.

Trayan understood what the man from the east had in mind and so he cleared the le and ushered Emma over to help. Daniel stripped and was left with only a towel to cover his pride revealing deep bruising on his arms, legs and back. Emma held her hands to her mouth and her eyes welled with tears when she looked at him.

"If you please," Tien asked Daniel to lie down on the wooden table and then he went and stood at the side of him, closed his eyes and joined his hands together as if in prayer.

When Tien opened his eyes he took the jar of jelly and removed the lid, then he took out a small handful and rubbed it between his hands. Then Tien proceeded to massage every inch of Daniels body covered with the dark blue bruises. His hands were strong and firm and he moved them in elaborate patterns over Daniel's arms and legs. Every now and then, he would stop and pray and then he would take some more of the jelly and replenish his hands.

After fifteen long minutes, Tien had finished and he now called over to one of the stewards to bring him a bowl of water. When the steward arrived Tien placed the bowl on the le and took out a small jar from his bag, he removed the lid and poured a little of the contents into the bowl. The water changed to a yellowy colour and then returned to its original colourless form. Tien then washed his hands in the bowl, dried them and bowed to Daniel as he lay on the le. "I have restored my honour; you will feel a great burning which will last for thirty minutes, now I must go." Then the young man bowed to Daniel and turned to leave but Daniel raised his head from the le to speak, "Thank you Tien, you know I will always consider you my friend and who knows one day we may meet again." With that Tien smiled and then turned and left not only the area but the stadium and the land of Arnorst itself.

Daniel dressed and then he walked out into the arena to summon Braer. When the animal appeared, Daniel went over and stroked the smooth silvery fur on his side and then he took out the small vial and gave it to his friend, "it will help with the pain, it was given to me by Tien out of respect for you." Then Daniel asked Braer to disappear and ready himself for the final hurdle.

Daniel returned to the waiting area and it was then that it started; the searing heat began in his left arm and then travelled around his body until he felt as though he had been immersed in a vat of boiling oil, and he screamed out in agony. The young man dropped to the floor and curled himself up into a ball and the sweat rose and poured out of pores on his face and skin. Emma rushed over and tried to douse him with a cloth that had been soaked in some cool fresh water, but it had little effect. Daniel tossed and turned on the floor and he called out in constant pain, there was little Trayan or Emma could do for him; the young man just had to ride it out.

It took the best part of thirty minutes for the pain to ease and slowly but surely, Daniel recovered his composure until finally he could sit up at the table on his own. He was immensely thirsty and downed two whole tankards of water one after the other and as he drank the sleeve of his shirt slipped down revealing his lower arm. Trayan reached over and grabbed Daniel's arm and pulled back the sleeve right to the top of his arm, the bruising had disappeared.

Daniel stood and removed his shirt, he stood and inspected every inch of his upper body, it was as though he had never been attacked at all. Tien had been true to his word and now Daniel turned and with a fierce look on his face he looked over at Trayan and Emma, "it is time to finish this"

The crowd had once again returned to their seats and now they waited for the final event of the day.

There was no pomp or ceremony, even the podium had not been re-erected and there were no trumpeters, Torek had insisted on it all and now as the sun began to sit a little lower in the sky he stood on the grass in the centre of the arena near to the south stand. He was dressed in a fine white silk shirt and black trousers, his sword hung elegantly at his side, and his black hair had been combed and tied back with a ribbon of fine black silk.

Daniel walked out into the warm summer's air and at once, the crowd erupted as they all stood as one and cheered. Daniel looked every inch the hero, his blonde hair sat scruffy on top of his head, his white linen shirt was muddy and unkempt, and as he waved to the crowd, he walked with an arrogance that Torek hated.

Daniel stopped at the point at which he had fought his earlier battles and now he stood and waited for the noise of the crowd to abate and for them all to sit back into their seats.

Suddenly there was utter silence in the stadium as Torek stood at one end, Daniel stood at the other, and then Daniel shouted across to his enemy. "It is time we finished this you and I." and with that he summoned the mighty Braer.

The pains had disappeared from Braer's limbs, all that remained were the scars to his face and limbs, his fur shone in the late evening sun, and he looked like a veteran warrior ready for his final battle. Daniel looked up at him and spoke, "everything has come down to this, all your pain and all your effort, right here right now. Just one more fight, one more step that is all I ask of you."

Torek smiled to himself he knew that Braer had fought four times to reach this fight, he knew it was tired and scarred and beaten and he knew he was no match for his two powerful animals and so now he drew his sword and pointed it to the sky. A grey cloud began to form above his head and then out of the cloud a bolt of lightning shot out and struck the ground not more than five feet from where Torek stood and then there standing next to him was the powerful Bull.

It stood fifteen feet tall, its legs, arms and torso were muscled, and it carried a huge wooden club in its right hand. The head of the beast was that of a Bull with two fierce looking horns perched on top of a bull's face that covered in grey leather like skin and it poured hot steam out of both its nostrils as it stood and looked over at Braer.

Torek turned and looked up at his huge beast, he spoke to it, and his voice was strong and unflinching in its conviction, "I want you to inflict as much pain as you can, beat it to the floor and leave nothing for the Kaldeira."

No starter appeared from the sides and there was no announcer to proclaim the fight, Torek would have none of it, the great Bull simply started to move forward and the battle had begun.

Braer roared to the heavens and then he too walked out to meet his foe. The two animals reached the centre of the arena and every step that the Bull took shook the floor that it walked upon. They circled each other for a while eyeing each other up, looking for a weakness, an opening, an advantage.

Suddenly the Bull charged at Braer with all of its power and fury, but Braer was ready and he met him with a charge of his own. The bull put his head down just as the two mighty beasts clashed in a frenzy of muscle and fur but Braer had kept his eyes on the Bull and he caught the horns of the great animal with his front paws.

The two animals' heaved and pushed against each other, their rear legs digging into the grass churning up great sods of earth as they tried to gain a foothold.

Braer pushed against the horns of the Bull but that left his body unprotected and now the Bull lashed out with his club and caught Braer across his middle not once but twice in rapid succession. Braer flinched against the blows, and then he managed to release one of the horns and swiped at the Bulls head with his free claw catching it across the face. The two animals separated for just a second, the Bull bled from the cuts on his face and Braer winced at the pain in his ribs.

Braer now disappeared and re-appeared behind the Bull and then lashed out twice with mighty swipes from both his front paws. He caught the Bull across the back, tearing two sets of gouges in its thick skin. The Bull raised its head to the sky and bellowed and then it struck out wildly with its club. It was a wild strike, born out of pain and instinct, but it was also a lucky one for it caught Braer across the joint on his right elbow, dislocating it.

Braer pulled back out of harm's way just as the Bull turned and lashed out once more with his great club, that weapon was causing havoc and Daniel knew it.

Blood ran down the back of the Bull and he also bled from the wounds on his face but as he looked at his foe standing there before him, he knew that Braer was his for the taking.

Daniel spoke to his friend through his mind and as he did, the Bull charged. The great beast bellowed and then ran at Braer with all his power. Braer stood up on his hind legs and readied himself for the impact and just as he was on top of him, the Bull lowered its horns forward to skewer him. Braer waited for the last possible moment and then as the

Brannai

Bull was right on top of him he dropped to the floor and moved his huge bulk to the right, skilfully leaving a trailing paw behind.

The Bull eyes were pointing to the floor, he did not see the move, and he tripped on the trailing leg and went flying to the ground.

As the Bull hit the floor, the club was jarred from his grasp and it was tossed across the grass, Braer saw his opportunity and now he disappeared and re-appeared on top of the fallen beast where he now pounced on top of him and attacked the back of his unprotected neck with his powerful jaws. The fight was over as Braer bit through the tough skin into the vertebrae, killing it instantly.

The whole crowd went wild with emotion as the great Bull disappeared in a shower of silver light.

Daniel punched the air with delight Braer had done it and he ran over to congratulate his injured friend. Braer limped back to Daniel as the crowd cheered and clapped, his arm was dislocated and he had several broken ribs but Daniel did not care and now he went and hugged him.
Trayan was not one of the ones cheering because Torek's second beast was his most powerful and now Braer was too injured to carry on and from now he could only see defeat for his brave young friend.

Torek surprised the whole crowd and began laughing. At first, it mingled with the noise of the cheering and clapping and no one noticed, but slowly and surely, the noise of the multitude died down leaving Torek laughing, alone.

Daniel released Braer and the two of them turned and faced their enemy.
Torek's laugh died down and then he looked over at Daniel and began to clap; he then bowed to Daniel before shouting out to him. "You have done extremely well my boy, to come so far with just one beast is truly remarkable, but as you can see your animal is finished. He cannot move with a broken arm and probably, from the look of him, broken ribs as well. It quite simply would not be a fair contest; I will save you from any embarrassment by calling this contest over."

Daniel walked to the front of Braer and looked up at his friend, he placed his hands on Braer's soft face and stroked his skin moving his hands softly over the cuts and gouges and then he pulled his head down and whispered in his ear.

"Your work is over, thank you my friend, we will be together shortly."

Braer then vanished amid gasps from the crowd, leaving Daniel standing alone. Torek shouted over to him, "That was a wise thing to do boy." However, Daniel had not finished and now he raised himself up and there was fire in his eyes.

"This contest is not over, MURDERER! A long time ago my father faced you and beat you with his beast, but that was something you could not stomach and so you set your beast on him and killed him."

There were gasps and cries from the crowd and Trayan looked across at Emma and then back to the arena. Torek had turned red with fury and now he began to step toward the boy drawing his sword as he went.

However, Daniel raised his hand to stop Torek, "There is more, I believe that this contest is the best of three and as you so rightly put it my animal cannot continue, however there is someone I would like you to meet, and yes he is mine."

With that, Daniel turned and walked back to his starting position, there he closed his eyes and summoned an old friend, the mighty Taitu.

The animal appeared next to him; it was fifteen feet tall and covered in jet-black fur. Taitu stood in the perfect pose of the great apes and there was ferocity on its face as it snorted hot air through its nose.
Torek took a step back he could not believe what he was seeing, the mighty arms and legs, the jaws; it was he the only animal to defeat him, back from his haunted dreams.

The crowd cheered for Daniel and Trayan sat back on his seat and laughed, so that is where he has been, and he looked up at Emma who was smiling down at him.

"You knew didn't you?" he said to her. "But how has he managed to evolve him so quickly."

Emma sat beside the old man, "If you remember back to when you left Daniel and I in the wood before we entered Narat, it was there that I decided to become a trainer like you. Well, before the tournament began I said goodbye to Taitu but before he left I asked him if he would become Daniel's Brannai, he turned and looked over at him and then said yes. After that, every chance he had Daniel trained Taitu by pitting him against Braer but always away from prying eyes, he wanted the world to think he only had one Brannai."

Trayan sat amazed at the young girl before him and now he placed an arm on her shoulder. "You have both exceeded all expectations."

The noise grew from the crowd, they were in a frenzy of excitement, there was going to be at least one more battle and now Trayan and Emma both stood to watch.

Torek could not turn and run, he had nowhere to go, he had to make his stand now, and so he pointed his sword up to the skies once more and in a fury he screamed out loud. A bolt of lightning shot to the floor and there next to him stood Kaldeira.

The beast was huge, it was a man heavily muscled in body and on the arms but the lower half joined to that of an insect like structure that was held up by six legs. Attached to the sides were two enormous claws like those of a crab and on the end, curled high above it was a tail with a curved sting.
Daniel looked up at Taitu and spoke to him with just enough intensity that only he could hear. "Remember your training my friend and we will be fine, you look magnificent."

Taitu spoke back to Daniel, his voice was strong, and deep, "It will be an honour to fight for you. I will not disgrace my brother, Braer."

The talking was over and now Torek shouted aloud to his Kaldeira, "Kill him."

The Kaldeira set off and the noise of its feet on the floor echoed around the arena as it ran. Taitu always possessed the skill to know were an attack was going to come but only if he was not attacking himself and the Kaldeira knew it and so he prepared himself. However, that was not Daniels plan and Taitu now set off and ran hard at his opponent churning up grass and earth as he went. The Kaldeira saw the attack coming and now brought himself up to his full speed. The two adversaries roared at each other as they met in the middle of the arena. However, Taitu did not engage him, as they closed to within a few feet, Taitu jumped high in the air twisting his huge body as he went; showing unbelievable agility. The Kaldeira could only look on as the great ape somersaulted over its head and once over, Taitu grabbed hold of the Kaldeira's sting between his two powerful hands.

In one acrobatic movement Taitu twisted and tore the sting right off the end of the beasts body and then landed gracefully on the floor where he spat at the sting in his hands before nonchalantly tossing it away.

Kaldeira screamed out in pain as the blood dripped from where his sting had been attached, and now it turned and ran at Taitu. The Kaldeira struck out with one of its giant claws but Taitu caught it with his hands and as he held on the Kaldeira hit out with his two powerful arms pounding into the sides of the great ape.

Taitu managed to jump backwards in a sort of flip but the Kaldeira continued forward and was once again on top of Taitu. This time it lashed out with both of its claws and it took all of Taitu's skill to avoid them, however the huge beast continued going forward and forcing Taitu back. Daniel called out to his new friend, "remember it is weakest from the back."

Kaldeira's objective was to grab hold of an arm and therefore immobilise it whilst he was then free to pound away with his huge arms, but Taitu kept on deflecting its attacks until as it backed up it tripped on a pothole that had been left partly repaired from the previous fights and he fell to the floor.

Like lightning, the Kaldeira pounced and struck Taitu across the head with one of its huge claws causing a huge cut to appear above his right eye. The ape gathered himself quickly as another claw came toward him; he managed to duck out of the way then caught by two blows from the hands of the Kaldeira that struck him across the middle, around the ribs.

Taitu was under pressure but he reacted with intelligence and skill. As the Kaldeira attacked with another of his claws, Taitu moved to the right and then bounced off the floor aiming for the other claw. He jumped into the air, wrapped both his hands around the claw, and then skilfully used it to spin himself around and land on the back of the giant beast.
Once on top it spelt the end for the Kaldeira for it had no sting to protect it and its huge claws could not reach, and so Taitu started to hammer blow after blow down onto the head of his enemy. The Kaldeira was beaten to the floor until finally Taitu grabbed hold his head. The Kaldeira tried to twist Taitu's hands away with its own but Taitu was too strong and finally there was a loud crack as he broke the beast's neck.

Taitu stood and pounded his chest with his hands in victory and the crowd went into raptures.

Daniel ran over screaming and shouting as the Kaldeira vanished in a shower of silver light.

Torek dropped to his knees, it was over, his reign had ended, and he watched as Emma ran out from the crowd toward her conquering hero.

However, Emma's run took her close to where Torek was and in a fit of pure anger and hate he jumped up and grabbed the girl as she ran past him.

Brannai

The crowd suddenly went quiet and Daniel froze next to his mighty animal as Torek took out a dagger from his belt and held it to Emma's throat.

Daniel stood and held out his hand in front of him, "Torek don't do this, the games are over, let her go."

Torek was in a mad rage, his world had fallen apart at the hands of a farm boy, but he would have the last laugh and now he pressed the blade of the dagger into the skin on the girl's neck until blood began to seep from the small wound.

"TOREK, leave the girl, you know it's me you want, it has always been you and me."

With that Daniel stepped clear of Taitu and asked his friend to leave. Taitu roared over at Torek and then simply disappeared.

"Look, my animal has gone, it is just you and I now let the girl go."

Torek composed himself and then he tossed Emma to the ground and drew his long silver sword. Daniel called over to him once more, "would you fight an unarmed man, here in front of your people/"

Torek looked around him, at the crowds of faces that now stared at him and he now walked toward the boy until his sword was but a few inches from his throat.

Trayan had raced out of his seat to Daniels horse where he found his sword attached to its side in a leather case, he pulled it out and ran back into the stadium and there he tossed it to the floor to where Daniel now stood.

Daniel slowly bent down to pick up his sword and Torek kept the point of his blade held to Daniel's head as he did so.

Daniel then stood and faced Torek, who bowed and then smiled at him. Torek attacked swiftly and it took all of Daniels skill to fend him off as the blades clashed and the sound of metal on metal rang out around the arena. Daniel parried as Thomas had shown him but Torek's skill was great.

Daniel attempted to parry and then lunge forward with a thrust of his own But Torek saw it coming and turned quickly out of the way and as he did he thrust forward and drove his blade into Daniels other arm. Daniel managed to spin out of the way to avoid another thrust but now the pain rose in his arm and the blood dripped onto the dry grass, staining it red.

The two men then circled one another gaining some respite and filling their lungs with fresh gulps of air. Torek had regained his composure for he knew he had the measure of the boy and now he attacked once more. The blows rained down in quick succession but Daniel managed to fend them off and even thrust forward himself, this time with good balance, but Torek parried the attack easily. Torek was moving forward as he cut and swiped, driving Daniel back all the time, suddenly Daniel tripped and fell to the floor and his sword fell from his hand.

Torek seized his chance and ran at the boy raising his sword high above his head ready to bring it down like an axe. Daniel fumbled around trying to feel for his blade, Torek swung his sword down, just in time Daniel found the handle, and now he thrust up and drove it into the chest of Torek.

Time stood still for just a moment with Daniel sitting up on the floor and Torek impaled on the end of his blade, and then Torek fell to the floor and all life left him.

Emma ran over and, crying she grabbed Daniel around the neck. Trayan appeared and stood over the couple as they hugged, "my boy that was too close," he said and then he held out his hand and lifted Emma and Daniel to their feet and it was only then that the crowd erupted and cheered for their new hero.

A presentation ceremony had been planned, however due to the circumstances the atmosphere was somewhat subdued, and the crowd had been subject to a scene of violence.

Torek's body was removed and the arena cleaned up and after a meeting with representatives of the Brannai council, it was decided to go ahead with the presentation.

Gregory walked onto the arena and addressed the people, "Due to the unforeseen circumstances of the past hour we have decided to go ahead with the presentation ceremony, and so if you could be patient for the next fifteen minutes." With that, he turned and left the field.

The podium was erected and decked out in the blue and white of the Brannai, and the trumpeters emerged, also in blue and took up their positions, making a path from the waiting area to the podium.

Gregory wore a long gown of blue and silver and was escorted onto the arena by three other members of the council; there they were clapped all the way up to the podium as they carried the ceremonial silver sword with its golden handle inlaid with the words lord of all Brannai written down the length of the blade, aloft.

Gregory then addressed the crowd, "Ladies and gentleman a new era has dawned, and the light from that era is shining brightly down on you and your champion. The dark clouds have been cast aside and now it just leaves me with the honour of presenting to you your champion, Daniel."
The crowd stood and cheered as Daniel walked out onto the arena, he was lined at either side by trumpeters who now rang out a fanfare to celebrate his victory. As he walked, he was accompanied on either side by Trayan and Emma and their faces beamed with joy, all the darkness had been lifted from their lives and their future looked bright.

Emma and Trayan stayed at the bottom of the podium and stood in front whilst Daniel walked up the steps on his own. Gregory greeted him at the top and shook his hand, before he went and presented the sword to Daniel.

Daniel bowed to Gregory and then accepted the sword into his hands, but before he raised the sword into the air, he turned and addressed the crowd. Gregory had to wave them to silence before Daniel could begin and then he stepped forward.

"My dear friends, this is a dream come true for me, a dream that would not have been possible without the help from my dearest friends Emma and Trayan."

There was loud clapping from the audience as the two friends turned and waved and then Daniel continued. "I feel that through my friend Trayan I have come to know my father, and it is he, Philip to whom I now dedicate this title."

The crowd once more clapped and cheered at the boys respect for his deceased father.

Daniel waited for the noise to die down and then he continued, "through all my endeavours I would be nothing without two of the finest, bravest and most honourable creatures I have ever laid eyes on and it is them that I now honour as my friends and protectors."

Daniel then closed his eyes and summoned Braer and Taitu who appeared in front of the podium in all their glory and splendour.

The crowd erupted and they all stood in unison and cheered for the magnificent beasts, as Daniel finally lifted the silver sword high in the air.

**

Printed in Great Britain
by Amazon